D1180207

Dear Reader,

Have you ever gone on a scavenger hunt? When I was growing up, scavenger hunts were a popular game at birthday parties. We'd be divided into two or three groups, given a list of items to find, then sent off in search of those items. We'd go on a mad dash, from door-to-door, asking for a piece of red yarn, or a postcard, or a cinnamon stick. Most of our neighbors would happily contribute, and once we'd gathered all the items on the list, we'd race back to the party, hoping to be declared the winner. The prize didn't really matter; it was the thrill of the hunt that was so much fun.

Maybe that's why I enjoy writing—and reading—mysteries so much. They're a type of treasure hunt for clues that will eventually lead to solving the mystery. In *Tea Is for Treasure,* Jan and Elaine embark on a different kind of hunt—one that will lead to both surprises and secrets. So settle in for a delicious cup of tea and enjoy another mystery at Chickadee Lake.

Blessings,
Kristin Eckhardt

Tearoom Mysteries

TEAROOM
mysteries

Tea Is for Treasure

KRISTIN ECKHARDT

Guideposts

New York

Tearoom Mysteries is a trademark of Guideposts

Published by Guideposts Books & Inspirational Media
110 William Street
New York, New York 10038
Guideposts.org

Copyright © 2017 by Guideposts. All rights reserved.

This book, or parts thereof, may not be reproduced, stored in a retrieval
system, or transmitted in any form or by any means, electronic, mechanical,
photocopying, recording or otherwise, without the written permission of the
publisher.

The characters and events in this book are fictional, and any resemblance to
actual persons or events is coincidental.

Acknowledgments

Every attempt has been made to credit the sources of copyrighted material used
in this book. If any such acknowledgment has been inadvertently omitted or
miscredited, receipt of such information would be appreciated.

Scripture quotations are taken from *The Holy Bible, New International Version.*
Copyright © 1973, 1978, 1984, 2011 by Biblica, Inc. Used by permission of
Zondervan. All rights reserved worldwide. www.zondervan.com

Cover and interior design by Müllerhaus
Cover illustration by Ross Jones, represented by Deborah Wolfe, Ltd.
Typeset by Aptara, Inc.

Printed and bound in the United States of America
10 9 8 7 6 5 4 3 2 1

Tea Is for Treasure

CHAPTER ONE

J an had a secret.

She didn't like keeping secrets, especially from her cousin Elaine, who was now busy preparing the tearoom for opening. It was a cozy Tuesday morning in March, and the kitchen smelled of cinnamon and cloves. She'd gotten up early to start the baking, and the cooling racks on the kitchen island were full of mini maple croissants, a favorite among their guests at Tea for Two.

Rose Young, one of the tearoom's two employees, had arrived a short time ago and tied on her apron before getting started on the tearoom's cookie of the day. The young server and baker stood at the kitchen counter, carefully measuring sugar for the lemon meringue cookies. She wore a butter-yellow apron over her tan slacks and white polo shirt, her wheat-blonde hair pulled back into a neat ponytail.

Rose had never made meringue cookies before, but she'd wanted to give them a try. And Jan had encouraged her, pleased at how Rose's confidence in the kitchen was growing each day.

Then Jan turned her gaze back to the window over the sink, reaching out to part the lace curtain. Gray clouds hung heavy in the sky, but a hint of sunlight shimmered behind them.

It had rained in Lancaster for the last three days, a soft spring rain that had slowly soaked the ground, leaving it wet and spongy. She and Elaine had laid out extra throw rugs in the entrance hall between the tearoom that comprised the double parlors, so their guests could wipe off any moisture or mud they might carry in on their shoes.

Raindrops still dripped from the porch roof beyond the kitchen window, but Jan sensed the sunlight struggling to break through the clouds foretold a clear day ahead. The daily high temperatures in March could range from the low thirties to the mid sixties, and today was a chilly one. So she'd dressed in a heavy-knit blue turtleneck sweater and gray slacks, along with a long silver pendant necklace.

Jan leaned closer to the window but didn't see any sign of the mail truck on the road. She'd hoped the postman would arrive before the tearoom opened at ten o'clock so she could intercept him. She didn't want Elaine or Rose to see the letter she was expecting.

"Oh no!" Rose exclaimed.

Jan turned around to see the younger woman standing in front of the oven and pulling out a cookie sheet. "What's wrong?"

"My meringues look more like little pancakes," Rose said with a groan. She set the cookie sheet on top of the stove, then removed her oven mitts. Frustration flared in her blue eyes. "I don't understand—I followed the recipe to the letter!"

Jan gave her an empathetic smile as she walked over beside Rose and took a look at the flattened cookies. "Meringues can be a little temperamental. Even the weather can affect them."

Rose glanced at the window. "But it stopped raining last night. Is there still too much moisture in the air?"

"No, I don't think that's the problem," Jan told her, placing her hands on her hips. "Did you let the eggs come to room temperature before you beat the egg whites?"

"Yes," Rose said with a nod.

"And you made sure the mixing bowl was spotless?"

"I wiped it clean." Rose turned and leaned against the counter. "And I used a glass bowl, because you taught me that fat particles can get into the microscopic cracks in plastic bowls and diminish the volume of the egg whites."

"You've got a great memory." Jan chuckled. "That was my next question."

Rose was an avid learner with natural talent. She'd recently started attending culinary school at night to hone that talent, giving her a busy schedule.

"The most common reason for egg whites to deflate," Jan explained, "is overbeating them or beating them too quickly."

"Oh," Rose said slowly, "that might be what happened. I set the mixer at the highest speed because I wanted to get these into the oven quickly so I could get started on the next batch."

Jan picked up the turner spatula and slid it between a meringue cookie and the parchment paper, lifting it off the pan. Then she took a bite, savoring the sweet, lemon flavor of the delicate cookie. "It's delicious," she proclaimed. "So just take it a little slower beating the egg whites on the next batch, and I'm sure they'll turn out just fine."

"Will do," Rose said, looking ready to take on the challenge. "Should I throw these out?" she asked, pointing to the flattened cookies.

"Absolutely not," Jan said a smile. "They might not look good enough to serve to our customers, but there's no reason we can't enjoy them in the kitchen. Half the fun of baking is eating the flops."

Rose laughed as she headed off to make the next batch while Jan scooped the deflated meringue cookies onto a plate.

A few moments later, Elaine walked into the kitchen. "We're all set in the tearoom. How's it going in here?"

"Great," Jan told her, putting a kettle on to boil. "Rose is working on the lemon meringue cookies and I just finished mixing up another batch of tea leaves for our Hello Spring tea."

She and Elaine loved mixing their own special tea blends, as well as serving the classics. Now that March had arrived, they'd decided to celebrate spring with a lighter tea combining the flavors of orange peels, lavender, and rose hips.

"At least the rain's finally stopped, so I'm expecting a bigger crowd than we've had the last few days." Elaine smiled. "As soon as Archie arrives, we'll have all hands on deck."

Jan nodded, taking another peek out the kitchen window. Archie Bentham worked part time at the tearoom. An older British man with the air of a distinguished professor, Archie had earned multiple degrees and traveled the world before retiring and settling down in Lancaster with his wife.

Jan was about to drop the curtain when she saw a flash of light from a windshield on the road. A few seconds later, the mail truck came into view.

"Mail's here!" Jan called out, her voice sounding shrill to her ears. "I'll get it." She hurried to the back door even though Elaine was closer. But when she glanced back at her cousin and Rose, she was relieved to see both women placing pastries on the silver serving trays and paying no attention to her as they chatted happily together.

"Calm down," Jan whispered to herself, slipping a windbreaker off the hook by the door before stepping onto the screened porch. She closed the door behind her, then saw Earl Grey snuggled cozily on a plump yellow cat cushion.

Now that the weather was warming up, the stray feline spent less time in the little home they'd made for him out of a Styrofoam cooler covered with Mylar and filled with straw to keep him warm during the winter.

He opened one sleepy green eye as she walked past him, then closed it again, undisturbed by the imminent arrival of the postman.

Jan stepped outside and started walking toward the front of the house as the mail truck pulled up in the driveway. Then she waved to the postman, Orin Bond. "Hello there! You're here early today."

Orin smiled as he grabbed his mailbag and stepped out of the truck. "I got an early start." A stocky man in his fifties, Orin had been born and raised in Lancaster. After enlisting in the army right out of high school, he'd served twenty years before returning to Lancaster and taking a job at the post office. During the tourist season, he shared mail duties with Russell Edmonds, who delivered mail by boat to the cottages along Chickadee Lake.

"At least the sun's peeking out today," Jan said, happy to see the clouds dispersing as the sunbeams skated across the icy lake. "Maybe it will dry up some of this mud."

Orin chuckled as he walked toward her. "I sure hope so. I got stuck yesterday. Gavin Richardson had to pull my mail truck out with his tractor."

"Oh dear, that's not fun."

His blue eyes twinkled. "Well, it wasn't all bad. He towed me to his dairy farm so I could hose the mud off the tires, then Annie sent me on my way with a piece of peach pie right out of the oven."

Jan laughed. "Sounds like you should get stuck more often." Then she leaned closer as he dug into his mailbag. "I'm expecting a letter."

"Well, let's see what we have here." Orin gazed down at the stack in his hand, separating out a few pieces of mail and dropping them back into his bag. Then he handed the stack to Jan.

He stood there while she thumbed through it, his gaze curious.

"Looks like mostly bills," she said, trying not to sound disappointed. It wasn't there. Her secret would have to wait another day.

She took a deep breath and smiled. "Thanks, Orin. I don't have any pie for you, but we do have some lemon meringue cookies." Her smiled widened. "They are flops, but they taste delicious."

"I better pass." Orin stepped toward his truck. "I'm not really supposed to eat on my route, with the exception of peach pie," he said with a grin. "But I might get in trouble if they find cookie crumbs in my mailbag." Then he slapped one hand to his forehead. "I almost forgot. I have a package for you."

"You do?" she said, wondering if it was the tea leaves they'd ordered yesterday.

Orin walked to his truck and pulled out a cardboard box about the size of a bread box. "Sorry to say, it must have fallen in a mud puddle sometime during transport. The label got a bit dirty." He handed the box to her. "I made an incident report, so you can file a report if there are any damages."

She stared down at the label, noticing the return address was unreadable.

Then her gaze moved to the postmark. "Looks like it came from New York City."

"Sorry again about the water damage," Orin said.

"No problem. It doesn't look as though the package itself got wet, just the label." She tucked the package under her arm.

Orin gave her a wave then climbed into his truck. "Have a nice day, Jan."

"You too!" she called back, watching as he pulled out of the driveway. Then she saw three cars heading toward the tearoom, recognizing one of them as belonging to Macy Atherton, a regular customer at the tearoom. She hurried back to the house, giving Earl Grey a quick pat as she walked through the screened-in porch and into the kitchen.

"There you are," Rose exclaimed, standing by the stove with an oven mitt on her hand. "The cookies are almost ready and Elaine wants us to make an extra pot of the Hello Spring tea. Macy called ahead and said she's got quite a crowd coming today."

Jan nodded, turning into Elaine's office and depositing the mail and the package on the desk before slipping off her windbreaker and heading back into the kitchen. As she tied on her apron, she made a mental note to tell Elaine they'd received a package addressed to the tearoom. Then she pushed up her sleeves, washed her hands, and got to work.

JAN CARRIED A silver tray into the tearoom. She'd been on the run since the tearoom opened and more people kept walking through the door. Archie and Elaine were serving customers in the west parlor while she and Rose tended to customers in the east parlor.

Macy Atherton frowned as Jan approached her table. "I was beginning to think you'd forgotten about me."

Jan smiled as she set the tray on the table. "I could never forget you, Macy."

One of their most frequent and loyal customers, Macy's communication style was more vinegar than honey. And today, for some reason unbeknownst to Jan, Macy was in an especially sour mood.

"And I think you're going to enjoy these lemon meringue cookies," Jan told her.

Macy looked doubtful as she picked up one of the meringue cookies and took a bite. She chewed thoughtfully for a moment, her dour expression slowly clearing. "Why, yes, they do have a nice, sharp flavor." Then she looked at the remaining cookie in her hand. "Perhaps next time you could work a little more on presentation. They should all have a nice dome shape. As you can see, this one has a tiny dimple in the top."

"I'll pass that along," Jan said, keeping a cheery note in her voice. The sound of the front door opening behind her made Jan glance over her shoulder. Two women she didn't recognize walked inside. She turned back to Macy. "My, we're certainly busy today. Not that I'm complaining."

"You have me to thank for that," Macy said, sitting proudly up in her chair. "I have several new guests staying at the cottages and recommended Tea for Two to them. So you and Elaine need to be at the top of your game."

Macy ran the Green Glade cottages on the shores of Chickadee Lake, along with her son, Shane, and daughter-in-law, Zale.

"It's not even tourist season yet," Jan said, glancing around the room. She'd noticed several new customers sitting among the regulars and had just assumed there was a gathering of some kind happening in town. "Are they here for some kind of reunion?"

"No," Macy said, leaning closer and lowering her voice. "They're actually part of a club and call themselves Finders Keepers. Apparently they like to travel together around the country looking for treasures—rare antiques and collectibles, I suppose."

Jan smiled. "That sounds like fun. And there are plenty of places around here to find nice antiques and vintage pieces.

They'll love Oldies But Goodies, Gift Me, A Little Something, and the Sugar Plum..."

"There is also another couple staying at Green Glade to celebrate their anniversary." Then Macy frowned. "And I can't forget the ornithologist."

"Oh, you have a bird-watcher?"

"Yes, and he's quite a persnickety fellow," Macy said with a sniff. "Always complaining that his cottage is too hot or too cold. Or that someone parked in his spot." She shook her head. "I just don't understand people who find fault with everything."

Jan stared at her, trying not to smile at the irony. "Yes, it is a mystery." She picked up Macy's teapot. "I'll make some more tea for you and be right back."

"Make sure it's hot enough this time," Macy called after her.

Jan carried the empty teapot to the kitchen, enjoying the hum of conversation emanating from the tearoom. Moments like this reminded her why she and Elaine had decided to open a tearoom together almost a year ago: to bring people together in conversation and fellowship—while enjoying delicious teas and treats.

"Ho, there," Archie said, almost running into Jan as they met at the swinging door leading into the kitchen. The tray in his hands was piled high with maple croissants, lemon meringue cookies, and raspberry biscotti. "We almost had a bit of a spill."

"Almost," Jan agreed, laughing. "Macy misses you, by the way. She's more cantankerous than usual today."

He chuckled. "Well, I have my hands full," he said, nodding toward the tray as he walked away, "with some hungry customers."

Elaine appeared behind her, carrying an empty tray. "Looks like we have a traffic jam."

"We sure do," Jan said, laughing. Then she remembered the mail. "Oh, Elaine, I wanted to tell you we got a package in the mail addressed to the tearoom."

"Is it the tea leaves we ordered?" Elaine asked, following Jan into the kitchen.

"No, it's from New York City, but there was some water damage on the label, so I couldn't tell who it's from."

"That's interesting," Elaine said cheerfully, setting the tea tray on the counter. Then she turned back toward the tearoom. "Let's take a look when we have a spare moment, shall we?"

"Sounds good." Jan set down the empty teapot, then looked over at Rose. "Your lemon meringue cookies are a hit. Even Macy likes them."

Rose beamed. "That's high praise indeed." She placed her hands on her hips. "I just put the last batch in the oven. As soon as those are done I can help you out in the west parlor."

"Perfect," Jan said, putting on some water to boil and wondering how long it would take before they could open that mysterious package from New York.

As it turned out, Elaine and Jan's spare moment didn't arrive until they'd closed the tearoom at four o'clock.

"The last customer just left," Elaine said, walking into the kitchen. "We were hopping today!" She smiled as she untied her apron. "I'm surprised we didn't run out of tea."

Jan laughed as she washed the last teapot while Archie and Rose finished wiping down the counters. "It was almost as busy as tourist season. I guess folks wanted to be out and about after all the rain we've had for the past few days."

"The more the merrier as far as I'm concerned," Elaine said, placing a lid on the bowl of raspberry biscotti. "Although I feel as if I haven't had time to sit down all day."

Archie pulled out a chair, then gave a formal wave of his hand toward Elaine. "Your throne, milady."

They all laughed as Elaine took a seat. "Now that's more like it. Why don't we all sit down and enjoy a break? We've earned it after a day like today."

They all followed Elaine's lead, taking a seat at the table and sharing a pot of tea and the lemon meringue flop cookies that Rose had baked early in the day. Jan enjoyed the light crunch of the meringues and the tart bite of the lemon flavor.

After a few minutes, Elaine turned to her. "What about that package you mentioned earlier?"

"Oh my, I almost forgot," Jan said, rising from her chair. She walked into the office and retrieved the package, then carried it back to the kitchen table. She set it down, then reached for the kitchen scissors and cut the parcel string holding it together.

Elaine pulled it toward her and studied the label. "It's just addressed to Tea for Two. I guess that means it's for both of us."

"Then you should open it together," Rose suggested.

Jan nodded, intrigued by the mystery of it all. She and Elaine both began to pull apart the brown paper covering the box. Then Jan used one blade of the scissors to slice through the packaging tape holding the cardboard lid flaps together.

Elaine pulled the lid open, revealing layers of bubble wrap and loose newspaper scraps. "Something fragile must be inside."

Jan reached into the box and carefully pulled out the large ball of packaging material, bound together with plastic tape. "The sender sure isn't making this easy for us."

Elaine leaned closer, her blue eyes wide with anticipation. "I wonder what it is?"

"So do I," Rose chimed in, her hands wrapped around her teacup.

Jan and Elaine began peeling away the packaging. "I think it might be a teapot!" Jan exclaimed as she finally glimpsed white bone china through the bubble wrap and plastic tape.

"I believe it is." Elaine removed the last of the packaging to reveal a lovely white china teapot adorned with an exotic floral design in vibrant shades of coral and sage green.

Jan looked up at her cousin. "Are you sure you didn't order this?"

"I'm positive," Elaine replied, looking equally perplexed.

Jan looked over at Archie, who had friends and connections all over the world. "Perhaps one of your friends sent it to you, now that you work here. But how would they have our address?"

Archie's mouth curved into a sheepish smile. "I've told quite of few of my mates about this place. In fact, an old school chum, Nigel Fox, is on his way here from England right now.

We've kept in touch all these years and now he's renting a cottage at the lake and planning a nice visit."

"If he's coming by way of New York, maybe he sent it," Rose said.

"I doubt it. Nigel is a collector, but has never been interested in pottery or dishware of any kind." Archie chuckled. "In fact, all of my mates have ribbed me a bit about working in a tearoom. But I quite enjoy my time here."

"And we're lucky to have you," Jan told him as Elaine nodded in agreement.

"Well, whoever sent this teapot has wonderful taste." Rose stood up and lifted the dainty lid off the teapot. "It's so pretty." Then her eyebrows arched in surprise as she stared into the teapot. "There's something strange inside."

CHAPTER TWO

Elaine watched as Rose reached inside the teapot and pulled out a folded sheet of brown paper.

"That paper looks old," Rose said, handing the paper to Jan. "So I'm guessing it's not care instructions for the teapot."

Silence descended on the kitchen as Jan slowly unfolded the crinkled brown paper.

"It's a map," Jan said, setting the paper on the table.

Elaine released a breath she didn't know she'd been holding. "What in the world is a map doing in a teapot?"

"Excellent question." Archie moved the map to the center of the table, his brow furrowed as he studied it. "It's hand-drawn, but the only geographic area identified is Chickadee Lake."

"You're right," Elaine said. It was like no map she'd ever seen before. A large lake was drawn in the middle, with the words *Chickadee Lake* written in the center. "Those stick-like drawings could be a wooded area."

Around the large, shaded lake in the center of the map were several curved lines, some of them leading off the edge of the paper. Elaine couldn't tell if they represented roads or trails.

There were also some quarter-inch squares drawn in different places on the map, and three triangles, two of them shaded.

The map was about ten inches square and drawn with a thick black ink. But the strangest thing about it was the series of numbers, letters, and symbols that were written on the map in a way that made no sense.

Elaine studied the map for a long moment, then noticed a familiar odor. She lifted the map to her nose and sniffed. "It smells like tea."

"Tea?" Jan echoed.

"I think someone stained the paper with tea," Elaine explained, "to make it look old."

"Must be the same person who wrote gibberish on it," Archie said.

Rose reached into the teapot. "There's something else in here." Then she pulled out a scrap of paper and handed it to Jan.

Elaine saw Jan's eyes widen when she opened the note.

"It's a poem," Jan said, then began to read it out loud.

> *"Two ladies serve tea and more,*
> *In a house built by a shore.*
> *A secret treasure is buried there,*
> *And you might find it, if you dare."*

Elaine stared at her cousin. "Is this supposed to be a treasure map?"

"That, or it's some kind of joke," Jan said, shaking her head. "I can't make heads or tails of it."

Neither could Elaine. But as the four of them sat at the table staring at the map, a sizzle of excitement shot through her. There were few things she liked better than a mystery—and this one was a doozy.

She took a bite of her lemon meringue cookie and chewed thoughtfully. She almost hoped it wasn't a joke so they could decipher the map and see where it led.

The four of them spent the next half hour chatting about the map, the poem, and the teapot as they finished their cookies and tea.

Then Elaine reached for the mystery teapot, a new possibility occurring to her. They did have tourists come through all the time and many of them remarked on Jan and Elaine's collection of teapots on display. "You know, this could be from someone who spent time vacationing here—a fellow tea lover. We did have a lady send us some tea leaves from India once. Remember that, Jan?"

"Yes. It was a sweet gesture." Jan smiled. "And she signed the note with only her first name: Mary. Neither one of us could quite place her."

Archie rubbed his chin. "But fellow tea lovers usually don't include a treasure map and verse in their gifts, do they?"

Jan laughed. "No, this is definitely a first. But I *am* intrigued by it."

"Me too," Elaine admitted, meeting Jan's gaze.

Rose walked over to the door and pulled on her jacket, her blue eyes gleaming with amusement. "Well, I wish whoever sent that teapot had signed their name to the note. We may never know who it's from."

"Don't be so sure," Archie said, following Rose to the door. "Something tells me that these two will try to solve this newest mystery."

Elaine laughed. "You know us too well."

After Rose and Archie left, Elaine got out her cell phone and snapped a picture of the map. "I'm going to send this picture to Jared. He used to enjoy cartography when he was a teen, so maybe he can figure out what the numbers, letters, and symbols mean."

"Good idea," Jan said, carrying the dishes over to the sink. "I was always surprised that was one of your son's hobbies. Most teens are into music or video games at that age."

Elaine chuckled as she slipped her cell phone into her pocket. "Oh, he loved those too. But with Ben's army career, we moved around a lot." She breathed a wistful sigh, remembering Jared and his father huddled together over a map at the kitchen table. "Jared began collecting maps of each country we lived in, so a hobby was born."

The memory made her smile as she began gathering up the scraps of packaging paper that had filled the box. Then part of a newspaper headline caught her eye. "Montana."

Jan stopped what she was doing and stared at her. "What did you say?"

Elaine dropped the pile of bubble wrap and crumpled newspaper scraps back on the table. Then she pulled one of the newspaper scraps from the pile. "I can see part of a headline on this newspaper scrap. It reads: 'Montana Wildlife Advocates...'" Her voice trailed off as she held up the scrap to show Jan. "It's torn here, so I can't see the rest. But this is from a

Montana newspaper—so how did it end up in a package from New York?"

"This just got even more interesting," Jan said, her face lighting up. She scanned the table. "There are lots of newspaper scraps here. It will take some time, but we might be able to put the scraps together like a puzzle and figure out where they're all from." Then she frowned. "Only they're so crinkled, they're almost unreadable."

"I have a solution for that." Elaine said with a smile, a plan forming in her mind. "Let's finish cleaning the tearoom. Then you can warm up that leftover clam chowder in the fridge for dinner." She held up the crinkled scrap of newspaper in her hand. "While I do some 'ironing.'"

LATER THAT EVENING, Elaine stood at the ironing board in the second-floor sewing room and carefully pressed the iron down. She'd sandwiched one of the pieces of newspaper between two tea towels to keep the ink from transferring to the ironing board or to the iron itself. The towels also protected the newspaper from burning.

After a few moments, Elaine set the iron down and then lifted the tea towel to reveal the flat newspaper fragment underneath. Elaine picked it up and placed it carefully with the other newly ironed pieces, then she reached for another crinkled scrap from the box beside her.

It was a tedious process, but Elaine smiled to herself as she picked up the iron once more, remembering how she used to starch and iron Ben's shirts for his military uniforms. She'd listen to a book on tape while she worked, making it an enjoyable task. And her husband had been so proud of the way she'd made his shirts so crisp and neat.

They'd shared three decades together before Ben's death. The deep ache of losing him had started to ease, soothed by so many wonderful memories. And she knew the best way to honor him going forward was to live her life to the fullest.

By the time Elaine finished ironing all the newspaper scraps and headed down to kitchen, Jan was setting the table for supper.

"The soup smells wonderful," Elaine said, her gaze moving to the soup pot on the stove. A delicate curl of steam rose from it, filling the air with a savory scent.

"You've got perfect timing." Jan ladled the soup into two bowls and then carried them over to the table. "Just let me get the butter for the rolls and we'll be ready to eat."

Elaine placed the box on one end of the table, then took a seat. She noticed Earl Grey's food bowl sitting on the counter near the sink. "Have you fed Earl Grey already?"

"Not yet." Jan carried the butter dish to the table and sat down. "I put together a safe, cat version of clam chowder—with just a tiny bit of cream and a few chopped clams. I thought he'd enjoy the treat, but it needs to cool a bit."

"He'll love it," Elaine agreed.

After they said grace, they began to eat. Elaine thought the clam chowder Jan had made yesterday was even better today. As she reached for a warm dinner roll, she said, "I can't wait to start putting the newspaper pieces together."

"Why wait?" Jan said, reaching for the box. "We can do it while we eat."

Elaine watched as Jan began laying out the newspaper pieces on the table between them. "We might as well get started now. It's going to take some time to match all of them."

Jan smiled. "I should have invited Avery and Kelly over to help," she said, referring to her granddaughters. "They love to put puzzles together."

"We may have to call them if we run into trouble," Elaine teased, her gaze scanning the newspapers. "There at least four different languages among them. Let's start by sorting them into language groups and go from there."

Jan set down her spoon. "Good idea."

They ate as they worked, moving the newspaper scraps over the table as they matched the languages. Elaine hoped they might be able to glean some clues from the fact that the newspapers had come from more than one country.

"You know," Elaine mused out loud, "we might be able to figure out the time span of the articles too—if there are articles about current events."

"You mean, like an earthquake in Peru would tell us the newspaper was from a month ago?"

Elaine nodded, finishing the last of her soup. She was eager to get started putting the scraps together. "Exactly. I'm not sure yet how that will help, but the more information we have, the better."

Jan stood up. "I'll wash the dishes, then we can start matching the pieces and taping them together."

Elaine nodded. "And I'll go feed Earl Grey. His chowder should be cool enough by now." She followed Jan to the sink and placed her supper dishes on the counter, then picked up the cat's food bowl and headed for the screened porch behind the kitchen.

Earl Grey sat waiting for her, his gray tail flicking impatiently behind him as Elaine closed the kitchen door. "Time for supper!"

She set the food bowl down. He hurried over to it and eagerly licked up the creamy chowder. Elaine walked over to the screen door at the back of the house and stepped onto the deck. Stars twinkled in the night sky and she could see the tree branches in the yard swaying slightly in the breeze.

She rubbed her hands over her arms, the cool breeze making her wish she'd grabbed a sweater before stepping outside. But she relished the fresh air, carrying the earthy scent of a spring thaw, and the sound of a loon calling in the distance. There might still be some chunks of ice left on the lake, but spring had officially arrived.

By the time she walked back inside the porch, Earl Grey had licked his food bowl clean and was purring contentedly on his cushion.

"You look happy," she told him, leaning down to scoop him into her arms.

The gray cat snuggled against her, rubbing the top of his head under her chin. Elaine spent a few moments softly stroking his silky fur and scratching gently behind his ears. Then she set him back on his cushion, where he promptly curled into a furry ball and closed his eyes for a nap.

She chuckled. "Sweet dreams, Earl Grey."

When Elaine walked back into the kitchen, she saw Jan had already finished the dishes and was sitting at the table, moving newspaper pieces around. She'd retrieved the tape dispenser from Elaine's office and was now taping two newspaper scraps together.

"I found a match," Jan exclaimed as her blue eyes scanned the other torn pieces of newspaper in front of her. "It's from that Montana paper."

Elaine hurried over to the table. Jan had taped three newspaper scraps together to reveal the article and full headline of the piece Elaine had found earlier.

"Montana Wildlife Group Files Suit to Protect Buffalo," Elaine said, reading the headline out loud. Then she silently scanned the article until she found a date. "This says that the wildlife group filed the suit six months after forming—and they formed in July of 2009."

"So this piece of newspaper is over eight years old?" Jan shook her head. "We save old newspapers, but not for that long. Could this be from a hoarder?"

"Someone who hoards newspapers anyway," Elaine said, moving the freshly pressed newspaper scraps around like puzzle pieces. Then she thought about that poem, the lines fresh in her memory.

Two ladies serve tea and more,
In a house built by a shore.
A secret treasure is buried there,
And you might find it, if you dare.

"You know, Jan, whoever sent us this teapot with the map and the poem inside wants us to find the treasure. But is it a treasure *they* buried or something that's been here for years?"

"That's a good question." Jan looked up at her. "And if they want us to find the treasure, why bury it? Why not just tell us where it is?"

Elaine stared down at the scraps of newspaper. "Maybe because it's a game, and they want us to play. I'm just wondering what kind of treasure we'll find." She looked up at her cousin. "*If* we find it."

"Oh, we'll find it," Jan assured her.

Elaine smiled. But would the newspaper scraps reveal anything helpful? *The only way to find out is to keep working at it,* Elaine told herself, reaching for the nearest scrap. Then she settled in for a long night of putting the pieces together.

ON WEDNESDAY, ELAINE hid a yawn behind her hand as she walked into the tearoom. She and Jan had stayed up late into the night matching the newspaper scraps and taping them together. Unfortunately, they hadn't discovered much more than when they started.

At the moment, she needed to get herself together and focus on the tearoom. She smiled as she approached a petite woman in her early sixties seated alone at a table. "Good afternoon," Elaine said. "Welcome to Tea for Two."

"Thank you, I'm happy to be here," the woman replied, her hazel eyes twinkling. Her shoulder-length blonde hair was curled in the back and artfully feathered over her temples in the front. Fit and attractive, she wore a blue chiffon blouse, a solitaire diamond necklace, and a long black skirt that looked more appropriate for a wedding than a tearoom. Her fingernails were perfectly polished and a large opal-and-diamond ring adorned her right hand.

"I was actually here yesterday," the woman told her. "And just fell in love with the place. I saw you working in the other parlor and my server, Rose, told me you're one of the owners."

"Yes, I am," Elaine said with a smile. "My cousin, Jan, and I own and operate Tea for Two."

"Well, it's just lovely," the woman exclaimed, taking a slow look around the room. Then she turned her attention back to Elaine. "My name is Astrid Shayne and I'm staying at one of the lake cottages."

"It's very nice to meet you. I'm Elaine Cook. And I hope you'll visit here often during your stay."

"Oh, I plan to," Astrid said. "Especially if you keep serving those luscious maple croissants. I've never had anything quite like them."

"They're a favorite around here. Would like to order one?"

"I'd much rather order two." Astrid's breathy laugh reminded Elaine of Marilyn Monroe. "Along with a cup of sweet tea please."

Elaine smiled. "Coming right up."

As she made her way out of the tearoom, Elaine smiled at sisters Elsa and Rachel Leon, and then gave a wave to newspaper reporter Candace Huang. She also recognized a few of the same tourists she'd seen yesterday.

"It looks like Macy is driving a lot of business our way," Elaine said as she entered the kitchen. "I think those antique club members are making Tea for Two a daily stop on their antiquing excursions."

Jan stood at the sink, hand-washing some delicate china teacups. "I'm glad to hear it," she said, rinsing a cup under the tap. "I heard about two of the club members yesterday as well, Jerry and Lawrence. Both men are retired, although Jerry said he keeps busy with some real estate investments."

They chatted about some of their other customers as Elaine prepared a pot of sweet tea for Astrid, then plated two maple croissants. A few minutes later, she carried the tray out to the tearoom.

When she turned the corner into the parlor she was surprised to see a man sitting at Astrid's table. He appeared to be about fifteen years younger than Astrid and had a deep tan that told Elaine he'd been traveling in a warmer climate recently—or making good use of a tanning bed. He wore a khaki shirt and jacket, along with a pair of blue jeans and hiking boots.

"Here we are," Elaine said, setting the tray on the table. She poured a cup of tea for Astrid, then placed the teapot on the table, along with the plate of croissants.

"Elaine, this is David," Astrid said. "He's staying at Green Glade too. In fact, he has the cottage right next to mine."

"That's right," David agreed, a boyish grin on his face. "We met last night when Astrid caught me after I climbed up her porch rafters. I'm lucky she didn't have me arrested."

Astrid giggled and blushed. "I knew you weren't a burglar. You don't look the part." Then she looked up at Elaine. "I'm an actress and an excellent judge of character."

"Oh," Elaine said, intrigued, "what kind of acting do you do?"

"Stage, mostly," Astrid said, "though lately I've done some voice work. That's more challenging than it sounds."

"Well, you do have a great scream," David told Astrid. "I almost fell off the roof when I heard it."

"I only screamed because I caught you sneaking around on my roof," Astrid said, her eyes shining with amusement.

While Elaine enjoyed watching the banter between them, she couldn't help but interject. "What were you doing on the roof?"

David smiled. "Trying to get a shot of a black-throated blue warbler. Astrid's scream scared it away though." He glanced over at the older woman. "Not that I blame you, Astrid."

"Of course you don't," Astrid said, reaching over to pat his hand. "And that bird might just like my roof enough to come back. I'll keep an eye out for it."

Elaine smiled at David. "You must be the ornithologist. I heard one was staying at Green Glade."

"Guilty as charged," he said, reaching out to shake her hand. "Dr. David Zabel. I also sell some of my bird photographs to nature magazines. I've traveled here hoping to capture some photographs of a gyrfalcon, golden eagle, or a black-headed gull. Or better yet, all three if I'm lucky."

"Well, you've come to the right place," Elaine said with a smile. "We've got lovely birds here year round—and even more in the summer."

"I've convinced David to have a cup of tea with me," Astrid told her, "but he wants to be on his way soon. We were wondering if he could take some of those delicious maple croissants to go?"

"Of course," Elaine said cheerfully. "We can box them up. We also have chocolate chip oatmeal cookies as our cookie of the day, along with some almond biscotti and sliced banana nut bread if you're interested," she told David. "They all travel well."

"I'll take two of each," David told her, "since I plan to be out on the trails most of the day."

"Let me get you a cup for your tea," Elaine told him, "and then I'll box up your pastries."

As she left to fill his order, Elaine stopped at Emmaline Cribbs's table to pick up her empty teapot, promising a refill, then headed into the kitchen, where Jan was transferring a fresh batch of cookies from a baking sheet to the cooling rack.

"Do you have time to refill this pot with sweet tea and take it to Emmaline's table?" she asked Jan. "I need to make up an order to go for one of Macy's cottage guests."

"Of course," Jan said with a smile. "I'm almost finished here."

While Jan brewed another pot of tea, Elaine retrieved one of the boxes they used to package leftovers for their customers. They stored them flat, so she took a moment to bend and fold it into shape, then walked over to the counter and began filling it with David's order.

"All done," Jan said, placing the teapot on the tray and then carrying it out to the tearoom.

"Thank you," Elaine called after her, before taking a quick inventory of the box. "Okay, I have the two maple croissants, two chocolate chip oatmeal cookies, and two almond biscotti." She looked at the counter. "All I'm missing is the banana nut bread."

When she didn't seen any banana nut bread on the counter, she headed for the pantry, where they stored quick bread and pastries overnight in sealed containers. After scanning the shelves, she still didn't see any banana nut bread and realized they must be sold out.

Then her gaze landed on a plastic tub full of scones at the back of a shelf. She reached out and picked up the tub, wondering why no one had told her about the scones.

Elaine carried the tub out to the kitchen island and peeled off the lid. She couldn't name the flavor just by looking at them, so she picked up a scone and gave it a sniff. It was the color of oatmeal, but she couldn't smell cinnamon or any other spices. However, the texture was perfect and they looked fresh. Then she took a bite just as Jan walked back into the kitchen.

"Oh no!" Jan cried, her eyes wide with horror. "Don't eat that!"

CHAPTER THREE

Startled by Jan's outcry, Elaine gasped and inhaled some scone crumbs into her windpipe. Choking, she began to cough and hurried over to the sink. She reached for a glass on the drying rack, still fighting for air.

"Elaine, are you all right?" Jan said, hurrying to her side and patting her between the shoulder blades. "Should I do the Heimlich?"

Elaine managed to shake her head in a silent no. Then she filled the glass with water and took a big gulp. The water washed down the remaining scone crumbs in her throat and she was able to breathe easier.

"I'm all right," Elaine croaked, her throat still dry and tight. She'd swallowed food down the wrong windpipe more than once in her fifty-five years and knew the discomfort would pass soon. She just needed to give it time.

"I'm sorry I shouted at you like that," Jan told her. "I just never meant for anyone to eat those scones."

Elaine took another long swallow of water, thinking the worst. "Please tell me I didn't just bite into a scone meant for Earl Grey?"

Jan blinked, and then chuckled. "No, those weren't cat scones! I promise."

"Good." Elaine managed a smile. "You had me worried there for a minute." Then she tilted her head as she looked at her cousin. "So why didn't you want me to eat it?"

Jan hesitated as she nibbled her lower lip. Finally she said, "I've been keeping a secret from you."

Intrigued, Elaine forgot about almost choking. "A secret? What is it?"

Jan took a deep breath and then met Elaine's gaze. "I entered a baking contest."

From the pained expression on Jan's face, Elaine had expected something much worse. Her relief made her laugh. "A baking contest? But why keep that a secret—especially from me?"

Jan shrugged. "Because I wasn't sure I'd make the cut for the contest and didn't want to disappoint you. It would be such good PR, after all." She pointed to the scones. "I made these a few nights ago, after you'd gone to bed. I thought it would be good practice for the contest, just in case, but instead it turned out to be a waste of good flour."

"The scone wasn't *that* bad," Elaine said. "It just tasted a little...soapy. But not horrible for a practice round."

Jan smiled. "Soapy wasn't the flavor I was going for, but thank you for being so nice about it. I tried to make honey lavender scones but must have used too much lavender. That's why it tasted soapy."

"So you just need to use a little less lavender the next time," Elaine said. "That sounds like an easy fix."

"There won't be a next time," Jan said evenly. "The contest is only accepting three entrants and since I haven't heard back from them, I'm assuming I'm not one of the three."

Elaine could see the disappointment reflected in Jan's eyes. "Only three?"

"Yes, it's going to be televised, so they're limiting the number of contestants. It's sponsored by a local morning show in Portland," Jan admitted. "They'll tape the two-hour baking contest there, then show parts of it each day during the following week." She rolled her eyes. "I must have been crazy to think of doing something like that."

"You still might get in," Elaine said, wanting to encourage her. "They haven't sent you a rejection letter, have they?"

"No, but it was stated on the application that they would only contact the applicants chosen for the contest. So in this case, no news *is* bad news." Then she brightened. "Or maybe it's good news, considering my soapy scone almost killed you."

Elaine laughed, then wrapped one arm around Jan's shoulders for a quick hug. "It didn't almost kill me, but why did you try to invent a new scone recipe? Our guests love your raspberry scones. And your pumpkin raisin scones are a big hit too."

"This baking contest is only open to pastry chefs working at local Maine restaurants and eateries," Jan explained, "so I'd be competing against the best of the best. I didn't think I could win with my old standbys."

Elaine placed her drinking glass on the counter, her throat feeling a little better now. "You may be overthinking this, Jan. Simple and classic flavors are a favorite for a reason. And I believe you're giving up on the contest too soon. Your acceptance letter could be on its way right now. So I'll be happy to taste-test any other practice pastries you make."

Jan laughed as she walked over to the counter and began transferring the cookies from the cooling rack into a plastic tub. "There's no need. If I haven't received an acceptance letter by now, I'm never getting into the contest."

"Nana always told us *Never say never.*"

Amusement gleamed in Jan's eyes. "When we were little, that was usually in response to you announcing that you were *never* going to bed."

"Maybe so," Elaine chuckled. "But it still applies." She turned her attention back to the take-out box. "I need to get this out to Dr. Zabel. He's waited long enough."

"Here, let me do it," Jan said, taking the box from her. "You can rest a bit more and finish your water."

Since Elaine still wasn't feeling one hundred percent, she decided not to argue. "Okay, I will. But we need to add two more pastries to the box. I promised Dr. Zabel some banana nut bread, but I couldn't find any in the pantry."

"Yes, we just ran out," Jan told her. "Bill Bridges stopped at the back door earlier," she said, referring to the local contractor who had worked on their house, "and bought the rest of the loaf. He's got a job in Augusta today and wanted to sneak in for a snack to eat on the drive."

"Well, half a loaf of that bread should fill him up." Elaine looked over the rest of the pastries on the counter. "So what should we substitute? Dr. Zabel is going to be out bird-watching all day, so nothing perishable."

"How about hazelnut shortbread?" Jan suggested, carrying the box over to the counter. "It travels well."

"Perfect." Elaine took a seat at the small kitchen table as Jan placed the shortbread in the box. It felt good to take a break.

"Now describe this guy to me," Jan said. "And tell me what table he's at."

"He's wearing a khaki shirt and jacket, and jeans. And he's sitting with a platinum blonde in her sixties, dressed to kill. Her name is Astrid and you can't miss her."

"Got it." Jan folded the lid of the box, and then tucked it securely in place.

"Thanks, Jan. I'll be out there soon," Elaine promised.

"Take your time," Jan said, giving Elaine a wink as she left the kitchen.

WHEN JAN WALKED into the tearoom, she was happy to see that all of their customers seemed content. A light, cheerful chatter filled the air and the clinking of spoons in teacups was music to her ears.

She spotted the platinum blonde right away and was surprised to see *two* men sitting at her table. One fit the description Elaine had given her of the ornithologist. The other man was about Astrid's age, early sixties or perhaps a few years older. He had a short, slight build but looked quite dapper with his neatly combed silver hair and perfectly trimmed silver mustache. He wore a white dress shirt under a gray cashmere sweater vest, along with a pair of black slacks.

"Sorry it took so long," Jan said when she reached their table. She set the take-out box in front of the younger man. "You must be Dr. Zabel."

"Yes," he replied, "but please call me David."

Jan smiled. "I hope you enjoy your pastries, David."

"Thank you," he said with a nod. "I'm sure I will."

"And you must be Jan Blake!" Astrid exclaimed, beaming at her. "Macy told me all about you and the wonderful pastries you make."

Jan doubted Macy had used such a glowing term, but she was charmed by Astrid's sunny disposition. "Yes, I'm Jan," she said. "It's nice to meet you."

"Nice to meet you too." Then she turned to the gentleman beside her. "And this is Lawrence Peacock. He's a dear friend of mine."

"Hello," Jan, smiling at Lawrence. "Are you an antique collector too?"

Lawrence considered her question for a long moment. "I guess you could call me that." Then he glanced over at Astrid. "It appears our reputation precedes us."

"I blame Millie for that," Astrid said, with a mischievous smile. "She's such a blabbermouth."

Lawrence's brow furrowed. "Millie is a very private person, Astrid. I don't believe blabbermouth is an accurate description of her."

"Oh, Lawrence," Astrid said, rolling her eyes. "You *must* know I was joking."

"Oh." His brow cleared. "Yes, of course."

Astrid's gaze moved back to Jan. "Millie is another member of our club, but she likes to keep to herself. We're sharing a cabin together at Green Glade, but I've hardly seen her. She's always off on a long walk somewhere."

Dr. Zabel rose to his feet. "And I should follow her lead if I want to get any work done today." He reached for his billfold, but Astrid held up her hands to stop him.

"It's my treat today, David," she said. "You've been such lovely company."

He nodded his thanks. "I never argue with a beautiful woman. I hope I can return the favor soon, Astrid. You have a nice day."

"You too," she chirped, waving to him as he left the tearoom. Then she turned to Lawrence. "You simply must try some of this tea. It's just divine."

Lawrence looked up at Jan. "I'll have a cup of strong black tea please."

"And bring him a couple of those yummy maple croissants," Astrid added.

Lawrence gave a small shrug of his shoulders. "Yes, very well. And put my order on a separate check please."

"Coming right up," Jan told him, inwardly amused at the dynamics between Astrid and Lawrence. Their personalities were so different from each other.

She stopped to chat with some of the other customers along her way back to the kitchen. Macy was just finishing the last of her tea as Jan approached her table.

"How was everything today, Macy?"

Macy put down her cup. "Just fine. Although I wish you'd use a lighter hand with the cinnamon. A little goes a very long way in some of these pastries. And the chocolate oatmeal cookies were quite chewy. Too much brown sugar, perhaps?"

Jan smiled, quite used to Macy's critiques. "I appreciate your input," she said, also used to taking Macy's opinions with a grain of salt.

But listening to her now, Jan decided that maybe it was a good thing she *hadn't* been accepted into that baking contest. It would be televised, after all, and the judges might be a lot harsher than Macy in their critiques. She certainly didn't want to risk humiliating herself—or worse, giving Tea for Two a bad name due to her poor performance.

"Well, the good news is that my guests seem to really enjoy your tearoom," Macy told her. "I've let them gather in my clubhouse for their little meetings, and I've heard them mention this place once or twice. Given the age of this house, though, it's not surprising that it intrigues them. They apparently like old things."

Jan smiled at Macy's description of their Victorian home. She and Elaine had worked long hours to fully restore this lovely house. And she loved every inch of it. "We're very happy to have them here," she said, picking up the empty teapot before heading back to the kitchen.

"How's it going out there?" Elaine asked as she placed a teakettle on the stove.

"Just fine," Jan said, setting the teapot on the counter. "I need a pot of strong black tea for Astrid's table, where another man has now joined her. They're both members of that antique club."

"I can make it," Elaine offered, walking over to retrieve a tea canister. "Since Rose is coming in this afternoon, I might drive over to the Richardsons' dairy. We're a little short on cream and honey."

"Sounds good." Jan chose a Dresden-style china dessert plate and placed two maple croissants on it, then used a clean dishcloth to wipe away a few stray crumbs on the rim. She placed the dessert plate on a tray, and a few minutes later added the pot of black tea that Elaine had just brewed.

"Thanks a bunch," Jan told her cousin.

"You're welcome." Elaine added a small pot of honey to the tray. "Say, when does Bob get back from his trip?"

"Tomorrow night." She'd been dating Bob Claybrook for a few months now and really enjoyed his company. He'd been gone for the past week on another business trip to Baltimore—he'd gone there about a month ago as well—so she was anxious to see him again.

"I think I just heard the mail truck," Elaine said, picking up the tray. "I'll let you go out and get your contest letter while I take this out to Astrid's table."

"I didn't make the cut," Jan called after her, laughing at how stubborn Elaine could be sometimes.

But as she moved toward the back door, her heart gave a little leap. "Don't get your hopes up," she warned herself as she made her way outside to greet Orin for the second day in a row.

And for the second day in a row, she came away disappointed.

THAT EVENING, JAN sat with Elaine at the small game table in the upstairs sitting room. They'd purchased a rosewood antique table and four matching chairs at an estate auction last week, thrilled that it matched the small rosewood desk that Jan had brought from her previous home.

They'd attended the estate sale with Nathan Culver and Bob Claybrook, who had helped them carry the set upstairs and place it in the perfect spot, next to the west window.

At the moment, the table was covered with the newspaper scraps they'd taped together last night.

"Here are the clues we have so far," Elaine said, sitting across from Jan with a notebook open in front of her. "All of the articles seem to be no older than 2009, and most of them are from the last year."

Jan nodded, looking over the columns in front of her. "We've got newspapers in four different languages. One newspaper in Portuguese, so it's most likely from Portugal or Brazil. One article is in French, but it's the official language in more than twenty-five countries."

"So the article could be from anywhere: France, Canada, or even someplace like Madagascar." Elaine sighed. "Or from countries in three other continents."

"I'm afraid so. And the translation program I used online didn't help me pinpoint the location." Jan shifted in her chair. "As for the rest of these articles, they're all in English, specifically from newspapers in Montana and New England."

"And two of them have *New York Times* printed at the top, so we identified the origin of those articles."

"But the *New York Times* is sold all over the place," Jan said, "so even that doesn't tell us much."

Elaine set down her pen. "Let's face it, Jan. We're no closer to finding out who sent us that mystery teapot than we were before. The newspaper scraps are a dead end."

Jan had to admit she was right. She loved puzzles, but this was one was frustrating. And she worried they might never solve it. Then another thought occurred to her. "Maybe we're investigating the wrong thing."

Elaine arched a brow. "Go on."

"We've been focused on the newspaper scraps to help us figure out who sent the teapot. What if we turn our attention to the teapot instead? The design is somewhat unusual. I've never seen it before."

"Neither have I. It's beautiful, but frankly, it was the map and the poem that caught my interest."

The doorbell rang before Jan could reply. "Hold that thought," she said, then headed for the stairs. When she reached the front door, she was surprised—and delighted—to see Bob standing on the other side.

He smiled. "Surprise!"

"Bob, you're back!" She reached out to give him a hug, pressing her cheek against the front of his black overcoat. "This is such a great surprise." Then took a step back and looked up at him. "I wasn't expecting you until tomorrow."

"I finished my business early," he said, "so I decided to head home. I thought we might have dinner together."

"Oh," she said, feeling disappointed, "Elaine and I already had an early dinner. But I'm happy to join you if you want some company." Then she had another idea. "Or you can have leftovers here. How does roast beef sound, with a side of potatoes and carrots?"

"Perfect," he said with a smile. "Shall we take a walk by the lake first? It's a beautiful evening. No wind, and just a slight chill in the air."

"I'd love to," Jan told him. "Just give me a minute to tell Elaine and grab my coat."

Bob waited for her in the front entrance hall as Jan hurried to the kitchen for her coat. She found Elaine there, studying the bottom of the teapot.

"It's a Lefton, and it's definitely vintage," Elaine told her, jotting notes in her notebook. Then she looked up at Jan. "Who was at the door?"

"Bob," Jan said, smiling. "He came home from his trip a day early. I invited him in for leftovers, but we're going to walk along the lake first if you'd like to join us."

"Thanks," Elaine said, her gaze still perusing the teapot, "but I want to do some computer research on this brand and see what I can find out. You two go ahead and have fun."

"Okay, we'll see you soon." Jan slipped her coat on as she walked out of the kitchen and met Bob in the entrance hall. "I'm ready."

He opened the front door for her and they both stepped outside. Then they headed for the wooded trail near the lake, which wouldn't take them too far from the house.

"It's not bad out here," Jan said, zipping up her coat, "although there's definitely a nip in the air."

The sun hovered on the horizon in the west, casting a glow on the low-hanging clouds. She loved taking walks during twilight, enjoying the sound of leaves and twigs snapping under her shoes and the shadows growing longer along the trail.

"So tell me about your trip," Jan said as Bob walked beside her, matching her shorter strides.

"It was productive, but I'm glad I finished early. I prefer my own home to a hotel room."

"I know you what mean, although it's fun to see new places." She hooked her arm through his. "Did you do anything fun while you were there?"

He smiled at her. "I watched a basketball game at a sports cafe one night." He hesitated, his smile fading. "And, well...I was offered a job there."

Jan's heart sank. "In Baltimore?"

He nodded, a look of wonder on his face. "They offered me a partnership at a very well-respected law firm." Bob chuckled. "Can you believe it?"

She could see he was not only flattered but also surprised by the job offer, but Jan wasn't surprised at all. Bob was still in his prime and one of the smartest men she knew. Any law firm would be lucky to have him. But the thought of him leaving Lancaster—and leaving her—made Jan's throat tighten.

"I don't know if I'll take it," he continued. "Although..." His voice trailed off, and then he smiled at her. "Let's save that conversation for another day."

Jan looked up at him. "But if you're planning to move to Baltimore..."

"I'm not planning to move anywhere," he said, meeting her gaze. "Not right now. I just want to enjoy this walk with you."

Jan smiled, telling herself she'd overreacted. "Well, then you might want to know you missed some excitement here."

He arched a dark eyebrow, looking grateful for the change of subject. "I did?"

She smiled up at him. "Someone sent us a strange package." Then she told him about receiving the teapot with the map and poem inside.

"Any ideas who might have sent it?" he asked as they walked.

"None yet," she replied, then told him about the steps she and Elaine had taken so far to investigate it.

He chuckled, shaking his head. "Well, if anyone can figure out this mystery, it's you and Elaine. But surely there's a reasonable explanation."

"And we're going to find it," Jan said, then laughed as a white-tailed rabbit bounded out of a bush and on to the trail in front of them before disappearing into the brush on the other side. As the trail curved toward the lake, Jan could see the many cracks already splitting the remaining islands of ice floating atop the lake.

"Looks like the ice will be gone soon," Bob said as they moved toward the shore.

Jan noted a hole in the ice a few yards from shore where locals had fished during the winter. Then she saw a woman sitting on a bench near the lake.

"Who is that?" Jan whispered to Bob.

His gaze narrowed on the woman. "I'm not sure. But she seems to be crying."

CHAPTER FOUR

As they moved closer to the woman, Jan could see that Bob was right: she *was* crying.

Her heart went out to the woman, who appeared to be in her mid sixties and wore a drab brown coat, beige slacks, and a pair of sensible brown shoes. She sat alone on the bench, shivering slightly as tears trickled down her cheeks.

Jan glanced up at Bob. "Should we?" she whispered.

He gave an affirmative nod and then they both walked up to the woman together.

"Are you all right?" Jan asked gently.

The woman looked up in surprise, dabbing a tissue at her red nose, as if she hadn't heard them approach. She had short-cropped black hair that curled slightly at her neck and temples. Tears shimmered in her big brown eyes behind a pair of black horned-rimmed glasses. Jan was certain her Grandpa Willard had owned a pair just like them.

"Oh yes, I'm fine," the woman said, then cleared her throat. "Thank you for asking."

"We apologize for intruding," Bob told her. "We saw you were upset and wondered if you needed any help."

In a flash, the woman dropped the tissue in her purse and rapidly blinked away her tears. "No, I'm fine. I had a weak moment," she told them, straightening her shoulders. "It happens, but, fortunately, they are few and far between. Thank you for your concern."

Her words sounded harsher than her tone. Jan could still hear a bit of a wobble in her voice, so she wasn't ready to walk away just yet.

Instead, Jan took a small step toward her. "I'm Jan Blake," she said warmly, "and this is Bob Claybrook. We're just out taking a walk. The lake is lovely this time of day."

"It is," the woman said, her expression softening a bit. "I'm Millie Cavett."

"Oh," Jan said, recognizing the name, "I believe I met your roommate at our tearoom today. Her name was Astrid."

"Yes," Millie interjected, a note of weariness in her voice "We're sharing a cabin. She's a very…exuberant woman."

Jan smiled. "I could tell. So you two must belong to the same club?"

"Yes, we do. How did you know?"

"Macy Atherton, the owner of Green Glade cottages, mentioned it," Jan replied. "I'm sure she told you that we have some wonderful antique shops in the area."

Millie nodded. "Yes, you do. In fact, today I found a lovely collector's edition book at a shop in Lancaster. The shop was called Oldies…something."

"Oldies But Goodies," Jan said with a smile, still wondering why Millie had been crying alone on the bench.

Jan and Bob might have moved on, but Jan sensed that Millie was enjoying their conversation. "Yes, Oldies But Goodies is a local favorite. What book did you find?"

Millie reached into her tote bag and pulled out a brown leather-bound book with gold accents, handling it like it was one of the most precious things she owned. "*Jane Eyre.* I was reading it right before you two got here. In fact, I'd just gotten to the part where Jane learns that Mr. Rochester, her one true love, has been lying to her."

Millie paused a moment, placing her hand to her chest. "To be honest, I love to read classic romances. They're so…enthralling." She said the last word with a catch in her throat and, for a moment, Jan thought Millie might start crying again.

Jan smiled, realizing that Millie had a tender heart. "Charlotte Bronte is one of my favorite authors," she confessed. "Do you collect a lot of books?"

"Oh yes, whenever and wherever I can." Millie gently placed the book back in her bag, then looked up at them. "Thank you for stopping to check on me. I don't want to keep you from your walk." She stood up and shivered. "And I best be on my way. It will be dark soon."

"It was very nice to meet you," Bob said, extending his hand.

Millie shook hands with Bob. "Nice to meet both of you." Then she shook hands with Jan before walking away.

Bob turned to Jan. "It is starting to get dark. Shall we head back to the house?"

"Yes," she said, curling one hand around his arm. "You're probably starving."

He chuckled. "I'm getting there."

An owl hooted in the distance as they turned around and started walking. The cold air made Jan pick up her pace, eager to enjoy a nice cup of hot tea in her warm kitchen.

"So what do you think about Millie's antique club?" Bob asked her as they moved along the trail. "Would you be interested in something like that when you retire?"

Jan considered the idea. "I love antiques, but they're a traveling club from what I understand, and while I enjoy traveling, I'm more of a homebody. I'd miss my family and friends too much if I was always on the road."

"Me too," Bob said, placing his hand on top of hers.

"I didn't notice Millie wearing a wedding ring," Jan said. "So perhaps she doesn't have those connections keeping her at home." She smiled up at Bob. "Or she's just got a travel bug. Elaine loved traveling around the world while Ben was in the military."

"Well, after just being away from home—and you—for the past week," he said, his voice low and tender, "I don't want to go anywhere."

Jan's heart warmed at his words and she sensed he was about to say more, but the moment soon passed and they began chatting about their favorite books until they reached the house.

ELAINE LOOKED UP as Jan and Bob walked into the kitchen. The savory aroma of roast beef filled the air. "Hello, you two," she said with a smile. "I've got dinner warming in the oven for Bob and a nice pot of hot tea ready to drink."

Jan chuckled as she removed her coat, her cheeks and nose pink from the cold. "You read our minds."

"Boy, that smells good," Bob said, peeling off his coat and gloves. "Thank you both for treating me to a home-cooked meal. This will be a nice change after eating in restaurants during my trip."

As Jan and Bob got settled at the kitchen table, Elaine opened the oven door and pulled out the roasting pan, then set it on top of the stove.

Steam escaped from the pan as she removed the lid, the juices bubbling on the bottom of the pan. She placed the roast beef on a serving platter, then spooned the carrots and potatoes around it before carrying it to the table.

"Dig in," she told Bob. Then she picked up the teapot and carried it to the table, where she'd already set two cups and saucers.

Elaine and Jan drank tea while Bob ate. He drained the glass of water Elaine had set on the table for him, then joined them in a cup of tea.

"So tell me more about this map," Bob said, after he'd finished his supper. "Jan told me a little about it on our walk and, I have to admit, I'm baffled as to why someone would put a map and a poem inside a teapot. Was it a prank of some kind?"

"We've considered that possibility," Elaine told him. "Although someone went to a lot of work for just an anonymous prank. I'll show you the map when you're done eating. I can't even begin to describe it accurately."

"What did you learn about the teapot itself?" Jan asked. "You mentioned that it was a Lefton."

Elaine set down her teacup. "Yes, and when I searched online, I learned that the Lefton China company formed in the early 1940s, so the teapot was made sometime after that." She got up from her chair and walked into her office to retrieve the map and the Lefton teapot.

"Here they are," she told Bob, setting them both in front of him on the table.

Bob pushed his empty plate aside and slid the map toward him. "It's hand-drawn. That's strange."

"Yes, we thought so too," Jan said. She leaned forward. "And look at the symbols. Those are not standard symbols you see on a map—so we're not sure what they mean."

He picked up the map and carefully turned it over. "It looks old—but it's not, is it?"

"No, we think someone just wanted to make it to look old by staining it with tea."

He chuckled. "Well, that's fitting." Then he read the poem out loud:

> *"Two ladies serve tea and more,*
> *In a house built by a shore.*
> *A secret treasure is buried there,*
> *And you might find it, if you dare."*

"Well," he said, setting the map on the table, "It sure looks as though someone is challenging you to a mystery. But it seems more playful than creepy." He looked between them. "It sounds like whoever sent it knows you two—and that you like to solve mysteries."

"Yes, it does," Jan agreed. "I've been racking my brain trying to figure out who it might be. But I'm stumped."

"So am I," Elaine agreed, settling into her chair. "And I can't help but wonder what kind of treasure is buried around here."

"And who buried it?" Jan added. "The same person who wrote the poem or someone else?"

"We need more information to answer that question," Elaine mused. "The map might help us answer that question, if we can figure out how to decipher it."

Bob's forehead furrowed as he studied the map. "Why does it have this mess of numbers and such in the first place? There doesn't seem to be any rhyme or reason to them."

Elaine smiled. "I think that's the point. Jan and I are supposed to solve the mystery of the map to find the treasure."

Jan nodded. "Yes, and that's why we decided to focus on the teapot, hoping it might give us some kind of clue." She turned to Elaine. "So we know the teapot could be about seventy-five years old. What else did you find out?"

"Nothing more yet," Elaine said with a sigh. "Nathan called shortly after you left on your walk, so my research was interrupted." Then she smiled, remembering how much she'd enjoyed her conversation with Nathan Culver, a childhood friend with whom she'd recently renewed a distinctly grownup relationship. Once they started talking, time always seemed to fly. "And then it was time to warm up the roast beef and vegetables. So I've got more research to do, but it will have to wait a bit."

"Well, there's no hurry," Jan said, "so I guess we can take our time."

Bob chuckled. "Somehow, I don't see you two taking a break from trying to solve this mystery."

Elaine laughed along with him. "You're right," she told Bob, exchanging an amused glance with her cousin. "And we *are* having fun, aren't we, Jan?"

Jan laughed. "We sure are. I just hope we don't come to a dead end."

"No chance of that, knowing you two." Bob stood up. "It's been a long day, so I'd better be getting home now. Thanks again for supper. It was delicious."

Jan rose from her chair. "I'll walk you out."

Elaine watched the two of them head toward the front door. Then she carried the dirty dishes over to the sink and set them inside. She began humming one of her favorite hymns, "In the Garden," as she filled the sink with hot water and added a generous squirt of dish soap.

A few minutes later, Jan walked back into the kitchen. "I can do those dishes," she said, pushing up the sleeves of her sweater.

Elaine stopped humming and turned to smile at her. "I've already got my hands wet," she said, plunging them into the foamy bubbles. "But you can wipe off the table and counters if you like."

Jan dipped a dishcloth into the soapy water, then gave it a squeeze. "Hearing that hymn makes me think about Easter. It's only a few weeks away."

"I know," Elaine said, washing the teacups first. "I can't wait. Will your kids be able to come over for Easter dinner?"

Jan wiped the dishcloth over the stovetop. "Yes, they're planning on it. Which means we'll need to plan an Easter egg hunt for the children in the afternoon." She smiled. "Maybe we can go shopping sometime soon to find treats for the baskets."

"I'd love that." Elaine put the roaster in the sink to soak, letting the other dishes air dry on the rack. "I also want to put some baskets together to mail for Lucy and Micah."

"So Jared and Corrie won't be able to make it for Easter?"

Elaine shook her head. "Not this year. They'll be spending it with Corrie's parents." She swallowed a sigh. "I'll miss them, of course. But since they spent Christmas here with us, I understand. Besides, we'll have a fun day with your grandkids here."

"Absolutely, and you know how much they love you."

"And I feel the same way about them." Elaine smiled as she dried her hands on a dish towel, then walked over to the table and picked up the map and teapot. "I'll put these back in the office. Then why don't we start putting together a menu for Easter dinner?"

"Great idea," Jan said, setting the wet dishcloth beside the sink. "Tara requested roast lamb with mint sauce, but I thought we might make two entrees." Jan's daughter loved mint sauce.

"Sounds good to me." Elaine made her way into the office. She set the teapot on her desk, then tucked the map into a bright-yellow folder before placing it inside the file cabinet.

Then she looked at the teapot, suddenly changing her mind. She picked it up and carried it back into kitchen, where Jan was pouring herself another cup of tea. "What do you think about displaying this teapot in our hutch?"

"That's fine with me," Jan said as she took a seat at the table. "We can even start using it for our guests, if you want."

Elaine considered the idea, then shook her head. "I don't know—it just doesn't feel right to use it when we don't know where it came from. It doesn't feel like ours."

"I know what you mean," Jan said. "Let's just display it for now. It's too beautiful to keep it hidden away in your office."

"Agreed," Elaine said with a smile. "I'll go find a place for it in the hutch now, then we can start on that menu."

"And I'll make us another pot of tea," Jan said as Elaine headed for the hallway. "Chamomile sounds good and will help us get a good night's sleep."

Elaine walked to the tearoom, carrying the Lefton teapot into the west parlor where the corner hutch stood. They used it to display some of their favorite collectibles and tea-related gifts they'd received, including sterling silver sugar tongs from Nathan Culver, whom Elaine had recently begun dating.

She set the Lefton down on the nearest table, then shifted some of the other teapots on display to make room for it. Since it was new, she wanted to give it a prominent place so all their guests could see it.

The doorbell rang. Elaine set the mystery teapot on the top shelf, then glanced at her watch as she moved toward the entryway, wondering if Bob had forgotten something. But when she opened the door, it wasn't Bob she saw.

A tall, handsome man who reminded her of a middle-aged Cary Grant stood on the other side. He wore an unbuttoned trench coat that revealed a neatly tailored black suit underneath. His thick, salt-and-pepper hair was parted on one side and hung low over his forehead, just above his chocolate-brown eyes.

"Hello," she greeted him. "I'm sorry to say we've already closed for the day."

"Good evening," he said in a posh British accent. "My name is Nigel Fox."

In an instant, Elaine recognized the name of Archie's friend from England. "Mr. Fox, this is a nice surprise!" She smiled and opened the door wider. "Archie told us you were coming to visit. I'm Elaine Cook. Please come in."

"Thank you, I..." His step faltered as he crossed the threshold and he reached one hand out to grab the door frame.

That's when Elaine saw the blood smeared over the tops of his broad fingers. Then her gaze moved to his pale face, where a trickle of blood now dripped slowly down his temple and on to his cheekbone.

"Are you all right?" she gasped.

He looked at her for a long moment, his brown eyes unfocused. "I don't think I am," he said slowly.

Then he collapsed on the floor.

CHAPTER FIVE

J an, help!"

Jan started when she heard Elaine's cry. She jumped up from her chair and dashed out of the kitchen and down the hall. She could see Elaine in the entryway near the door, kneeling beside a man crumpled on the hardwood floor.

"Oh my goodness, what happened?" Jan asked when she reached Elaine. "Who is that?"

"It's Archie's friend, Nigel Fox." Elaine held up both hands. "I don't know what happened. I saw blood on his forehead and then he just collapsed."

She reached out to gently part the blood-dampened hair at his temple, revealing a bloody wound on his scalp, about the size of a fifty-cent piece. "I think we should call an ambulance."

Jan hurried over to the phone and dialed the emergency number. A moment later, an operator came on the line. "What's your emergency?" she asked.

"A man collapsed in our home. This is Jan Blake." She gave the operator their address, then said, "His head is bleeding and he's unconscious. Please come quickly."

"An ambulance is on its way," the operator said. "Is the man breathing?"

Jan took a quick glance over at Elaine. "Is he breathing?"

"Yes," Elaine said, "but he's still unresponsive."

Jan relayed that information to the operator, who then instructed Jan to cover him with a blanket.

"The ambulance should be there soon," the operator told her before ending the call.

Jan hung up the phone, breathing a silent, fervent prayer for Archie's friend. She turned toward him, her heart sick at how helpless he looked. "I'll get him a blanket and pillow," she told Elaine before heading toward the stairs.

As she took the steps two at a time, Jan wondered what could have possibly happened to him. Had he been in a car accident? Tripped and fallen? Bumped into something? They'd have no way of knowing until he regained consciousness.

If he regained consciousness.

Jan pushed that unwelcome thought out of her head as she reached the second floor landing and headed for the linen closet. She pulled a thick wool blanket from the shelf, along with a spare pillow, then grabbed a roll of gauze from the bathroom medicine cabinet before hurrying back down the stairs.

"Here," she said, holding the pillow out to Elaine.

"Thank you," Elaine said, her face pinched with worry as she gently lifted Nigel's head just far enough to slide the pillow under it.

His eyes fluttered for a moment at the movement, then closed again.

Jan shook out the blanket and carefully draped it over him. Then she knelt down beside him and very gently pressed the gauze against his head, trying to staunch the blood seeping from the wound. "Why isn't the ambulance here yet?"

"It's coming!" Elaine peered through the window. "I see a flashing red light!"

A moment later, the wail of a siren penetrated the house. Jan breathed a sigh of relief, stepping away from Nigel and placing a worried hand over her mouth as she looked down at him.

Elaine moved to the door and opened it just moments before two paramedics rushed inside. They both wore name badges from MaineGeneral with just their surnames on them.

Jan watched as they knelt beside Nigel. The female paramedic, wearing a name tag that said Ames, checked his pulse while the male paramedic, Fullerton, gently removed the gauze on his head to and checked the wound underneath.

Ames looked over at them. "What's his name? And do you know what happened to him?"

"We don't know what happened to him," Elaine said, twisting her hands together, "but his name is Nigel Fox. He just arrived here from England, I believe."

"Nigel," Fullerton said, his head close to Nigel's face. "Nigel, can you open your eyes for me?"

Jan watched Nigel's eyes flutter open, then close again. But then Nigel spoke. "My head hurts."

Jan took that as a good sign and released a breath she didn't realize she'd been holding.

Elaine turned to her. "Should we call Archie?"

"Yes, of course," Jan replied, wishing she'd thought to do so earlier. She reached for her cell phone and walked into the hallway so she wouldn't disturb the paramedics.

Jan dialed Archie's number, then took a deep breath.

He answered on the second ring. "Hello?"

"Hello, Archie, this is Jan." She tried to sound calm. "Your friend Nigel is here, at our house. He's been hurt."

A long moment passed before Archie spoke. "What's that?"

She tried again, realizing this call must come as a shock to him. "Your friend, Nigel Fox, knocked on our door, then he collapsed inside. It appears that he hit his head. The paramedics are here now."

"But what happened?" he gasped.

"We don't know," she replied, gripping the phone tighter. "He's not able to tell us yet."

"I'll be right there," Archie said, followed by a dial tone.

Jan slipped her cell phone back into her pocket and then walked back into the hallway. During that short phone call, the paramedics had clipped Nigel's thick hair around the wound and cleaned the blood away, revealing a half-dollar–size swollen lump. "How's he doing?" she asked Elaine.

"Better," Elaine whispered.

Ames briskly shook Nigel's shoulder. "Nigel, open your eyes for me."

The motion made the Englishman wince, then he slowly opened his eyes. Jan and Elaine moved closer to stand near his feet. His gaze narrowed on them. Then he tried to speak, his words barely audible. "You're in danger."

JAN LET ARCHIE inside the house as the paramedics helped Nigel move from the floor to a sturdy chair in the east parlor. She led Archie to Elaine, who was standing just inside the doorway of the east parlor watching the paramedics work.

"He's conscious now," Elaine told them in a quiet voice, "but still a little woozy."

"What happened to him?" Archie asked, his face pinched with concern.

"We're not sure yet." Jan leaned a little closer to Archie so Nigel couldn't overhear them. "He's only spoken a couple of times since he collapsed. The last time, he looked at the two of us and said, 'You're in danger.'"

"'You're in danger'?" Archie echoed, looking between them. "But he doesn't even know you."

Elaine lifted her shoulders. "That's what's so strange about it."

"We wonder if he's just confused," Jan added, worry etched on her face. "He does have a head injury, after all."

Then Elaine looked at Archie. "Did you know he'd arrived in Lancaster?"

"I had no idea. I wasn't expecting him for a few more days, so he must have changed his travel plans." Archie shook his head with a puzzled frown. "I wonder why he didn't contact me when his plane landed in Portland. I would have been happy to pick him up and drive him to his cottage at Green Glade."

Jan watched as the paramedics began bandaging the wound on Nigel's head. His brown eyes were open now, though he winced slightly as the paramedics tended to him.

Archie slowly approached Nigel's chair. "Hello there, mate."

Nigel blinked. "Archie?"

"Yes, it's me. It's been a while, hasn't it?" Archie asked, kneeling down by his chair. "How are you feeling?"

"Rather wonky," Nigel said slowly. "Got a bit of a head-ache too."

Archie rose to his feet and turned to the paramedics. "Does he need to be hospitalized?"

"No, no," Nigel said, holding up both hands. "I will be fine after a good night's sleep."

"We've done a full assessment and you may have a mild concussion," the male paramedic told him. "We should transport you to MaineGeneral for observation."

"Rubbish," Niles said, sitting up in the chair. "I've had a concussion before, and this is not nearly as bad. Thank you for your assistance, but you may go now."

Archie looked up at Ames. "Can he just refuse like that?"

She nodded. "According to our protocol, a patient can refuse treatment if our assessment determines that he's mentally competent."

"And we do," Fullerton said, handing Nigel some papers to sign.

Jan watched Nigel quickly review the documents, then sign them.

Then Ames reached into her bag and pulled out a folded pamphlet. "Here's some information about concussion symptoms and treatment, including a phone number to call for a nurse to assist you."

"Very good," Nigel said, taking the pamphlet from her.

As the paramedics packed up their gear and prepared to leave, Ames approached Jan and Elaine. "I don't know his situation, but he really shouldn't be left alone tonight."

"He can stay in our guest room," Elaine told her. "We'll keep an eye on him."

Ames nodded. "That's a good idea. If you have any problems, you know our number." Then she and Fullerton walked out the door.

"I feel better knowing Nigel will be staying with us," Elaine said.

"Me too," Jan reached over to squeeze her cousin's hand, breathing a silent prayer of thanks that Nigel's injury wasn't more serious.

Nigel looked over at them. "What's that?"

Jan moved toward him, knowing how disoriented Nigel must feel being injured and so far from home. "I'm Jan Blake," she said, then motioned to her cousin, "and I live here with Elaine. We'd feel better if you'd stay here in our guest room tonight, Nigel. Just to make certain that you're okay."

"That's very gracious of you ladies, but not necessary," Nigel said, rising to his feet. He swayed for a moment before sitting back down. "Or perhaps it is."

Archie looked over at Jan and Elaine. "I can take him home with me. I don't want to cause you any inconvenience."

"We insist, Archie, and are happy to have him," Elaine said. "Besides, I'm not sure he's steady enough yet to handle a car ride anywhere."

Nigel sighed. "I'm embarrassed to say she may be right, Archie. I don't quite have my sea legs yet."

"Then I'll stay too," Archie looked between Jan and Elaine. "If that's all right with the two of you?"

"Of course," Elaine said, with a nod of understanding.

Archie pulled a chair up next to his friend and sat down. "What happened to you, Nigel? Do you remember?"

"No...it's all fuzzy," Nigel said, reaching a hand up to his forehead and gingerly touching the bandage there. His eyes shifted to the cousins. "I was walking in the woods toward your house—hoping to speak to both of you."

"How do you know about us?" Jan asked, curious.

Nigel looked over at Archie. "Because my good friend here wrote to me about his life in Lancaster, including the two kind ladies who had opened a tearoom and gave him a job here."

"I did indeed," Archie said. "But why were you in such a hurry to speak to them tonight?"

"Because I overheard something at Green Glade." Nigel lowered his hand and curled it tightly around the armrest. "Macy, the owner of Green Glade, gave me directions to the tearoom. Maybe I should have waited until tomorrow, because it was dark when I set out from my cottage." He paused for a moment, resting his head against the chair. "And after a bit, I heard something—or someone—moving in the trees. The next thing I knew I was on the ground."

Jan glanced between Elaine and Archie. "Do you mean someone did this to you? Assaulted you?"

"I'm not...sure," Nigel said, wincing again.

"If it's a possibility, then we should call the police," Elaine said, pulling her cell phone out of her pocket.

"Please," Nigel said, holding out one hand to stop her, "let's wait until tomorrow. I have a pounding headache and anyway I can't remember exactly how it happened."

Jan met Elaine's gaze and gave a slight shrug, torn as to whether they should contact the police tonight. From her cousin's expression, she felt the same way. While Jan wasn't sure that waiting until tomorrow was the right decision, she knew Nigel was hurting and still shaken.

"I suppose it can wait until tomorrow," Elaine said, slipping the phone back into her pocket. "You need to rest and, hopefully, your memory will be clearer in the morning."

Archie leaned forward, placing his forearms on his knees. "If someone *did* assault you, did they take your wallet? Your cell phone?"

"Not my cell phone," Nigel replied. "The battery was dead after the long flight, so I left it back at my cabin to charge." Then he patted the front of his jacket. "I still have my wallet." Nigel pulled up the sleeve on his left arm, revealing a gold watch around his wrist. "And my Rolex."

Jan found herself beginning to wonder if Nigel's injury had made him imagine hearing someone in the woods. Why would someone assault him, but not take any valuables? He'd just arrived in town, so it was highly doubtful he had any enemies here.

"Did you see or hear anyone after you were on the ground?" Jan asked him.

Nigel shook his head, wincing again. "No, but that was kind of a blur too. I was so dizzy. I just managed to make my way here before I passed out."

"Thank goodness you made it," Elaine told him. "If you'd collapsed before you got to our door, we might not have found you until morning."

Jan suppressed a shudder at the thought, aware that Nigel would have been in much worse shape if he'd spent the night outdoors. The fact that he'd pushed himself to make it to their house impressed her—and made her curious. "So you set out from Green Glade tonight to speak with us. And when you got here, you said we were in danger. What did you mean?"

Nigel sighed. "I may have...overreacted. Danger isn't the right word. But you could have...trouble."

Elaine looked perplexed at his words. "Why do you say that?"

Nigel was silent for a long moment, as if gathering his scattered thoughts. "As I said, I overheard something in the clubhouse after I arrived at Green Glade. Something I thought you should know."

"What's that?" Archie asked him.

"There's a group staying here," Nigel said. "You've probably met some of them already. They call themselves the Finders Keepers Club. I heard them talking about the two of you and this tearoom."

Jan stared at him. "We know there is a group of antique collectors staying at Green Glade. Is that who you mean?"

"Yes," Nigel said. "The Finders Keepers Club has several individual chapters all around the world. My neighbors in

London used to be members—so that's why the group caught my attention when I overhead them in the clubhouse."

"And you wanted to warn us about them?" Elaine said, looking confused.

"You need to understand," Nigel said. "They're not looking for antiques—at least not in the conventional way. They're treasure hunters. And some of them can be quite ruthless."

CHAPTER SIX

"Treasure hunters?" Jan echoed, surprised by his words. Then she thought about the map in the teapot, and the poem challenging them to find a buried treasure. Macy had told her club members traveled around together looking for treasures, only Macy had assumed they meant antiques and collectibles—and so had Jan. Until now.

Jan caught Elaine's gaze and she could see the doubt swimming in her blue eyes. Was Nigel's head injury making him imagine things?

Archie was strangely silent, and they saw the concern etched on his face as he looked at his friend.

Nigel fidgeted in his chair as a long, uncomfortable silence stretched between the four of them. Then he spoke. "I'm making a muddle of this, aren't I?" He looked over at Archie. "Let me start again."

Archie hesitated. "Perhaps you should rest, mate. We can talk more in the morning."

"No, I can do this," Nigel insisted, leaning forward in his chair. "After what happened to me, I think they should know."

"Know what?" Elaine asked.

"That people like to hunt for treasures—big or small. That's why hobbies like geocaching are so popular."

"That's where people hunt for a hidden object using GPS coordinates, right?" Elaine said.

"That's right," Nigel said. "There are all different kinds of treasure hunting too—some more dangerous than others. People go into the wilderness unprepared and some have had to be rescued. Some have even died. That's why people who liked searching for treasure but didn't like the risk decided to form a club."

"The Finders Keepers Club," Jan said.

Nigel nodded. "Yes, and now there are several small chapters all over the country—including the group at Green Glade. They're here to search for treasure—and you two are involved somehow." He took a deep breath, as if struggling to continue. "It's possible that one of them did this to me—thinking I might be a treasure hunter too and wanted to take me out of the competition."

"That seems...extreme," Jan said slowly, finding it hard to believe a group of retired folks would hurt a man just to stop him from finding a treasure.

"We did receive a teapot in the mail with a strange map inside," Elaine said. "And there was a short poem challenging us to find a buried treasure."

Nigel's brow furrowed, then he thought for a moment. "Sometimes," Nigel said slowly, "the club members take turns burying a treasure and then challenging their fellow club members to find it. But why include you?"

"We have no idea," Jan said, realizing the stakes had just gotten higher. If a member of the Finders Keepers Club found the treasure first, she and Elaine might never solve this mystery.

Jan looked over at Nigel, full of questions. But in that short time, he'd nodded off, his head falling forward. A moment later, he jerked awake again.

"So sorry," he said, wincing. "Jet lag seems to be catching up with me."

"We can talk about this more tomorrow," Jan said, worried about him. "Nigel should get some rest." Then she looked over at Archie. "Shall we take him upstairs to the guest room on the second floor? And then you can stay in one of the bedrooms on the third floor."

"Yes, that sounds perfect," Archie said, looking as if he had more questions too. But he kept them to himself as the three of them got Nigel safely to the second-floor guest room.

"Would you like something to drink?" Jan asked Nigel. "Perhaps a cup of herbal tea? We have a special decaffeinated blend with lavender and rose hips."

"That sounds grand," Nigel replied, sitting down on the side of the bed. "Thank you so much, Mrs. Blake."

"Please call me Jan," she told him.

"And I'm Elaine," her cousin added. "We're happy to help in any way we can."

Then Jan and Elaine walked out of the guest room, leaving Archie to help Nigel into bed as the two of them headed downstairs.

"I'll put the kettle on," Jan told Elaine, "if you'll grab that pamphlet the paramedics left for us. We should read it to make sure he's allowed to have some tea."

"Good idea," Elaine said, the two of them parting at the first floor landing.

As Jan moved toward the kitchen, she was certain Elaine was bursting with questions, just as she was. They hadn't wanted to talk about it in front of Nigel, but Jan still couldn't believe it was true.

Treasure hunters? At Chickadee Lake? Had one of them really assaulted Nigel? And were she and Elaine really in danger? Had one of the treasure hunters sent them the teapot and the map? And what kind of treasure was hidden here?

Jan filled the teakettle with water as those questions swirled in her mind. She wanted answers to all of them but wasn't sure where to start.

By the time the teakettle was whistling, Elaine had read through the pamphlet at the kitchen table and assured Jan that Nigel could have a cup of tea. They were also supposed to check on him periodically to watch for things like confused speech, lethargy, and blurred or double vision.

"Confused speech?" Jan interjected. "So it's possible Nigel *was* confused about dangerous treasure hunters?"

"Very possible. We both met Astrid. Does she seem dangerous to you?"

"Not at all," Jan replied. Then she told Elaine about running into Millie Cavett during her walk, and that she'd been crying over a scene in *Jane Eyre.* "Millie doesn't strike me as dangerous either—not in the least."

Jan poured the hot water into a teapot, then added the stainless steel strainer filled with the Hello Spring tea blend. When the tea was ready, she placed the teapot on a tray with a couple of cookies and then she and Elaine headed for the stairs.

That's where they met Archie as he descended the last step. "I'm sorry you went to so much trouble, but Nigel is already asleep," he announced, "so he won't be needing that tea."

"It was no trouble at all," Jan told him, "I'm just happy he's getting some rest."

He looked between them. "Thank you again for letting me stay here with him. I've called Gloria to let her know what happened and she's going to pack an overnight bag for me and drop it off."

"Good," Elaine told him. "Then let's sit in one of the parlors and enjoy the tea while we wait. I'll get cups for us while you and Jan choose a table."

Jan smiled up at Archie. "Where shall we sit? By the window in the east parlor?"

"Perfect," he said.

Archie switched on a lamp in the parlor while Jan set the tray in the center of the table. The full moon in the night sky provided even more light in the parlor, adding to the cozy atmosphere.

Elaine soon returned with the teacups, along with a plate full of cookies. "I thought we could all use a snack," she said, setting the cups and plate on the table before taking a seat across from Jan. "Archie, I'm so glad you decided to stay and have tea with us. We have a million questions."

"We certainly do," Jan said, pouring tea for each of them.

"I can imagine," he said dryly. "I'm just not certain how many I'll be able to answer."

Elaine reached for a cookie. "You can start by telling us about your friend. How long have you known him?"

A smile tipped up one corner of his mouth. "I first met Nigel at Oxford. He was studying architecture, but we had some classes together. We ended up becoming flatmates and then, after we graduated, we moved on to Cambridge to continue our education."

"So you know him very well," Jan said.

"Indeed." Archie's long fingers curled around his cup. "I even stood up for him at his wedding." He sighed. "Unfortunately, he lost his lovely wife, Flora, three years ago, shortly after he retired. And they never had any children."

"So what does he do now?" Jan asked, remembering Bob asking her if she might enjoy traveling after retirement.

"He has several hobbies that keep him busy," Archie replied. "He's independently wealthy, so money's not an issue. As an architect, he loves to travel to see old ruins and medieval castles. He's even done some side work by creating blueprints for centuries-old buildings that need remodeling." Archie took a sip of his tea, then smiled. "But that's not his only interest. He's quite a collector. I remember at Oxford, he became obsessed about collecting old clocks. He eventually sold them all for a pretty pound too."

As Jan listened to more of his stories, she could see why Archie considered him such a good friend. It sounded as if Nigel's life was as interesting and varied as Archie's own.

"Believe it or not," Archie continued, "his current hobby is collecting old Hollywood memorabilia—especially from silent screen stars. He's headed to California after his stay here to tour all the Hollywood mansions."

"He sounds like the perfect candidate for the Finders Keepers Club," Jan mused.

"Nigel's more of a lone wolf when it comes to his hobbies—and life in general, lately," Archie replied. "In fact, I haven't seen him since Flora's funeral. That's why I was so happy when he told me he was planning a visit here."

Jan took the last bite of her cookies, then brushed the crumbs from her fingers on to a napkin. "Well, I'm glad he's here and just hope he feels better tomorrow."

Elaine nodded. "So do I. And maybe he can tell us more about what happened to him—and this Finders Keepers Club. It can't just be a coincidence that they're here at the same time we received that mysterious package in the mail."

"But why bury a treasure around Chickadee Lake?" Archie asked, a glint of curiosity in his eyes. "There must be some connection to you or this area."

Jan nodded, thinking the same thing. "According to Nigel, some chapters of the club take turns burying treasures themselves and then challenging other members to find them."

"But why would they do that?" Elaine asked.

Archie smiled. "I assume they like the adventure of it, but there simply aren't enough buried treasures around for them to safely enjoy."

"So they invent their own?" Jan thought it sounded similar to the popular hobby of geocaching. "Nigel mentioned that some of the players were ruthless—but we certainly haven't met anyone who seems to fit that description so far."

Elaine met her gaze. "Unless someone really did assault Nigel in the woods. Maybe someone in the club noticed him eavesdropping at the Green Glade clubhouse."

Archie sighed. "And saw Nigel as competition." Then he glanced at the window. "Gloria's just pulling into the driveway. I'll run out and get my bag."

"She's welcome to come in and join us for a cup of tea," Jan told him.

He smiled. "Thanks, but she has an early day tomorrow, so she'll probably take a rain check." Then he headed outside.

Jan and Elaine sat together at the table, sipping their tea.

"I think we should encourage Nigel to call the police in the morning," Jan said at last. "Even if he's not sure what happened, they might find a witness to what happened to him."

"Yes, I agree." Elaine shuddered as she began collecting the empty teacups and placing them on the tray. "You and Bob were walking in that same area earlier this evening. What if someone had attacked you?"

Jan hadn't thought about that, but it made her uneasy. Chickadee Lake was a safe, happy place for residents and tourists alike. And she'd do everything in her power to keep it that way.

THE NEXT MORNING, Jan emerged from her bedroom fully dressed and trying not to make too much noise as she walked to the guest room door in her brown leather knee-high boots.

The boots were partially hidden by a floral maxi skirt that she'd topped with an olive-green tunic sweater cinched at the waist with a brown belt.

It was just past seven o'clock and she could hear Elaine moving around in her bedroom, but the guest room was silent.

Both Jan and Elaine had peeked in on Nigel during the night, just to make certain he was resting comfortably and in no distress. They hadn't heard a peep from him since Archie helped him to bed the night before and Jan hoped that was a good sign.

Now, Jan leaned her ear closer to the door and when she didn't hear any noise inside, she cracked open the door to check on their guest.

He was gone.

The sound of a door opening behind her made Jan turn around just as Elaine walked out of her room and into the hallway.

"Good morning," Elaine said with a smile. "How's our guest?"

"He's gone," Jan said, pushing open the guest room door as a wave of worry washed over her. The bed was neatly made, and there was no sign that Nigel had even been there.

Elaine frowned. "Gone? I didn't hear him get up. Did you?"

"No." Jan headed for the stairs with Elaine on her heels. She hoped that Nigel had just awoken early and felt well enough to head back to his cabin at Green Glade. But she had visions of a dizzy and disoriented Nigel wandering outside in the cold alone.

"We'll check downstairs first, and if he's not here, we'll wake Archie and start searching for him."

Elaine nodded. "I heard Archie checking on Nigel around three o'clock last night, so I'm sure he's exhausted."

"That's why I don't want to wake him yet," Jan said. "Let's hope we don't have to."

When they reached the first-floor landing, they headed to the front door. "It's locked," Elaine said. "He might still be here."

"Maybe he's in the kitchen," Jan said, praying it was true. But when they reached the kitchen, the light was off and the room was empty. The morning sun lit the room enough to show that nothing had been disturbed from the night before.

"He's not here," Jan said her heart sinking.

Then Elaine tapped her on the shoulder. "Look."

She turned to see Elaine pointing to the kitchen window. That's when she saw Nigel seated at a table outside on their side porch.

"He must have gone out the back door," Elaine said, heading in that direction.

Jan followed her, first taking a moment to say hello to Earl Grey on the screened porch, then walking toward the door that led to the side porch.

"Good morning," Nigel greeted them as Elaine and Jan approached his table. He was dressed in the clothes he'd worn the evening before, but his hair was neatly combed and it looked as if he'd freshened up. A shadow of dark whiskers covered his jaw and cheeks, giving him a rakish appearance.

"How are you feeling today?" Elaine asked him.

"Tip-top," he said with a smile. "My headache is gone and I got a wonderful night's sleep." His gaze moved toward the lake. "It's so peaceful and quiet here. So different from London."

Jan slid into the chair across from him. "Is that where you live?"

"Yes, it is," he said, turning his attention to her. "And don't mistake me, I love it there. After living all over the world, there's still nothing like the hustle and bustle of London to get my heart pumping."

Elaine smiled. "Well, I'm so glad you're feeling better. Archie will be happy to hear it too." She checked her watch. "I'm sure he'll be down soon."

"Perfect," Nigel exclaimed. "I can't wait to catch up with him."

"What can I get you for breakfast?" Elaine asked. "We have pastries, toast, eggs…"

"A cup of tea and a slice of buttered toast would be excellent," he told her. "Although I really shouldn't trouble you." He stood up. "There's no reason I can't go back to my cabin and make my own breakfast."

"There's a very good reason," Jan told him, hoping he'd stay. "We want to hear more about this Finders Keepers Club."

He hesitated. "I hate to be any trouble."

"Not at all," Elaine assured him. "But it is a bit chilly out here. Shall we have breakfast inside?"

"That would be lovely," Nigel said with a smile. "It is rather nippy out here, but the view is breathtaking."

By the time they were seated at the kitchen table enjoying tea and buttered toast, Jan and Elaine had learned more about Nigel's life in London and some of his excursions through England and Scotland's oldest castles.

"You have a magnificent home here," Nigel said, looking around the kitchen. "And brilliant architecture, actually."

"Thank you," Elaine told him. "We think so too."

"I'd love to have a more thorough tour sometime," Nigel said with a smile, pushing his empty plate away. "There's nothing I like better than exploring old homes and manors."

"Of course," Jan promised. Now that he'd finished eating, she couldn't wait any longer. "So what more can you tell us about the Finders Keepers Club?"

He leaned forward, folding his hands together on the table.

"My neighbors in London, William and his wife, were charter members. They planned and enjoyed their amateur treasure hunting trips for years." A smile curved his mouth. "They enjoyed hiding treasures too, and then handing out the same clue to each of their fellow club members to aid in their search."

Elaine nodded. "Like the map in the teapot we received. So you're saying each of the Finders Keepers members staying at Green Glade got an identical map?"

"Yes, that's how it works," he said. "May I see your map?"

"Of course." Elaine stood up and headed for her office.

Jan's mind whirled as she stood up to make another pot of tea. Out of the corner of her eye, she saw Nigel rub his forehead, taking care not to disturb the bandage. She hoped his headache wasn't coming back, although his color was definitely better this morning.

By the time Elaine returned to the table, Jan was pouring a fresh cup of tea for Nigel.

"Here you go," she said, setting the map and the poem in front of him.

Nigel picked up the poem first. "This is known as the invitation to the hunt. Each member received this same poem, along with the map."

"Well, that explains why the Finders Keepers members keep showing up at our tearoom," Jan said. "The poem specifically mentions it, along with the two of us."

Nigel nodded. "And that's an indication to the other members that you two might be playing the game as well." Then he studied the map in front of him. "Yes, this looks complicated. The clues William and his wife showed me were just as... baffling."

"Because they don't want us to solve it too quickly," Jan surmised.

"Exactly," he replied, taking a sip of his tea. "That way it draws out the game so the members can enjoy whatever locale they're visiting. But some of the chapters began experiencing problems—including William's group. The value of the hidden treasures kept climbing higher and people started cheating—and even breaking some laws—in their efforts to win."

"That doesn't sound fun," Elaine said.

"Too right." Nigel said, nodding. "When a fellow club member broke into William's home hoping to find some answers to the clue puzzle, he and his wife quit on the spot." He looked up at them. "So you can understand why I was concerned when I overheard Finders Keepers Club members at Green Glade talking about a treasure hunt here and mentioning your tearoom."

"Yes, I can." Jan looked over at Elaine. "We're part of this game whether we like it or not."

"If you have anything valuable here," Nigel said, "I'd suggest putting it in safekeeping—just in case."

Jan thought for a moment. "Most of the things we own have sentimental value rather than monetary value."

"Wait," Elaine said, staring at him. "Do you believe one of the club members would actually steal from us? I thought they just wanted the treasure?"

Nigel shrugged. "I can't say for certain. According to William, there were some scoundrels among them. But this lot might be perfectly harmless."

"The sapphire ring," Jan said suddenly, looking at her cousin. "That does have value—and would be easy to carry out of here without us knowing about it."

Then Elaine looked over at Nigel. "We found a ring here when we moved in. It was in quite an unusual place."

"Ah, I think remember Archie mentioning it to me once. It was found under a floorboard, wasn't it?"

"Actually, it was behind a wall," Jan said, smiling at the memory. "That was months ago, but we still haven't found out how it got there."

"So you've hung on to it?" Nigel said. "I would have thought you'd sold it by now."

"Oh, I don't think we'll ever sell it," Elaine said with a smile. "Even if we never find out how it got here, it's not ours to sell."

Nigel smiled. "Well, then I suggest you keep it in a good hiding place. At least until the Finders Keepers Club members leave town."

"I still want to know why someone is including us in the treasure hunt," Jan said.

A long silence fell between them as Nigel stared at the map. "Perhaps someone you know is a Finders Keepers member, even if they haven't mentioned it."

Jan turned to Elaine. "Remember when we thought a former customer might have sent it to us? Well, that could be true—if that customer is also a Finders Keepers member."

"And if they visited here as a tourist," Elaine said, "then they might know how much we enjoy solving mysteries."

"Then it makes even less sense that the Finders Keepers members would try to harm us—or harm Nigel. They don't even know him."

At that moment, Archie entered the kitchen through the back door. "Good morning." He smiled when he saw Nigel seated at the kitchen table. "You're looking much better today, mate."

"I'm feeling better," Nigel replied, then motioned to the map in front of him. "Jan and Elaine were just telling me about the strange package they received."

"So what do you think about all this?" Archie asked him. "And what happened to you last night?"

Nigel took a deep breath. "I think it's time to call the police."

CHAPTER SEVEN

This is about where it happened," Nigel said, stopping near to a large fir tree along the trail.

State Trooper Daniel Benson stood next to Nigel, in full uniform, taking notes on his notepad. He'd arrived about twenty minutes earlier and had taken down some preliminary information before asking Nigel to show him the site where he was injured.

Elaine, along with Archie, had accompanied them, while Jan had stayed behind at the house to help Rose prepare for the opening of the tearoom at ten. Rose had been full of questions when she'd arrived, surprised to see the state trooper's SUV in the driveway. Jan had promised to explain everything as the rest of them had walked out the door.

Daniel slipped his notepad and pencil into his shirt pocket, then looked at Nigel. "Can you point out exactly where you fell?"

Nigel hesitated, his gaze narrowing as he studied the trail in front of them. It wove around trees and bushes and was covered with dried leaves and grass flattened by the winter snows and the many hikers and cross-country skiers who had trod over it.

Then he walked a few feet forward, near a large tree root that had broken the surface of the dirt. "Here," he said, pointing to the thick root. "That's where I hit my head."

The trooper followed him, then knelt down near the root and studied it closely. He pointed to a dark smear. "Yes, that looks like blood." He glanced up at Nigel. "That must have been a nasty fall. You're lucky you were able to make it to Mrs. Cook's house."

Nigel nodded. "Very lucky indeed."

They had walked about ten minutes from the house to get to this spot on the trail. Elaine shuddered to think what would have happened if Nigel had been unconscious and alone out here so close to nightfall.

In March, the days were warmer, but the nights were still cold. Definitely low enough to possibly cause hypothermia in someone unable to seek shelter.

Even now, the cool morning breeze chilled the tips of Elaine's ears as she stood still on the trail. She'd worn her spring jacket over her black denim jeans and cream-colored turtleneck, along with a pair of sturdy hiking shoes.

Daniel rose to his feet again, his gaze moving over the thick copse of fir trees on either side of the trail. "So you heard someone moving through these trees? Are you sure it wasn't an animal?"

"I don't think so," Nigel replied, furrowing his brow. "It sounded like footsteps but, as I told you earlier, I didn't actually see him."

"*Him?*" The trooper arched a dark brow. "If you didn't see anyone, how do you know it was a man?"

Nigel blanched. "Well, I can't imagine a woman doing such a thing."

Elaine couldn't help but smile at his chivalrous—or some might say, antiquated—answer, especially since she knew of at least two women who belonged to the Finders Keepers Club: Astrid Shayne and Millie Cavett. From Jan's description, Millie didn't seem like the violent type. Although neither did Astrid, Elaine thought to herself.

"But you didn't hear or see anything that would definitely identify your alleged attacker as a man?" Daniel asked.

"No," Nigel replied. "I heard rapid footsteps behind me and the next thing I remember is waking up on the ground." He pressed his mouth into a firm line, then said, "If someone did push me, I suppose it *could* have been a woman."

Daniel nodded. "Let's start from the beginning and walk me through exactly what happened from the moment you arrived at Green Glade."

Nigel folded his arms across his chest, his expression thoughtful. "I checked in with the owner, Mrs. Macy Atherton. She was very efficient and showed me the way to my cabin. I was quite impressed with it, actually, since I didn't know what to expect."

Daniel nodded. "So I assume you got settled in your cabin before heading out for your walk?"

"Yes," Nigel replied, "but first I took a nap. I was quite jet-lagged after my flight—London is several hours ahead of

Maine on the clock, so it was the middle of the night, London time. I slept for about two hours."

Elaine was glad to hear that Nigel remembered the events before he left Green Glade.

"When I awoke, I was feeling a bit peckish, so I headed to the clubhouse. Macy had told me there'd be some biscuits and tea available there." He met Elaine's gaze. "That's when I heard a group of people talking near the fireplace. They hadn't noticed me come in and I caught enough of their conversation to realize they were members of a Finders Keepers Club here to look for treasure."

Elaine noticed the skeptical expression on Trooper Benson's face, but he kept taking notes as Nigel told his story.

"That's when I got the idea to visit Tea for Two and let them know about it—since I'd heard someone in the group mention the tearoom. And I was hoping to catch Archie there as well." Nigel shook his head. "I realize now that notion was quite wonky, since he'd left a few hours earlier."

Archie smiled. "Yes, it was, mate. But I'm familiar with jet lag, so it's no surprise your timing was off."

Daniel flipped to a new page on his notepad. "Go on."

"Well, I'd seen the tearoom sign on my drive to Green Glade, so I knew which direction to walk."

Daniel stopped him. "It was dark by then. Why walk instead of drive?"

Elaine had wondered the same thing, especially for someone so unfamiliar with the surroundings.

"I wanted to stretch my legs after spending so many hours cramped on an airplane. And there was a full moon, so there was enough light to see my way to the house." Then he shrugged. "And to tell you the truth, I'm not sure I'll ever get used to driving with the steering wheel on the wrong side of the car."

Daniel nodded, appearing satisfied with his answer. Elaine was impressed with the amount of detail that went into the trooper's interview. Given the fact that Nigel hadn't seen who might have assaulted him, even the tiniest of clues could lead him to a culprit.

"Actually," Nigel said, holding one finger in the air, "I did have to go back to my cabin before setting out on my walk. I'd only gone a short way when I realized it was colder outside than when I arrived at the clubhouse. Not surprising, of course, since the sun had gone down. So I grabbed a coat from inside my cabin and headed out again."

"Did you see anyone?" Daniel asked.

Nigel thought for a moment. "Why, yes. A man was parked outside of the clubhouse. But he walked inside before I could get a good look at his face."

Daniel's pen was poised over his notepad. "Can you describe him?"

"He was a short, stocky fellow," Niles said. "About my age, I suppose." He smiled. "I'm sixty-five, by the way, although people say I look younger."

Daniel smiled as he wrote, obviously enjoying Nigel's personality. "Got it. Anything else?"

"Well, as I said, he was quite a portly fellow. And balding on top, with just a fringe of gray all around."

"And did he see you?"

"No, I don't think so," Nigel said. "I was behind him and could see his profile, but I never saw him turn my way."

"So then you continued on your walk?" Daniel prodded.

"Yes, and I was walking quite fast, as I didn't want to miss Archie. It was when I reached this part of the trail that I heard the footsteps behind me." His eyes widened. "I do think someone pushed me." He looked over at Archie. "And I've always been a bit of klutz, haven't I? So it didn't take much for me to lose my balance. Then everything went black."

"You remember a push?" Archie said.

Nigel gave a slow nod. "Yes, I think so. It's still fuzzy, but…" His voice trailed off as he looked at the trooper. "I can't say for certain."

"That's not unusual with a head injury," Trooper Benson replied. "It might come back to you—or it might not. For now, I'm going to treat this as a possible assault."

Elaine breathed a sigh of relief at Daniel's words, though she was not happy about the possibility that an assault might have happened so close to their home.

"Thank you," Nigel said to the trooper. "Anyway, that's the long and short of it. By the time I was on my feet again, there was no one around."

"But you could hear someone running through the trees," Daniel asked. "That's what you said earlier."

"I think so, but my head was throbbing and I was in no shape to give chase."

Daniel nodded his approval. "I think that was a wise decision."

"That's about it," Nigel said with a sigh. "I managed to make my way to Jan and Elaine's house, although it was a tough go. Then everything went black again."

Daniel's mouth twisted to one side as his gaze moved over his notepad. "Why didn't you make a report last night?"

Nigel opened his mouth to answer, but Archie spoke first. "He was in no condition for an interview. When I got here, he was woozy and somewhat incoherent. I'm not sure he even recognized me at first."

"I should have called you as soon as I arrived at Green Glade," Nigel told Archie. "And I probably should have gone to the hospital too, but I just didn't feel up to it." He turned toward the trooper. "Is there anything else I can do to help your investigation?"

"Probably not," Daniel admitted. "There's not much to go on, honestly, since you can't identify a possible suspect. I know you just arrived in the States, but do you know anyone who would want to hurt you?"

"No one," Nigel said, shaking his head. "That's why I think it might be a member of that Finders Keepers Club I told you about earlier. They don't know me, but one of them might have noticed me eavesdropping on their conversation. Maybe they thought I heard too much—or even believed I was a treasure hunter too."

Daniel arched a brow as he looked at the three of them. "Do all of you really think there's a treasure buried around here?"

"I don't know," Elaine replied. "It could be some kind of elaborate prank, but that doesn't really make sense either. We showed you the map, Daniel, and the poem."

"All I know," Nigel added, "is that there's a group here that believes a treasure is hidden around Chickadee Lake—even possibly in or around Jan and Elaine's house. And perhaps one of them thought I was looking for it too and wanted to stop me."

Daniel's gaze narrowed. "That's the motive?"

"Maybe," Nigel said. "Now, whether there is a treasure or not, I have no idea. But it's the only explanation that I can think of at the moment."

Elaine wondered if Daniel would confiscate the map for possible evidence. If so, it would sit in a file drawer collecting dust. Something told her the only way to find out who had hurt Nigel was to decode the secret message on the map.

"I can send you a photograph," Elaine said, ultimately coming to her senses and deciding not to conceal possible evidence from the police, "of the treasure map. It could be related. And the poem, if that would help."

"No, that won't be necessary." Daniel said, closing his notebook and slipping it back into his shirt pocket. "Keep me posted if you get any more information. And in the meantime, Mr. Fox, I'll interview Macy at Green Glade to see if she's seen or heard anything suspicious."

Nigel nodded. "Thank you, Trooper. I appreciate it."

As the four of them walked back to the house, Elaine was glad that Daniel would be interviewing Macy at Green Glade. If someone did assault Nigel—which seemed likely now that his memory was returning—then seeing the police there might deter the culprit from harming anyone else.

AFTER THE TROOPER drove off, Elaine, Archie, and Nigel walked through the back door and into the kitchen. Jan stood at the counter, lining up a row of teacups. Elaine glanced at the stove clock, realizing the tearoom was due to open in few minutes. No doubt Rose was attending to the double parlors, getting all the tables ready to go before opening the front door.

"How did it go?" Jan asked as soon as they were inside, her blue eyes wide behind her glasses. "Were there any clues on the trail?"

"None that we could find," Elaine told her. "Daniel asked Nigel a lot of questions."

"He certainly did," Nigel agreed. "The man was very thorough. But he didn't seem too optimistic about catching the ruffian who pushed me."

"Pushed you?" Jan echoed, looking at Elaine.

"Nigel remembered someone pushing him," Elaine said. "That's how he fell and hit his head."

Nigel nodded. "It helped to be at the spot and walk through it with the trooper. That's when I remembered someone giving me a shove."

"And we talked to Daniel about the map," Elaine said to Jan. "He's skeptical about a possible treasure hidden in Lancaster." She gave the three of them a rueful smile. "I don't really blame him."

"Neither do I," Nigel said. "But as long as people believe the tearoom may be connected to the treasure, you need to careful." He pointed to Archie. "And you as well. They may find it strange that a man of your background and experience would work in a tearoom in a small hamlet in Maine."

Archie smiled. "Do you find it strange?"

Nile laughed. "Not a bit! I know you well enough to believe it. Others, though, may think you have ulterior motives for hanging around here."

Elaine looked up at Archie, wondering if he took any offense to that possibility. His expression remained unchanged but she saw a steely glint in his keen hazel eyes that she'd never noticed before.

"Let them think whatever they want," Archie said. "I don't care as long as my friends are safe." Then he frowned, his gaze moving to Nigel's head wound. "And, unfortunately, it's too late for that."

Rose walked into the kitchen. "Everything is ready to go." Then she looked over at Nigel. "Oh, hello. You must be Mr. Fox."

"And you must be Rose. " He smiled. "Call me Nigel please."

Rose smiled. "Nice to meet you, Nigel."

"Likewise," he said with a nod. "Archie's told me wonderful things about all of you, and about his life here at Chickadee Lake. That's another reason I was so keen to visit. He made it sound like the perfect holiday locale."

"It's even nicer in the summer," Elaine said, pleased to hear how much Nigel liked their community. "How long will you be staying?"

"I've reserved the cabin for two weeks," Nigel told her. "Then I'll be on my way to California for another two weeks before flying back to London from there."

Elaine could sense that Nigel was ready to return to his cabin. "What can you tell us about the club members you overheard at the clubhouse? How many were there?"

"Four," Nigel said, "two men and two women. But I didn't catch their names."

"That would be Astrid," Elaine began counting them off on her fingers. "Lawrence, Jerry, and..."

"Millie," Jan added. "Bob and I met Millie. She seems quiet and a little shy—not the type of person I'd expect to be a treasure hunter."

"They've all visited the tearoom—except for Millie," Elaine explained, "so we've gotten to know them a little."

"Astrid told me she's a former actress," Rose said, "mostly at community theaters. She mentioned that she also does some seamstress work now and then."

"And Lawrence is quite well traveled," Archie added, "and speaks three or four languages. He comes from money, so I'd guess this club is a bit of a lark for him."

"And Jerry is retired," Elaine said, "and has some real estate investments. They all seem perfectly normal."

"And yet," Archie said, pointing to Nigel, "one of them may have done that."

His words sent a small chill through Elaine, reminding her that looks could be deceiving.

Nigel glanced at his watch. "It's almost time for your tearoom to open, so I should be on my way."

Archie moved toward the door. "I'll give you a lift."

"I don't want to keep you from your work, mate," Nigel said.

Jan smiled. "No worries. Archie isn't actually scheduled to work today."

Nigel clapped his hand on Archie's back. "Then how about we see the sights together? You can show me around your new home."

"Sounds good to me," Archie said, waving to Jan, Elaine, and Rose as the two of them headed out the back door.

"Nigel seems like a nice man," Rose said after they left. She walked over to the counter to remove the plastic wrap around a loaf of lemon pound cake.

"He does," Elaine replied, staring after them. She liked him as well and hoped he wasn't putting himself in further danger by continuing to stay here.

AFTER THE TEAROOM had closed, Jan walked into the Bookworm, eager to enjoy the cozy atmosphere, browse some books, and just relax after all excitement and activity of the last few days. A cheerful blaze burned in the stone fireplace at the back of the store, inviting Jan to the perfect spot to spend the next hour or so. Then she saw Katelyn Grande shelving books on the other side of the shop and waved to her. The thirty-year-old worked part time at the Bookworm and also wrote crossword puzzles.

The shop's owner, Bristol Payson, emerged from the backroom. "Hello, neighbor," she greeted Jan. Bristol had dark-blonde hair that hung to her shoulders and friendly blue eyes. She wore a denim jacket over a white peasant blouse along with a chunky silver necklace. She and her husband, Mark, both in their early forties, were fellow congregation members at Lancaster Community Church.

"Hi, Bristol," Jan said, walking over to the front counter. "Has my magazine come in yet?" She loved puzzle magazines so much that Bristol had started carrying the monthly issues of *Cryptograms* in her store.

"Not yet, Jan," Bristol replied as she placed a new shipment of books, still shrink-wrapped, on the counter in front of her. "It should arrive by next week though."

"That's what I thought, but I just wanted to check." Jan leaned closer, her smile widening. "Plus, it gives me an excuse to come to your shop more often."

Bristol laughed. "You don't need an excuse, Jan. You can visit as often as you'd like."

"Oh, that would be a dream come true," Jan said, laughing, "so don't tempt me."

They chatted a few minutes more and discussed the upcoming sunrise service at church on Easter morning. Then another customer arrived to pick up a book order, so Jan made her way over the wide-planked wood floor to the table full of new and used cookbooks, looking for something to read while she sat by the fire.

"See any cookbooks you like?" Katelyn asked, walking toward her. She wore a pair of navy slacks with an ivory knit top and a matching cardigan.

"Too many," Jan said with a smile. "I wish I had time to read all of them."

"I know the feeling," Katelyn said, laughing as she turned away. "Let me know if you need any help."

"Thanks, I will."

After browsing for a few more minutes, Jan finally selected a used cookbook from the 1970s, smiling at the fondue pot on the front cover. She was old enough to remember when fondue parties were all the rage. Her parents had even hosted one for their circle of friends at her house, letting Jan have her own fondue forks to join in the fun.

After pouring herself a cup of hot chocolate, Jan breathed a happy sigh as she carried the cookbook and her cup to a chair by the fire. No one else was seated there, which was unusual at this time of day.

She settled into an overstuffed chair, then placed her cup on the table beside her. As the fire crackled in the hearth, she slowly turned the pages of the cookbook, the 1970s-style photos and recipes bringing back so many memories. She'd been in high school during the latter seventies, and worn her share of bell-bottom pants and peasant blouses. It all seemed so long ago.

As she drank her hot chocolate and paged through the cookbook, her mind kept wandering to more recent events. The assault on Nigel just made it even more important for her and Elaine to get to the bottom of this mystery of the map and the teapot. She still didn't want to believe that Astrid, Millie, Lawrence, or Jerry had anything to do with it, but she barely knew them.

Maybe that's where she could start.

She drained her cup, feeling reenergized after her trip down memory lane. Then Jan got up from her chair and made her way to the front counter.

"Did you find something good?" Bristol asked as Jan set the cookbook on the counter.

"I sure did. This cookbook brought back a lot of fun memories. Elaine's mom's birthday is coming up soon and I think she'd get a kick out of it." Then her gaze landed on the stack of identical books on the counter. Bristol had cut away the shrink-wrap and now she could see the title.

"*Through My Eyes: Chickadee Lake and the Great Depression*," she read out loud, picking it up. "Is this by a local author?"

"Yes," Bristol said with a smile, "and you actually know her. Diane Blanchett had it self-published recently, based on some recorded interviews she had with her great-grandmother years ago."

A wave of excitement swept over Jan. She and Elaine had been looking for any tidbit about the Great Depression in Lancaster, hoping to discover some clues about the sapphire ring. Since finding it behind the wall, they'd collected bits and pieces of information, but still didn't have enough to complete the puzzle.

Jan grinned as she handed the book to Bristol. "I'll take it."

CHAPTER EIGHT

When Jan walked into the kitchen a short time later, she saw Elaine and Rose waiting for her. Rose stood next to the kitchen table wearing an ash-gray apron over her dark jeans and light-pink top. Elaine stood a few feet away, rocking slightly on the heels of her shoes, her hands behind her back. They both stared at Jan as she closed the door behind her.

"What's going on?" she asked, setting her purse and the bag from the Bookworm on the counter.

A smile flirted on Elaine's mouth. "Something came in the mail for you." Then she swung one hand from behind her back to reveal a white envelope. She held it out to Jan. "We've been on pins and needles waiting for you to get home to open it."

When Jan saw the return address on the envelope, her heart skipped a beat. "It's from the baking contest?"

Elaine grinned. "It sure looks like it." She walked over to Jan and pushed the envelope into her hands. "Let's open it and find out."

Jan swallowed, her heart beating fast as she turned the envelope over and slid a fingernail underneath the flap, breaking the seal.

The she pulled out the single sheet of paper inside and unfolded it.

"Dear Mrs. Blake," she began reading out loud as both Elaine and Rose leaned closer. *"We are pleased to inform you that you have been selected as a contestant in our Maine Dessert Competition."*

"Woo-hoo!" Elaine exclaimed, then reached out and hugged Jan. "You made it!"

Rose clapped her hands together, delight shining in her blue eyes. "This is so exciting! You're going to be on television!"

Jan couldn't stop smiling, even as a quiver of anxiety ran through her. She'd never been on television before—and certainly never baked anything in front of such a large audience. But she tamped down her nervousness and decided to enjoy the moment. "I can't believe it! I thought for sure they'd rejected my application."

"Well, you've been checking the mail every day." Elaine chuckled. "And we should know better than anyone what they say about a watched pot."

Jan laughed. "You're right about that! I finally stopped expecting a letter to arrive, and here it is!"

Rose leaned toward her, tilting her head slightly. "What else does it say?"

Jan took a deep breath, calming herself as she turned her attention back to the letter. She licked her lips, then began to read it out loud. *"Congratulations. You have been accepted as one of three contestants for the Maine Desert Competition. Please find detailed instructions below, as well as directions to the TV station. You are permitted to wear clothing identifying the name of your eating establishment. However, all cooking equipment and ingredients will be supplied by the contest sponsor."* She looked up from the letter. "That means I can wear my apron with *Tea for Two* cross-stitched on it!"

Elaine smiled. "That will be perfect. And we can arrange to have your hair and makeup done too, if you want."

"Maybe," Jan said feeling another flash of nerves as she continued reading the letter. *"There has been one change to the contest since you submitted your application. We will now be giving each contestant a surprise basket of ingredients with which to prepare a baked dessert of his or her choice—and two hours to prepare it. The judges will then evaluate each dessert and choose the winner."*

Jan's throat suddenly went dry as she looked up at Rose and Elaine. "That's a big change."

Elaine's brows rose. "So you'll have no idea what ingredients you're baking with until the day of the contest?"

Jan scanned through the rest of the letter, including the rules and regulations listed at the bottom. "Yes, they make it quite clear that we won't know what's in the basket until the cameras start rolling."

Rose grinned. "That sounds perfect for you, Jan. You know desserts inside and out. You'll knock those other contestants on their trivets!"

Jan laughed, finding Rose's enthusiasm contagious. "It does sound fun, doesn't it? I'll have to practice, of course, especially since the contest is coming up so soon."

They chatted about the contest a few minutes more, then Rose took off her apron. "I'd love to stay and talk about this, but I'd better scoot since I have class tonight."

"Don't worry," Jan told her, so proud of Rose for going to culinary school. "I'm sure we'll be talking about it plenty in the days to come."

After Rose left, Elaine breathed a happy sigh. "Just think of how excited your grandkids will be to see their grandma on television."

"I hope I do them proud. I'll admit that the surprise basket has me a bit nervous."

"Just think of it as a puzzle," Elaine told her. "You're great at solving those. All you have to do is fit the ingredients together in a way that make a wonderful dessert."

"You're right," Jan said, hoping it would be that easy. Then she remembered her trip to the Bookworm. "And speaking of puzzles..." Jan walked over to the counter and pulled a book out of the bag. "Look what I found."

"*Through My Eyes: Chickadee Lake and the Great Depression*," Elaine said, reading the title. She looked up at Jan. "The author is Bertha Sullivan. I've never heard of her, have you?"

"No, but Bristol told me she's Diane Blanchett's great-grandmother." Diane Blanchett was a thirty-year-old computer whiz who owned Computer Gal in Lancaster and helped residents with all their personal information technology needs. "The book is a series of interviews Diane did with her. Do you think it's possible that she knows something about the sapphire ring?"

Elaine's eyes widened. "Maybe. And if not the ring, something about the woolen mill or the Wood family. I can't believe you found this!"

"Neither can I," she said with a smile. "It's going to take me a while to go through it, but I'm hoping we find out once and for all how that ring got into our wall."

LATER THAT NIGHT, Jan climbed into bed and propped the feather pillow behind her. It was past eleven o'clock, a little later than she'd planned to retire, but she and Elaine had talked late into the evening.

She breathed a contented sigh, grateful once again for the close relationship she shared with her cousin. Living together and opening Tea for Two had been one of the best decisions of her life.

Jan opened the book in her hands, then settled in to read, the bedside lamp casting a bright pool of light on the pages. The room was cool, but the heavy coverlet on the bed provided plenty of warmth as she began to read the introduction.

My grandmother, Bertha Everett Sullivan, lived at Chickadee Lake in Lancaster, Maine, from 1927 until 1940. The only child of Lester and Mary Everett, Bertha moved there with her parents when she was ten years old. Her father was a lawyer, and her mother, a homemaker, often held charity events at their home to raise money for the local orphanage.

They lived a quiet life and enjoyed the prosperity of the 1920s. Then the Depression hit and they, like so many of their friends and neighbors, lost almost everything.

This book is written from the point of view of my great-grandmother, who was patient enough to sit with me for hours on end as I asked her questions about growing up at Chickadee Lake and her life there.

This is Bertha's story, seen from the eyes of a child growing into adulthood, and witnessing one of the darkest economic times in American history. She passed away ten years ago, and it took me some time to compile the recordings and turn them into a book. She loved her family unconditionally and was always my biggest cheerleader. I know she would be proud of me.

So it is with much love and admiration that I give you her story. I hope you enjoy it as much as I do.

Diana Blanchett

Jan smiled as she turned the page, feeling the love Diane had for her great-grandmother in her words. Something told her that Diane would have taken great care to present Bertha's story as accurately as possible.

She took a moment to thumb through the pages, noting that the book ended on page 150. That meant she wouldn't get through the story tonight, especially as her eyelids were already getting heavy. She thought about looking for specific references to the woolen mill, but knew that by skipping passages, she might miss something important.

Besides, she was truly interested in what Bertha had to say. After adjusting the pillow under her head again, she began to read the first chapter.

I loved Chickadee Lake the moment I saw it. Little did I know, at ten years old, the moments of both joy and grief that I would experience there. We didn't realize how much we had in the late 1920s, before the stock market crash on Black Thursday in 1929.

We just lived our lives, not knowing what lay in store for us—and for the country.

Jan's eyelids grew heavier as she continued to read about Bertha's first year at Chickadee Lake. She barely made it to the end of the chapter before she fell fast asleep.

ON SATURDAY, JAN smiled at Dr. Matt and Dr. Andrea McInnis as they walked through the front door of the tearoom. "Good morning! So happy you could stop in."

"I've been looking forward to a maple croissant all week," Andrea said, patting down her hair. Tall and lithe, with dark hair and eyes, Andrea moved with a grace that Jan envied. "That wind is really blowing today."

"It sure is," Jan said as she escorted them to an empty table. "How's this?"

"Perfect," Matt told her, pulling out a chair for his wife before taking a seat across from her. "We love looking out over Main Street."

Both Andrea and her husband were family practitioners at Lakeview Medical Clinic in Lancaster. They'd taken over the practice from Matt's father, Dr. Tyson McInnis, who was a frequent guest at Tea for Two, along with his lovely wife, Claudia.

"No kids today?" Jan asked, referring to the couple's two children.

Andrea smiled. "They're spending the day with Matt's parents, so we're on our own."

"Which is pretty rare for us," Matt said with a chuckle.

Jan could only imagine how rare it was for two married doctors to find time alone together, and felt honored that they were spending part of their morning here. "So how many maple croissants can I bring you?"

"Two for me, along with a pot of vanilla chai tea." Andrea reached out to squeeze her husband's hand. "How does that sound?"

"Vanilla chai sounds great," he replied, his gaze moving from Andrea to Jan. "And I'll have two croissants as well."

"Great minds think alike," Jan told them, finding their smiles infectious.

As she turned away from their table, she quickly scanned the other occupied tables in the west parlor. Macy sat by herself, enjoying a raspberry scone and a pot of jasmine tea. Two young college students were sharing a pot of green tea and a plate of black forest cookies, each topped with whipped cream and a bright-red cherry. The Murphys had arrived a few minutes ago and Elaine had taken their order and disappeared into the kitchen.

Jan's gaze moved to the east parlor, where Nigel sat at a table near a window, a book open in front of him as he sipped his oolong tea. Elaine had waited on him earlier, but Jan had been too busy to stop and say hello.

She had started to move in his direction when a familiar voice called her back.

"Jan!" Macy waved her hand in the air. "A little help here please."

Jan swallowed a sigh, then walked over to Macy's table. "Yes, Macy, what can I do for you?"

Macy folded her hands in front of her. "I'd like to talk to you about marzipan."

"Oh," Jan said, aware of the front door opening and seeing Astrid, Millie, and Lawrence walk inside.

"Are you listening?" Macy asked, tapping on the table to get her attention.

Jan focused on Macy. "Yes, of course. Marzipan."

"You should start serving it." Macy reached for the teapot in front of her and poured the last of the brew into her cup. "I think your customers would enjoy it and someone with artistic talent, perhaps Rose or Archie, could easily shape it into something decorative. Maybe Easter eggs or flowers or whatever suits their fancy."

"We'll have to give that some thought," Jan said diplomatically. While she was always open to suggestions for the tearoom, she hadn't missed Macy's little dig. She forced a smile and asked, "Would you like some more tea?"

"No, I've had enough," Macy said, waving her off. Then she peered into the other parlor. "I see Nigel is here. He's been an excellent guest at Green Glades. And such a gentleman. Perhaps I'll have a word with him on my way out."

"He is very charming," Jan agreed before picking up the empty teapot and heading for the east parlor.

"Good morning," Jan greeted the three Finders Keepers members, now seated two tables away from Nigel. She still found it hard to believe that any one of them could be danger-ous. They looked so harmless. "I just want to let you know that our cookie of the day is a black forest cookie. Along with maple croissants and our traditional pastries. I'll be happy to bring out a sample tray, if you'd like."

"Oh my, so many choices," Astrid said, rubbing her hands together. "Why don't you give us a few minutes to decide, dear? We're in no hurry."

"Of course," Jan said with a smile. They might not be harmless, she reminded herself as she moved toward Nigel's table. Or at least *one* of the treasure hunters wasn't harmless—whichever one had assaulted Nigel the other night.

"Hello there!" Nigel said, looking up from his book as Jan neared his table. "My, this is fine tea." He picked up his cup and took a sip, closing his eyes for a moment. "Just as good as any I'd find in England, I must say."

"That is a high compliment," Jan replied, happy to see that Nigel seemed fully recovered from his head wound—even the bandage was gone now. "Were you able to spend time with Archie?"

"Yes, I had a lovely dinner with Archie and Gloria at their home last night. We had a grand time. Archie and I nattered on about old school memories and some of the pranks we played on each other." He chuckled. "How young we were then."

"It's always fun to get together with old friends," Jan said. Then she glanced at his book. "What are you reading?"

He smiled, closing the book to reveal the cover. *"Angel Eyes: The Amelia Howe Story.* She's a starlet from the silent film age—not well-known now, of course. But quite a talent in her day."

"Oh yes, Archie mentioned you collected old Hollywood memorabilia."

He nodded. "I do indeed. That probably seems strange for a chap from across the pond, but my wife was American—a film studies major, actually. She did her master's thesis on the silent screen era, so naturally I learned all about it as well." He turned his gaze back to the book cover. "Amelia Howe was one of her favorite actresses, along with Claire Windsor and Lillian Gish."

Jan was reminded of a long-ago conversation with her grandfather, Willard. "My grandpa always used to say that movies were never as good once the actors started talking."

Nigel laughed. "My Flora would have agreed with him."

Jan saw Macy headed toward them, her purse slung over her arm. "Well, I have an order to fill, so I'd better get going on it. Enjoy your book."

"Thank you, I will."

Jan turned to leave, not wanting to get caught in a conversation with Macy again, and saw another customer walk through the door.

It was Jerry Huston, another member of the Finders Keepers Club. Funny how he'd seemed so *normal* before she knew he was a treasure hunter.

"Hello, Jerry," she greeted him.

He gave a short nod. "Hello."

"You're welcome to sit at whichever table you choose and someone will be along to take your order."

"Jerry!" Astrid called out, waving to the man from her table. "Come join us."

Jerry frowned and hesitated for a long moment before pulling a folded newspaper out his jacket and holding it up in the air. "Thanks," he called to Astrid, "but I just want to do a little reading this morning."

Then he headed for an empty table as far away from Astrid's table as he could get.

Intrigued, Jan headed into the kitchen to start the McInnisses' order and met Elaine coming out of the kitchen door, a tray in her hands.

"Hold on," Jan said, before Elaine could pass her. "All four members of the Finders Keepers Club are here—only Jerry refused to sit with the other three."

Curiosity flashed in Elaine's blue eyes. "Really? Why?"

"I'm not sure. He said he wanted to read his newspaper—but maybe they're not all as friendly with each other as they seem."

"Well, they are in competition to find the treasure," Ellen mused. "Where is he sitting?"

"At a table in the east parlor," Jan said, keeping her voice low. "Do you mind taking his order?"

"Not at all," Elaine said. "I'll do it as soon as I deliver this to Des and Jo," she said, lifting the tray in her hands.

Jan nodded. "And I'll have Rose start the order for Matt and Andrea, then head back to Astrid's table."

The two women set off in opposite directions. Jan walked into the kitchen and saw Rose putting the kettle on to boil.

"I need a pot of vanilla chai tea and four maple croissants, two on each plate," Jan said, carrying Macy's empty teapot over to the sink.

"Sure thing," Rose said, moving toward the pantry.

Jan rinsed out the teapot, then set it aside to be washed later. Then she took a moment to gather her thoughts as Rose emerged from the pantry with a tea canister in her hands.

"Is Archie coming in today?" Rose asked.

Jan checked the stove clock. "Yes, he should be here any minute."

As if on cue, the door between the kitchen and the screened-in porch opened and Archie walked inside. "Good morning," he greeted them. "How goes it today?"

"I'd say things are moving at a pleasant pace," Rose replied, placing tea leaves into a silver tea infuser.

"Nigel is here," Jan told Archie as he hung up his coat and tied on an apron. "Don't worry about taking some time to sit down and visit with him. Elaine and I can cover the tearoom."

Archie smiled as he moved to the sink. "I may do that if I find a spare moment." Then he rolled up his sleeves. "Let me have a go at these dishes first."

Jan left the kitchen, certain Astrid's table would be ready to order by now. Macy was still standing at Nigel's table, chatting away. As Jan passed Jerry's table, she could hear Elaine telling him the different pastries available.

"There she is," Astrid's voice pealed, seeing Jan approach them. "Right on time."

Jan smiled. "What would you like today?"

Astrid motioned to Millie. "You go first, dear."

Millie cleared her throat. "Ginger tea and two black forest cookies."

"Excellent choice," Jan said, then looked at Astrid. "And for you?"

"I'll have the same." She winked at Lawrence. "Care to make it unanimous?"

Lawrence shook his head. "No cookies for me, thank you. I'll just have a cup of Earl Grey and one of those raspberry muffins, if you still have them."

"Yes, we do," Jan said as she watched Macy leave through the front door. Then she glanced at Jerry's table. "Is Jerry all right? I noticed he isn't sitting with you."

"Likes to keep to himself," Lawrence said, looking over at Millie, who nodded in agreement. "Which works out well for all of us."

Astrid laughed. "Oh, Lawrence, that's taking it a bit far. Jerry's just very cerebral. Like Millie here." Then she looked up at Jan. "Millie is a very smart woman—and I'm talking genius level." Then she glanced over at Millie. "Oh, look at her blush."

Jan could see Millie shift uncomfortably in her chair at Astrid's words.

"Perhaps we should change the subject," Lawrence said, then turned toward Jan. But before he could speak, a loud scream tore through the air.

"Help!" cried a woman's voice from outside the house. "Help me!"

CHAPTER NINE

Elaine froze when she heard the loud scream, followed by cries for help.

Then she bolted into action, hurrying toward the front door at the same time as Jan and Nigel, with Matt and Andrea McInnis following close behind.

Elaine reached the door first and pulled it open. Then Nigel raced past her as another cry for help, weaker this time, emanated from the front lawn.

That's when she saw Macy, sprawled on the ground. She was propped up on one elbow, the other hand reaching down toward her black shoes, each accented with a gold buckle.

"My ankle," she groaned, wincing as she tried to move.

Nigel removed his suit coat and laid it over her, then tucked it around her shoulders. "What happened?"

"I stepped in a hole and twisted my ankle," Macy said, her face pale. "I think it's broken."

Matt and Andrea hurried to her side.

"Which ankle?" Matt asked as he gently supported Macy, carefully turning her all the way on her back.

"The right one," Macy said, then groaned, her eyelids fluttering shut.

Andrea knelt down at Macy's feet and gently rolled up the cuff of her black slacks a couple of inches to reveal the black sock underneath. Then Andrea began gently probing her ankle.

"Ouch!" Macy scowled at Andrea. "You're making it worse!"

"I'm sorry, Macy," Andrea said evenly, her gaze still on the ankle. It was already beginning to puff up under the sock. "I'm checking for any broken bones."

"You don't have to torture me in the process," Macy cried, the color returning to her cheeks as a crowd began to gather on the front porch. "I'm telling you it's broken."

"Tell me exactly what happened," Matt said to Macy, obviously trying to distract her from Andrea's exam. "Did you hit your head when you fell? Do you feel any dizziness?"

"No and no," Macy said crisply. "Like I said before, there's a hole in the lawn. I was cutting across it to get to my car quicker and down I went." She looked up at Elaine. "It was like a booby trap."

Archie walked toward them while Rose trailed a few feet behind. "What happened here?"

"Oh, Archie," Macy said, leaning her head against Matt's arm, "I'm so glad you're here. Please tell Dr. Andrea to stop poking at me."

"She stepped in a hole," Elaine told him, while Nigel rubbed one hand over his chin, his face etched with concern, "and twisted her ankle."

Andrea rose to her feet. "Well, the good news is that your ankle is not broken," she told Macy. "The bad news is that you have a severe sprain."

"Just a sprain?" Macy echoed. "Are you sure?"

"Yes, but a sprain can be just as painful as a broken bone," Andrea said. "You're going to need to be on crutches for a few days—maybe even a week."

Matt nodded. "We can get you a pair from the clinic and..."

"No need," Macy interjected, holding one hand in the air. "Shane broke his leg when he was a teenager and we bought a pair of crutches for him then. They're adjustable, so they should work for me too." She sighed, wincing again. "Good thing we kept them around, I guess."

Andrea rolled the cuff of Macy's slacks back down, then rose to her feet. "We've got a medical bag in our car. I want to wrap that ankle to stabilize it before we try to move you."

"Are you cold?" Elaine asked Macy as Andrea walked toward her car.

"No, Nigel's coat is keeping me nice and warm," Macy said, smiling up at the Englishman.

"Glad to be of service," Nigel told her.

Elaine was grateful the weather was in the high fifties already, and climbing, although rain was predicted for later that evening. Then she turned around and said, "You can go back inside, folks. Macy will be fine."

"Yes, go," Macy called out, waving them away. "Enjoy your tea. I don't want anyone else falling into a hole out here."

The crowd slowly moved back inside, with Rose promising hot tea for anyone who wanted a fresh pot. When the front door closed, Elaine turned to Jan. "We need to fill that hole in."

"I'll do it," Archie offered as Andrea carried her medical bag over to Macy. "Where is it?"

"Over there," Macy said, motioning toward an area near her feet. Then she squeezed her eyes shut and sucked in a deep breath as Andrea began to carefully wrap an ACE bandage around her swollen ankle.

Elaine, Jan, and Archie moved in that direction, the brown grass and leaves flattened by the spring rains. Then Elaine saw a clump of earth sticking part way out of the ground. "Here it is," she said, pointing it out.

Archie leaned down and easily pushed the clump of dirt aside to reveal a hole about eight inches wide and six inches deep—big enough to trip someone up.

Elaine picked up the clump of dirt, grass and leaves still clinging to it. "This was probably loose enough for Macy to stumble on."

"And this hole was made by a spade." Archie pointed out the smooth, hard-packed sides inside the hole. The he looked up at Jan and Elaine. "Someone was digging here."

Elaine looked at the clump in her hand again, turning it over. That's when she saw a faint line of fluorescent orange paint among the blades of grass. "Look at this," she said softly, moving closer to Archie and Jan. "Remember last summer when that utility worker marked the lines leading to our house before they began to work on the power poles?"

Jan nodded. "Most of them faded away." She looked up at Elaine. "Do you think some thought this marked the treasure so they started digging?"

"It seems so." Elaine sighed, realizing the implication. "Macy was right. There could be more holes around here—especially if there are any orange stripes left on the grass. We'll need to walk the lawn just to be sure it's safe."

But she was worried about more than holes in her lawn. This was just another sign that the treasure hunters could create havoc—even without realizing it. She doubted they meant for Macy to fall into a hole and get hurt, but was that the consequence of their treasure hunting? It appeared so.

First Nigel was hurt, and now Macy. She watched as Matt, Andrea, and Nigel slowly helped Macy stand up, taking great care to keep all weight off her swollen ankle.

"All right, now let's walk you slowly to your car," Matt told her, with him and Nigel on either side of her helping her take slow steps to her car. "I'll drive your car to Green Glade and Andrea will follow. We'll get you settled in, and talk to Shane and Zale about your care."

"Yes, I'll call them on the way," Macy said. "I hate to be a bother."

"I'm sure they won't mind," Andrea assured her.

"And I'll be happy to help in any way I can," Nigel said. "I'll be right behind you in my car," he told Matt. "To help get her into the house."

"You're so kind," Macy told him, now wearing Nigel's suit coat draped over her shoulders.

Elaine watched them with Jan at her side, feeling helpless and a little guilty that Macy had been hurt at their home. "Is there anything we can do for you, Macy?" she asked, walking toward the driveway.

Macy shook her head, her expression tight as she moved slowly along, obviously in too much pain—or too angry—to answer.

Jan sighed. "We'll check on her tomorrow," she said to Elaine. "Maybe take her that basket of goodies."

"We'd better make it a big one," Elaine said, placing her hands on her hips. "And figure out how to decipher that treasure map before someone else gets hurt."

THAT EVENING, ELAINE stood in front of her bedroom mirror, putting the finishing touches on her makeup. She was meeting Nathan for dinner at the Pine Tree Grill and felt as nervous as a teenage girl. Which was silly, she told herself, carefully applying a final coat of mascara to her eyelashes. So why did she feel like she'd downed three cups of espresso?

She thought about their first date on Valentine's Day, when he'd been about to kiss her and she'd turned away.

Elaine had regretted it almost immediately. And Nathan hadn't tried to kiss her since.

Maybe tonight will be different.

"Here's the bracelet you wanted to borrow," Jan said, walking through the open door of Elaine's room. Then her eyebrows rose. "Wow, you look so pretty! I love your top."

Elaine smiled as she looked down at her cobalt-blue boat-neck sweater with three-quarter sleeves. "Thanks, I found it in the back of my closet. I haven't worn it for so long, I think it came back in style."

Jan laughed. "I love closet shopping—especially finding clothes I don't remember buying." She handed the bracelet to Elaine. "Maybe that's a sign that I should clean out my closet more often."

"Me too," Elaine agreed, slipping the cuff-style bracelet over her wrist. Then she picked up the tortoiseshell brush that had belonged to their nana and ran it through her short brown hair. "There, I think I'm ready."

Jan tilted her neck, wincing a little.

"Does your neck still hurt?" Elaine asked, concerned. Jan had mentioned something about a sore neck this morning.

"I just have a crick in it," Jan said with a smile. "That's what I get for falling asleep over a good book. It will work itself out soon enough."

"Find anything interesting in Diane's book yet?"

"Not yet," Jan replied, "but I'm just getting started. It's quite good so far though."

"I'd like to read it after you're done." Elaine applied a light coat of lipstick, then grabbed her jacket off the bed. "I'd better get moving if I don't want to be late."

"Have a wonderful time," Jan said, then placed her hands gently on Elaine's shoulders. "And don't be so nervous."

Elaine laughed. "Is it that obvious? I don't know what's wrong with me."

"Nothing's wrong with you," Jan said gently. "Dating again after a long marriage is hard—and uncomfortable. But I can't think of anything better than dating a man you've known your entire life—especially a man like Nathan."

"You're right," Elaine said, calming a little. "After that mud pie fight we had in fifth grade, he's definitely seen me at my worst."

Jan smiled. "That's the spirit. Now off you go."

Elaine gave Jan a quick hug and then headed for the stairs, ready to spend a fun evening with one of her best friends.

By the time Elaine arrived at the Pine Tree Grill, the eatery was already full with the dinner crowd. A favorite spot in Lancaster, the Grill served sandwiches and burgers year round. She scanned the crowd but didn't see Nathan.

"Hey there, Elaine," Bianca said, wearing her signature gold bangle bracelets that sounded like wind chimes when she was on the move. She owned the Grill with her brother and had the gift of gab, always making both friends and strangers feel at home. "If you're here for dinner, you've come on the right night. We've got French meat pie for our special this evening and I know it's one of your favorites."

"It sure is," Elaine replied, her mouth watering. A variation of shepherd's pie, the French meat pie was made with ground pork and beef and seasoned with spices like cinnamon and cloves, all wrapped up in a flaky pastry.

"I'm meeting Nathan, so I'll wait to order until he gets here." Elaine looked around. "Are there any tables available, or should we sit at the counter?"

"I believe there's a small table open in the back," Bianca said as another customer approached the cash register.

"Thanks," Elaine said, heading that way. She saw several familiar faces in the restaurant, greeting them with smiles and waves and pausing for a quick chat with Rue and Ned Maxwell before claiming the empty table for two.

She took a seat, slipping her purse on to the back of her chair. The older man sitting behind her pushed his chair back slightly, bumping against hers.

"Pardon me," he said, glancing at Elaine over her shoulder.

"No problem," she told him. "We're a little squished here, aren't we?" She moved her table a few inches away, then scooted her chair forward to make more room between them.

Then she saw Nathan walk through the door and her heart gave a little bounce. She saw him look around for a moment, then they made eye contact. Elaine waved her hand in the air. He flashed a smile as he walked toward her, wearing dark jeans and a cobalt-blue shirt on his lean frame.

She laughed when he reached the table. "We match!"

He chuckled as he took a seat. "I guess we do, although you look better in blue than I do."

"And I think blue suits you better, but I guess we'll have to agree to disagree," she told him. "I'm so glad we could get together. Your busy season is starting up."

"It sure is." Nathan worked as an auctioneer, specializing in antiques. With the weather getting warmer, he'd already started working jobs at estate sales, many of which would be held outside. "I'm getting calls every day now for upcoming sales."

They chatted easily together for a few minutes before Bianca arrived at their table. They both ordered the French meat pie and a beverage.

"Coming right up," Bianca said, giving them a wink as she walked away.

Then Elaine heard the man behind her say, "It took you long enough, Peacock. I thought you chickened out."

She froze. *Peacock?* The only Peacock she knew was Lawrence Peacock, a member of the Finders Keepers Club.

"I'm here, aren't I?" replied a male voice that Elaine immediately recognized. Yes, it was definitely Lawrence. And the man behind him definitely sounded like Jerry. She hadn't noticed before, when his chair had bumped into hers. But why the animosity between the two men?

"Is something wrong?" Nathan asked her.

She blinked, realizing she'd been so distracted by the men at the table behind her that she'd been ignoring Nathan. Not wanting to tip them off, Elaine held up one finger, then pulled a pen out of her purse and scribbled a note on her paper napkin. *Two members of the Finders Keepers Club are at the table behind me. I want to hear what they have to say.*

Elaine slid the napkin across the table toward Nathan. When he'd called to make their date, she'd filled him in about the mystery teapot with the map inside and everything that had followed its arrival.

Nathan turned the napkin slightly, then his light-brown eyebrows rose on his forehead. He met her gaze, giving a slight nod, his blue eyes lit with curiosity.

"Come now, Lawrence," Jerry growled. "No need to be like that, especially in a place like this. You like these small, quaint towns, don't you? I expected to find you happy as a clam."

"What do you want, Huston?" Lawrence replied, his voice terse. "You have a lot of nerve coming here after what happened in Albuquerque."

A snort of laughter sounded behind her. "You're still mad about that? You're getting soft, Lawrence. Maybe if you stopped mooning over a certain lady and concentrated on playing the game, you'd win more often."

Astrid? Elaine wondered if the two men were fighting over her. Lawrence had joined Astrid and that ornithologist at their table the other day. Maybe he was the jealous type.

"Let's keep the lady out of it, Jerry," Lawrence said tersely. "Why did you want to meet me here?"

Nathan jotted a note on the other side of the napkin, then slid it toward Elaine. *They really dislike each other.*

She gave a nod of agreement, then looked up as Mel, Bianca's brother, approached their table. Flecks of gray peppered his neatly trimmed mustache and beard, and threaded through his receding hairline.

"Here you go," Mel said, lowering the tray in his hands. "Two French meat pies. And they're piping hot, so be careful."

Elaine momentarily turned her attention away from the two men behind her and chatted with Mel as he placed their plates and drinks on the table. Mel wasn't as talkative as his sister, but he had a solidness about him that folks in Lancaster admired.

Then, as Nathan and Mel began chatting, she risked a quick glance over her shoulder, hoping the two men wouldn't recognize her and clam up. Lawrence was dressed in a dark suit and tie with a crisp white shirt, as if he was attending a business meeting. And perhaps he was, in a way, she thought to herself. The two men indeed seemed hostile, so what else could bring them together but some kind of business proposition—even if that business involved stealing the map?

Jerry sat in his chair like a bag full of pudding—cinched in the middle with a belt. He wore a black dress shirt and tan khakis, but despite his more casual style he projected an air of authority. Jerry looked about Lawrence's age, somewhere in the mid sixties, although his short hair was coal black and combed into place with some kind of stiff gel.

"Let's get to it, shall we?" Lawrence said. "I have things to do."

"As do I," Jerry replied.

Elaine looked over at Nathan, suddenly realizing that Mel was gone. She felt a stab of guilt, but Nathan gave her an encouraging smile as he sliced into his meat pie, releasing a curl of steam from the flaky crust.

Then the conversation between Huston and Peacock caught her attention once again.

"Let's work together," Jerry said, his voice lower now. "We can split the bounty fifty-fifty."

Lawrence sniffed. "Why in the world would I want to do that?"

"Because the tea ladies are involved now—and that complicates things."

Elaine strained to hear them over the noise of chatting customers and clinking silverware. The two men kept their voices low and intense.

"Yes, I know," Lawrence confirmed. "Millie saw a state trooper's vehicle parked at Tea for Two the other morning during her walk. Then Macy told me a cop interviewed her about one of her guests getting attacked."

Jerry made a sound between a sniff and a snort. "Yes, her son, Shane, told me the same. Hit over the head, or some such thing."

"That's more your style than mine," Lawrence said.

Elaine looked over at Nathan, her shock reflected in his eyes. Had Lawrence just accused Jerry of assaulting Nigel? Maybe these club members *were* dangerous. But so far neither man had actually admitted to anything she could take to Trooper Benson.

Then Lawrence chuckled. "You think I have part of the map figured out. That's why you want us to work together."

"Or perhaps I've figured out the entire map and already know where the treasure is," Jerry countered. "And just need some assistance in unearthing the booty."

Booty? Elaine smiled at the word. Did these two men think of themselves as modern-day pirates? One thing was clear, they didn't trust each other.

"So what do you say?" Jerry asked him. "Shall we work on this one together?"

"Sorry, Jerry, but I'm going to pass," Lawrence told him. "You'll have to find someone else to play your fall guy this time."

The sound of chair legs scraping against floor made Elaine look over at Nathan. He gave her a signal that Lawrence was standing up now—obviously preparing to leave.

"Let me know if you change your mind," Jerry told him, sounding amused.

"You're on your own," Lawrence replied, then emitted a wry chuckle. "You should be used to that."

Elaine stiffened as Lawrence walked past her table, keeping her head down so he wouldn't recognize her. After he'd walked out of the Grill, she heard Jerry mutter something under his breath before taking his leave as well.

"Well, that was fascinating," Nathan said.

Elaine looked up at him. "Do you think they know we have the map?"

He shrugged. "Hard to tell—they said you were involved now, but they might have just been referring to what happened to Nigel." Then he reached his hand across the table and grasped her free hand, giving it a warm squeeze. "Are you worried?"

"No," she said, a little surprised at her answer. Despite the conversation she'd just overheard between Jerry and Lawrence, they'd only made her more determined to find the treasure before they did. "But the treasure must be valuable, if Jerry wanted to 'split the booty' [she made motions with her hands like quote marks] with Lawrence. What do you suppose it could be?"

"Money, jewels, rare coins?" Nathan ventured.

She nodded. "It can't be anything too big, or it would be difficult to hide."

Nathan gave her hand another squeeze then released it. "Your pie is getting cold."

She looked down at the golden crust of her meat pie and suddenly realized she was starving. She picked up her fork and dug in, the conversation she'd just overheard still swirling in her head.

"One thing is clear," she told Nathan, "we'll need to keep a step ahead of those treasure hunters if we want to find what they're looking for."

He nodded. "Just be careful, Elaine. From the sound of it, those two guys are dead serious about winning this game of theirs."

She thought about Nigel, collapsed and bleeding on the floor and knew Nathan was right. "Then we need to figure how to beat the players at their own game."

AN HOUR LATER, Nathan walked Elaine home. The tearoom was about two buildings away from the Grill, so it had been a short and quiet walk.

On the porch, she didn't see any other people around. A light mist hovered in the air, giving the street lights an ethereal glow.

"Thank you for a wonderful evening," Nathan said, reaching for her hand.

Elaine smiled up at him, her stomach fluttering. Her earlier nerves had disappeared during dinner, but now they were back with a vengeance.

There was something about the mist. The sense that they were the only two people in the world at this moment. The look in Nathan's eyes as he took a step closer to her.

Then he reached out to gently caress her chin, tipping it up with his fingertips.

Elaine's nerves melted away as he hesitated, as if giving her an opportunity to slip away. But she wasn't afraid anymore of Nathan or her growing feelings for him. She wasn't going anywhere.

Then he kissed her.

CHAPTER TEN

Jan sat at the kitchen table on Saturday night, all her cookbooks open in front of her. Jazz music played softly on the radio as she jotted notes on the notebook in front of her.

The baking competition was only a few days away and she needed to study up if she wanted to compete with the other contestants. The idea of a surprise basket still made her nervous, but excited too. It would be like a game—and the best way to win was to use all the ingredients in the basket together in a way that would wow the judges.

Or she might fall as flat as a ruined soufflé.

"Think positive," she said to herself, flipping through the pages of her Nana's old cookbook. She wanted to study the popular desserts of the past, as well as the present, to gather together as many ideas as possible.

She'd need to be able to think on her feet once the time clock started. Two hours wasn't really long at all to prepare a dessert course—especially if she needed to cool baked items before adding frosting or sauce.

Jan tapped her pen against the table, hoping she'd be able to keep this all in her head. She didn't think she'd be able to take any notes into the contest with her, but she'd check the rules listed on the letter again, just in case. She was about to do just that when the door to the kitchen opened and Elaine walked inside.

"My, it's wet out there," Elaine said, pulling back the hood of her raincoat. "But the rain is finally letting up. It's a good thing Archie filled in that hole for us, or it would be full of water."

Jan looked at her. "You're smiling."

"Well," Elaine said, her eyes shining, "Nathan and I had a wonderful time."

Jan chuckled. "I can tell."

Elaine's smile widened as she turned around to hang up her raincoat. Then she fluffed her hair before facing Jan once more. And she was still smiling.

Jan was happy Elaine's date had obviously gone well. She was about to ask her about it, then decided Elaine would tell her in her own good time.

Elaine pointed to the cookbooks on the table. "What's all this?"

Jan closed the book in front of her. "I was just cramming for the contest—taking notes and trying to come up with a strategy. It's more work than you'd think."

"I have every confidence in you," Elaine said, pulling out a chair at the table and taking a seat. "And speaking of strategies, you'll never guess who Nathan and I saw at the Grill."

Jan listened intently as Elaine told her all about Jerry and Lawrence's conversation. Hearing about Lawrence's refusal to conspire with Jerry made her like him even more.

"That's odd though, isn't it?" Jan said when Elaine had finished the story. "Jerry wouldn't even sit at the same table with Lawrence this morning."

"Probably because Astrid and Millie were there. And from what I've seen—and heard—from Jerry so far, he isn't what you'd call a people-person."

"Rough around the edges?" Jan said.

Elaine thought for a moment, then shook her head. "No, more like someone wearing a suit of armor. He doesn't seem to want people to get too close. Even when I was taking his order in the tearoom, he never actually looked me in the eyes."

"Guilty conscience, perhaps?" Jan ventured. "Maybe he's the one who assaulted Nigel."

"Maybe." Elaine rubbed her hands together. "I could use a cup of hot tea. Care to join me?"

Jan laughed. "I think you already know the answer to that question."

"You're right, I do," Elaine said with a grin. She got up from the table and retrieved the teakettle, then began filling it with water.

Jan glanced down at her notes, her mind jumbled with thoughts of the baking contest and the treasure map and a group of treasure hunters staying nearby. But all of that would keep until the morning. She closed the notebook in front of her, ready to relax and enjoy a cup of tea.

"So you've been studying all evening?" Elaine asked, retrieving two tea cups and saucers and carrying them to the table.

"Well, not the whole evening." Jan began stacking the cookbooks together. "But it's been fun looking through them—I love reading some of our old family recipes. Remember when Nana used to make hummingbird cake for us?"

Elaine smiled. "I sure do. Almost made myself sick eating it one time. Are you thinking of making that at the contest?"

"I don't know," Jan mused. "Maybe a variation of it, if I have the right ingredients. It would be nice to make something…unexpected. And with a wow factor, of course. No pressure there."

Elaine chuckled. "Speaking of a wow factor, what should we put in Macy's care package? I really do feel terrible about her accident."

Jan reached for the teapot and poured herself a cup of tea, inhaling the fragrant steam that rose from the cup. "*Hmm*, is this the new lavender-honey blend? It smells wonderful."

"It sure is," Elaine said, pouring herself a cup. "No caffeine in it either, so it won't keep us up." She smiled. "Not that we ever let that stop us before."

Jan took a sip of the tea. "Let's put some of this tea blend in Macy's basket, along with the Hello Spring blend."

"Okay, and what about pastries? Your maple croissants, of course."

"And I made marzipan," Jan told her. "Before her accident, Macy told me we should serve marzipan, so I thought I'd make some just for her."

"You had time to make marzipan while I was out?" Elaine asked, her brows lifting.

"Sure," Jan said with a smile. "It's just a mixture of almond paste, confectioners' sugar, corn syrup, and food coloring. Mix up batches in different colors, then mold them into the shapes you want. I made decorated Easter eggs."

"Fun!" Elaine exclaimed. "I hope Macy likes them."

"We'll see," Jan said. "You never know with her."

She didn't know what the judges of the baking contest would like either, but she pushed that thought out of her mind as she took another sip of her tea, knowing everything would look better in the morning.

AFTER CHURCH THE next day, Elaine drove to Green Glade while Jan stayed home and prepared Sunday dinner. As she pulled into the long driveway leading to Macy's two-story home, her mind wandered back to all those cookbooks Jan had spread across the kitchen table last night.

She knew her cousin wanted to do well at the baking contest and was even a little nervous about it. Maybe Elaine could find some way to help.

As she parked her car in front of the house and switched off the engine, the seed of an idea came to her—a way to help Jan and have some fun in the process.

She pushed it to the back of her mind as she grabbed the basket on the seat beside her. They'd filled it with small tins of tea leaves, cookies, muffins, and the marzipan Easter eggs Jan had made last night.

Elaine got out of the car and walked to the house, so happy to see the sun out today. The ground was still moist from last night's rain but the air smelled clean and crisp, promising a beautiful day ahead. Although Macy's house was much larger than the surrounding cottages, it fit in nicely in the community of Green Glade.

As she climbed the porch steps, she saw the front door partway open behind the screen door. She tapped on it, then heard Macy call out, "Come in."

As Elaine entered the tiled foyer, she saw Macy reclined on a sofa in the living room, half-propped up with pillows behind and another pillow under her sprained ankle. Her bare toes peeked out from the ACE bandage.

"Hello, Elaine," Macy said, adjusting the light-green afghan that lay over her. "Nice of you to stop by."

"I wanted to see how you're doing," Elaine said, setting the basket on the coffee table. "Jan and I made up a basket of goodies for you."

Macy leaned forward a few inches to get a better look at the basket. "Anything good in there?"

"We have a variety of teas, along with a small jar of honey. And some pastries, of course." Then Elaine reached into the basket and pulled out a small box tied with a pink ribbon. "And Jan made something special for you."

Macy took the box from her before sliding off the ribbon and then opening the lid. "Well, look at that."

Egg-shaped marzipan sat in a nest of spun sugar. The marzipan eggs, close to a dozen, had each been colored a pastel shade of pink, yellow, blue, or green. Then Jan had used royal icing and edible pearls to uniquely decorate each one.

"Jan mentioned that you liked marzipan," Elaine said, watching Macy pick up an egg and examine it.

"I didn't tell her I liked marzipan," Macy clarified. "I told her that I thought you two should serve it in the tearoom."

Elaine felt a twinge of frustration at her lack of appreciation—especially when Jan had gone to so much work.

Then she told herself that Macy was in pain and unable to walk on her own two feet, probably making her crankier than usual. "So you don't like marzipan?"

"I didn't say that either." Macy took a tentative bite of the small marzipan egg, chewing thoughtfully. "Not bad," she pronounced at last, then popped the rest of the egg in her mouth.

Elaine couldn't help but smile. For Macy, that was high praise. "Well, I hope you enjoy them. And I'm sorry you'll be laid up here for a few days. We'll miss seeing you at the tearoom."

Macy licked a smudge of white royal icing off one finger, then looked up at Elaine. "Don't worry, I'll be there tomorrow. Nigel has kindly offered to chauffeur me back and forth."

"Oh," Elaine said, surprised, "that's very kind of him." She wondered if Macy and Nigel were forming an attachment, but Macy quickly quashed that possibility.

"Don't get the wrong idea," Macy told her, picking up another marzipan egg. "There's nothing romantic between the two of us. He mainly talks about his dead wife—and I enjoy spending time with a man of his education and experience. Some say the art of chivalry is dead, but Nigel is a walking, talking example of it."

"Well, I'm glad you enjoy each other's company." Then Elaine looked down at Macy's foot. "Are you in a lot of pain?"

"It comes and goes." Macy studied the decorated egg in her hand, studded with tiny pink edible pearls. "Shane and Zale stayed with me last night and will be back after lunch. They'll handle everything at the clubhouse until I can manage on my own again."

Elaine peeked at her watch. "Well, I'd better get going. I hope you feel better soon."

"I'm sure you do, since it happened on your property," Macy said before taking a bite of the egg. "But don't worry—I'm not planning to sue, if that's what brought you here today."

Elaine caught her breath and stared at the innkeeper. "Macy, I'm here because both Jan and I were concerned about you," she said truthfully, although she was happy to hear Macy wasn't planning a lawsuit. "Please let us know if you need anything. We'll be glad to refill that basket for you until you're back on your feet."

"Thank you," Macy said, a little grudgingly. "Now I'm a little tired, if you don't mind."

"Of course. Take care, Macy." Elaine headed for the door, sensing that the woman was grateful for the basket and the visit, even if she'd been prickly about it.

As she walked toward her car, Elaine saw Lawrence Peacock strolling along the row of cottages in the distance. She hesitated, then walked past her car to catch up with him. The day was warm enough for brisk walk, and she doubled her pace to get closer to him before he could disappear inside his cottage.

"Lawrence!" she called out, slightly out of breath.

He turned around and smiled as she reached him. "Hello there, Mrs. Cook."

She smiled. "Please call me Elaine."

"Elaine," he said, nodding as he continued to walk, only at a slower pace. "Nice day for a walk, isn't it?" He looked up at the blue sky overhead. "The sun is out and the ice is melting on the lake."

They both turned toward Chickadee Lake, where chunks of ice bobbed in the water.

"It sure is," Elaine replied, eager to learn more about him and his treasure hunting friends. "How do you like Lancaster so far?"

"I love it," he said, looking around him. "There's something about it that reminds of home."

"Where is home?" she asked.

"Minnesota, originally," he said, a fond gleam in his pale-blue eyes. "The land of ten thousand lakes—so this place makes me feel right at home." He sighed. "I've moved around since then, but hope to settle there again—eventually."

"After you're done treasure hunting?"

He paused a step as he turned to look at her. "How do you know about that?"

She stopped walking, intrigued by the intensity of his gaze. She wondered if he'd seen her at the Grill last night and knew she and Nathan could hear their conversation. "Let's just say I have my sources." She lightened the moment with a smile. "It's just a game, right?"

He looked at her for a long moment. "Can I be honest with you?"

"Of course," she said. "In fact, I'd prefer honesty."

"Yes," he said, nodding. "Wouldn't we all?" Then he raked a hand through his silver hair. "To tell you the truth, Mrs. Cook— I mean, Elaine—I don't care one whit about treasures or hunting for them."

"Oh? Then what are you doing here?" she asked bluntly. "And why would you remain a member of the Finders Keepers Club?"

He arched a brow. "So you even know the name of our club? Those sources of yours are impressive."

She smiled. "Macy happened to mention the name of your club, so it must not have been too big a secret."

He shrugged, then stared out at the lake. "While I don't care all that much about the club or its purpose, I care very deeply about one of its members. She and I are charter members of the Finders Keepers Club and there are only four of us left now. This club means a lot to her."

Elaine blinked, surprised by the admission and the love she saw shining in his eyes. "You're in love with Astrid?"

"No, not Astrid." He turned to look at her, both frustration and longing etched on his aristocratic face. "Millie."

"Millie," she echoed, then suppressed a smile. So Lawrence had fallen head over heels for quiet, bookish Millie. Her opinion of the man just went up another a notch. "Does she know?"

"I...honestly don't know."

Elaine blinked. "You haven't told her?"

A muscle flexed in Lawrence's square jaw. "If I tell her and the feeling isn't mutual, then it's over. It may sound cowardly to you, and I suppose it is, but I'd rather be close to her than lose her altogether."

Elaine didn't know what to say. She could see the anguish in his eyes and understood his dilemma. Millie wasn't the type of person to reveal her inner thoughts or emotions. She was as closed as some of the books she liked to read. And yet Jan and Bob had caught her crying over Jane Eyre's love for Mr. Rochester.

Elaine looked at the lake, knowing how much life flowed under the icy sheet that covered it during the winter months. Maybe the same was true of Millie and the icy wall she'd built around herself.

"I'm not sure why I'm telling you this," Lawrence said at last, breaking the silence between them. "Perhaps I'm just tired of keeping it to myself for so long. Or maybe I want someone to tell me it's a worthless cause and to stop wasting my time."

She looked up at him, the bright sun making her squint. "Do you feel like you've been wasting your time?"

"Not at all," he said without hesitation. "Millie has a brilliant mind. We can talk for hours, about anything. And I've never won a chess match against her, although I believe she's let me come close a time or two." He smiled. "So maybe that's enough."

Elaine didn't know what to tell him, aware of how it felt to have your heart pulled in two directions. After she'd moved back to Lancaster and renewed her friendship with Nathan, he'd wanted more. But she'd held back. Her love for Ben had filled her heart for so long, she'd feared there wasn't room for anyone else.

Now she knew differently.

Then Elaine realized that she'd fallen silent again. Lawrence had been open enough to share his deepest feelings with her. But she wasn't sure if he was looking for advice or commiseration.

Or maybe he was trying to throw her off track by making her think he wasn't interested in the treasure? He sounded sincere, but she couldn't be certain. Still, she decided to speak honestly.

"I don't think it's ever wrong to follow your heart," she said carefully, not wanting to overstep. "I think Millie would be lucky to have you."

He smiled. "Well, that's nice to hear, at least." He checked his watch. "Looks like it's almost lunchtime. I don't want to keep you."

"One more thing," Elaine asked. "Since you're not interested in the treasure, can you tell me what it is?"

He blinked. "You don't know?"

"You do?" she asked, arching a brow.

"Well, for this particular treasure hunt we do, though that's not always the case. Whoever hides the treasure has the option of telling us what we're searching for."

Elaine wondered why a description of the treasure wasn't included in their mystery package. Perhaps it was spelled out in the secret code on the map. Or the sender wanted it to be a surprise.

"So what is it?" she asked, hoping he'd share the information.

"It's a ruby necklace and it's valued at about five thousand dollars."

Elaine stared at him in disbelief. "That's a lot of money." She thought about Nigel's head injury. "Enough to make someone desperate to have it, I suppose."

He smiled. "Our club has hunted for treasures worth more than that, and several worth less. It varies."

As he spoke, Elaine reminded herself that she couldn't be sure he was telling her the truth about anything.

She knew Jan would have dinner ready soon, but she wasn't ready to let Lawrence go yet. "Just one more thing."

He arched a silver eyebrow.

"We've had two incidents since your club has arrived in Lancaster," Elaine said. "Two people who have been injured, one by accident and the other, intentionally. I'm afraid something even worse might happen if we don't stop whoever is responsible for these incidents. Do you know...?"

"It's not me," Lawrence interjected. "As I've made clear, I'm not interested in the treasure." He hesitated, as if wrestling with what to say next. "I don't really believe a member of our club would hurt anyone. But, if I had to guess, I'd say watch out for Jerry."

THAT NIGHT, JAN lay awake reading in bed. She'd had a full day, starting with church and then enjoying Sunday dinner with Elaine. That's when she'd learned that Macy had liked her marzipan, the treasure was a ruby necklace, and that Lawrence suspected Jerry might be ruthless in his pursuit of it.

Most surprising of all, Elaine confided that Lawrence was in love with Millie. The matchmaker in Jan made her want to help facilitate a romance between them, but she was old enough to know that if two people were meant to be together, God would guide them. He'd helped her and Peter find each other and blessed their marriage with three beautiful children. And now He'd blessed her even more by bringing Bob into her life.

Jan had so much to be grateful for.

That's why it was silly to let the upcoming baking contest make her nervous. She'd spent the afternoon baking—creating practice cakes and tarts for the contest, and trying out a variety of different ingredients. Some of them had been flops, but she had a few successes too. Enough to give her hope that she might actually have a chance to win the contest.

The toughest part would be the timing. Once she opened the surprise basket, she'd have to decide very quickly what to make so she could use the full two hours to prepare all the elements of her dessert course.

The more she thought about it, the more her muscles tensed, until she finally had to sit up and stretch her stiff neck before adjusting the pillows behind her. Then she lay back down and took a deep, calming breath, focusing on the book once more.

She liked reading *Through My Eyes: Chickadee Lake and the Great Depression* even more than she'd expected, but had yet to read anything about the woolen mill or the Wood family.

As factories in Maine began to close and farms began to fail, people soon began to realize that life would get worse before it got better. My parents began to live more frugally, my father bartering his legal services for eggs and butter. With money tight, few people could afford a lawyer. And for places like Lancaster, which depended on tourists for a large part of its economy, the Depression hit hard.

I remember when my mother had a women's club meeting at our house. Only a few of the members attended and one, Mabel Wood, dropped out...

Jan gasped when she read the name. Mabel Wood. It was the first mention of the Wood family she'd come across. As her gaze scanned the rest of the page, she saw mention of the woolen mill. It was all starting to come together.

She settled back into the pillows and continued reading Bertha Sullivan's story.

I sat in the corner that day, quiet as a church mouse, hearing them talk about how the Wood family was bankrupt, and that it had happened even before the Depression hit. The woolen mill had shut down and even more people in town were out of work—

Suddenly, Jan heard a loud thud.

She sat up in bed, trying to gauge where the noise had come from. She put the book aside, a chill running through her that had nothing to do with the cold night air.

She got out of bed and grabbed her robe, worried that Elaine might have fallen. She padded over the hardwood floor to her door and opened it, then stepped out into the hallway.

A moment later, Elaine's door opened too. "Did you hear that?" she asked Jan.

"Yes," Jan replied. Just then they heard another thud, even louder this time.

Elaine paled as she moved quickly toward Jan and dropped her voice to a mere whisper. "I think someone is in the house."

CHAPTER ELEVEN

Elaine stood with Jan in the second floor hallway, the only light the dim glow of a nightlight plugged into an outlet at the end of the hall. Neither one of them said a word, the silence suddenly eerie and oppressive.

Elaine didn't move, her ears straining to listen for any more unusual sounds. They stood there together, not speaking for several minutes, but all she heard was the usual creaks and groans of the house—sounds so familiar they were like old friends.

Then Jan reached out and switched on the overhead light. As light flooded the hallway, Elaine's tension eased. What a difference it made not to be standing in the dark. She squared her shoulders and looked at her cousin. "I don't hear anything now, do you?"

"No," Jan said, her voice low. "But I don't think that sound was just the house settling either."

Elaine nodded, feeling the same way. Then she pointed to the sewing room that was directly across the hall from her own bedroom. "I think the sound came from in there."

Jan stared at the closed door for a long moment. Then she said, "Come with me."

Elaine followed her cousin into her bedroom, where Jan retrieved her cell phone and a can of hairspray. She slipped her phone into her pocket, then motioned for Elaine to follow her back into the hallway.

Elaine knew how silly they'd feel if the noise they'd heard turned out to have a reasonable explanation. She hoped they did feel silly. That would be better than the alternative.

"Should we call the police?" Jan asked, now hesitating outside the door of the sewing room.

Elaine shrugged. "What if it's nothing? Maybe it was the sound of a pipe clanking—now that the weather's warming up and the ground is thawing, it could be metal or wood expanding." Her logical explanations sounded good to her, but her heart still beat hard in her chest.

"Except it didn't sound like a clank to me," Jan whispered, her gaze still on the closed door. "It sounded like a thud. Like something—or someone—falling."

Then Elaine remembered something. "I left the iron out on the ironing board after I finished ironing those newspaper clippings," she whispered. "It could have fallen off."

"Maybe," Jan said, sounding doubtful.

Elaine realized that they could stand in the hallway speculating all night. Time for action. She reached for the doorknob and pushed the door open, while Jan stood holding the hairspray can in front of her. It wasn't mace, but a good blast of hairspray in the eyes might blind an intruder long enough for them to make a run for it.

Elaine thought of every horror movie she'd ever seen and how she'd called the actors crazy for investigating strange noises in the middle of the night. But when the noise was in *your* house, where you felt safe, it made sense. Especially because, most of the time, it turned out to be nothing.

She prayed this was one of those times.

The sewing room was dark, but the light from the hallway cast enough light for them to see inside the room. Everything looked normal.

Elaine breathed a sigh of relief. The iron still stood on the ironing board and nothing seemed to be out of place. They walked inside the room and she switched on the light.

Then Jan pointed to the closet.

Elaine really didn't want to look inside, but she knew if they didn't that she'd never sleep a wink the rest of the night. She walked over and pulled the closet door open.

"Well, that's a relief," Jan said, lowering the hairspray. "Maybe it was a pipe or something."

Then Earl Grey padded into the room.

Jan's mouth dropped open. "Earl, what are you doing up here?"

Elaine's skin prickled. "Jan, I gave him a cat treat right before I came upstairs and left him in his little shelter. And I made certain the kitchen door was locked before I turned out the light." Then she picked up the cat and cradled him in her arms. "I think we'd better call Trooper Benson."

"NOTHING'S MISSING IN my office or either parlor," Elaine announced, walking into the kitchen where Trooper Daniel Benson stood with Jan. "The sapphire ring is safe and sound too."

Jan breathed a sigh of relief. "Well, that's good news."

Daniel had made a thorough search of the house and yard, brushing off Elaine and Jan's apologies for calling him out so late at night. But he hadn't found any sign of an intruder.

"Are you sure the cat didn't find another way inside the house?" Daniel asked. "None of the locks have been broken and there's no broken windows."

Elaine had been asking herself the same question, even though she distinctly remembered locking the kitchen door after leaving Earl Grey on the screened porch.

Or did she?

It was well past midnight and she'd been half asleep when the loud thud had sounded outside her room. Could she have dreamed locking the door? "I'm sure Earl Grey was on the screened porch when I locked the kitchen door," she said at last, pushing away any doubts. "I'm worried it was one of the treasure hunters."

Jan nodded. "I've been thinking the same thing."

"You mean that retired persons' club?" Daniel asked, looking a bit skeptical.

"Yes, the members of the Finders Keepers Club are retired, but any one of them could be capable of breaking in, couldn't they?" Elaine said. "It's happened before, according to Nigel, with some of the chapters. Treasure hunters have broken into homes, or even risked their own lives in pursuit of a treasure."

"Sure, it's possible," Daniel agreed. Then he looked between Jan and Elaine. "But why would someone think the treasure was in your house?"

"Because the treasure could be hidden anywhere in this area," Jan said, "or they might believe we've already found it."

"And it's worth a lot of money—five thousand dollars, according to a member of the club." Elaine thought for a moment. "Or maybe the intruder wasn't looking for the treasure itself," she ventured. "Maybe they were looking for answers to the treasure map. Nigel said his neighbor's house was broken into by someone searching for a solved clue puzzle."

"Maybe the intruder believed we've decoded the map enough to lead to the treasure," Jan said, nodding. "Several people know we have a map and word gets around."

"Macy and Nigel have become friends," Elaine said. "Maybe he mentioned it to her, then she mentioned it to someone else…"

"Until everyone at Green Glade knows about it," Jan concluded. "But our map is safe, isn't it?"

Elaine had been too worried about the sapphire ring and the rest of their family keepsakes to even think about the map. "I'll go check."

She walked into her office and pulled open the file drawer. Then she drew out the yellow folder and opened it. The map was tucked inside, just where she'd left it.

She carried the folder into the kitchen. "The map is safe."

"Do you mind if I take a look at it again?" Daniel asked.

"Of course not." She pulled the map out of the folder and handed it to him.

His brows drew down as he looked at it. "This doesn't make any sense to me."

Jan chuckled. "Well, I'm glad we're not the only ones who feel that way."

Daniel shook his head. "Are these letters, numbers, and symbols some kind of secret code?"

"We think so," Elaine told him. "Although we haven't cracked it yet."

"But we're not going to stop trying," Jan added, "especially after what happened tonight. I'm going to need something stronger than a can of hairspray if someone is breaking into our house."

"Just be careful," Daniel warned. "I'm going make a report of the incident. And if you have any more trouble, just give me a call."

"We will," Jan promised, then walked him to the door.

After he left, Elaine looked at her watch. Despite the late hour, she was wide awake.

Jan locked the front door, then turned to Elaine. "I don't know about you, but I could use a cup of tea about now."

Elaine smiled, so thankful they were both safe and could count on people like Daniel to call on day or night. "Let's make a pot and then sit down and try to figure out this map."

While Jan made the tea, Elaine retrieved a notebook and pen from her office. Then she sat down at the table, pulling the map toward her.

Jan soon joined her, setting two mugs of tea on the table and moving her chair so they could both get a good look at the map. It had been almost a full week since they'd received the map in the mail and they were still no closer to figuring it out.

"Maybe our mistake has been trying to decode everything at once," Jan said. "The numbers, letters, and symbols. They're all muddled together." She pointed to the map. "Here's two numbers, followed by two letters, followed by a symbol. Then one number, followed by three letters, followed by a symbol, then six numbers in a row."

"It's perplexing," Elaine said, "but I know we can figure this out." She glanced at the clock and smiled. "Although we might not be at our sharpest at one o'clock in the morning."

"Maybe not," Jan conceded, "but I'm not tired enough yet to fall back asleep, are you?"

"Not at all."

Jan turned her attention back to the map. "Let's separate out the numbers, letters, and symbols from each other and see if that helps us decode it. Even if we figure out a small part, that might lead us to the next clue."

"Good idea." Elaine picked up the pen and drew two lines down the length of the notepaper, creating three separate columns. At the top of the first column she wrote the word *Numbers*. The second column was labeled *Letters*, and the third column *Symbols*.

"First, I'll read off just the numbers," Jan said, "starting from the top left of the map and moving to the right until we reach the bottom right of the map."

"And judging from the way Chickadee Lake is situated and labeled," Elaine said, "I think we can still assume the top of the map is north, the sides east and west, and the bottom edge is south."

"Correct." Jan cleared her throat. "Okay, reading across the top, the numbers are 2, 0, 1, 4, 103, 8, 11, 68, 10, 2, 5, 4, 26." Jan paused to take a sip of her tea. "The next row of numbers: 200, 4, 49, 11 . . ."

Elaine jotted down the numbers in the column as Jan recited them out loud. Soon, she started a new page with a new column, until all the numbers had been listed: forty numbers in all.

"Now, let's move on to the letters," Jan said. "There's only three of them." She took another sip of her tea. "In the first row, we have an *L* and then another *L*. Then below that is a *P*."

Elaine looked up from her notebook. "*LP* could stand for Lawrence Peacock."

"Yes, it could," Jan agreed, feeling a twinge of excitement. "So moving on to the symbols, we have an eye, an ace of spades, a heart, and an 'at' sign, like you'd find on a computer keyboard." She looked over at Elaine. "That's it."

Elaine studied the paper in front of her. "There are so many numbers compared to the letters and symbols. And we still don't know why some of them are on the lake portion of the map."

"Okay, so *LP* might mean Lawrence Peacock. But I'm not sure these letters, numbers, or symbols are directional. I think they're a message of some kind."

Elaine nodded, then rubbed her eyes. "It's been a long night."

"Let's go to bed," Jan suggested. "Then we can look at this again with fresh eyes tomorrow."

THE NEXT MORNING, Jan hid a yawn behind her hand as she walked into the kitchen just before nine. She and Elaine had both risen late after staying up way past their usual bedtime. They only had an hour to go until the tearoom opened, and Archie and Rose weren't due to arrive for another thirty minutes.

Elaine had made herself a cup of espresso for breakfast, what she liked to call "the hard stuff," to help her wake up. Jan's sleep had been marred by strange dreams of maps and cats and floating numbers, until she'd awoken this morning feeling as if she'd barely slept at all.

She moved around the kitchen, setting up for the day while Elaine prepared both parlors for their customers. Despite her weariness, she was more determined than ever to figure out the secret to the map and solve this mystery once and for all.

Then she heard someone walk in the back door of the screened porch and her heart skipped a beat. But it was only Rose, who came in wearing a stylish knit black dress with cute leggings and a pair of black boots.

"Good morning," Rose said with a smile, her blonde hair pulled back into a neat ponytail. "I hope you don't mind that I came in early."

"Mind?" Jan countered, chuckling. "You've got great timing." Then she told Rose everything that had happened the night before. By the time she'd finished the story, Rose's mouth was agape.

"That must have been so scary," Rose said, her blue eyes wide.

"It was," Jan admitted. "But we can talk more about it later. Right now I need some help getting ready."

The next hour passed in a blur. Soon they were busy serving customers and getting Archie up to date on the possible intruder. Like Rose, he'd expressed concern for their safety and seemed especially bothered by the incident. She assured him they'd be fine, then they all went back to work.

That afternoon, as Jan took an order from Sylvia Flood, she noticed Archie talking to Nigel at Macy's table. Suddenly, all three of them looked over at Jan.

She gave them a nod and a smile before heading back to the kitchen, wondering what they were talking about. A few minutes later, she carried a tray of tea and cookies toward Sylvia's table. That's when she saw Archie head toward the kitchen with Nigel following close behind him.

Macy remained at the table, her injured ankle resting atop the nearest chair and her crutches propped against the wall. She had a magazine open in front of her, paging through it as she sipped her tea. Nigel had been as good as his word by bringing Macy to the tearoom. But Jan couldn't help but wonder what he was doing with Archie in the kitchen.

"Here we go," Jan said, setting down the tray on Sylvia's table. She placed the teapot on the white tablecloth, along with a small pot of honey and a dessert plate with four butter-and-jam thumbprint cookies on it—the cookie of the day.

"This looks wonderful," Sylvia said, her black hair slicked back into a neat braid. The forty-six-year-old owned a vintage clothing shop called Sylvia's Closet and was a fashionable dresser herself. Today she wore a man's gray pinstripe suit, tailored to her slender figure, with a white silk blouse underneath and a black silk rosette at the white lace collar.

"Enjoy," Jan said with a smile, then picked up the tray and headed for the hallway, making room for Rose to pass by her with a loaded tray before she entered the kitchen.

When she walked inside, she saw Archie and Nigel standing at the kitchen table with Elaine. "What's going on?"

"I'm not sure yet," Elaine told her. "They wanted to wait for you so they could talk to us at the same time."

Archie nodded. "I may have overstepped my bounds," he told the two of them, "but given the circumstances, I thought it was necessary."

Jan and Elaine exchanged a glance. Then Jan said. "You told Nigel what happened last night?"

"I did," Archie confessed. "And I think he might be able to help."

"We don't mind that you told him," Elaine said, "do we, Jan?"

"Of course not," Jan said, smiling at Nigel. "It's not like we're keeping it a secret. In fact, the more people who hear about it, the better chance we'll catch the culprit."

In her mind, the most likely witness would be someone at Green Glade, since most of the treasure hunters were staying there. Astrid, Millie, and Lawrence were currently in the east tearoom, enjoying a large plate of pastries and their second pot of white tea, making her wonder if they'd worked up an appetite digging more holes.

You're getting paranoid, Jan told herself, trying not to jump to conclusions. She needed to keep a clear head and heart to solve this puzzle.

Jan did notice that Jerry wasn't with them. She'd be curious to see if he showed up later this afternoon.

"So how can you help?" Elaine asked Nigel.

"Well, it's just a hunch," Nigel began, "but I noticed something a little strange when I spent the night in your guest room."

"What was it?" Elaine asked him.

"Well, the next morning, I opened the closet to retrieve the clothes I'd hung up there. I don't know if you've noticed, but that closet is shallower than a standard closet. In fact, my fingers brushed against the back wall while I was getting my clothes out. And that's when something was off."

"Off?" Jan had no idea where he was going with this, but couldn't wait to find out. "How so?"

"The wall was cold," Nigel replied. "Much too cold for a heated space."

She looked at him, still not sure what he was trying to say. "And?"

He hesitated, glancing at Archie before saying, "It might be best if I just show you. Do you mind taking me upstairs?"

Before either Jan or Elaine could answer, Rose walked through the door. "We've got another order," she said. "Two maple croissants and a pot of blackberry tea."

Archie stepped forward. "I'll help Rose down here. The two of you can accompany Nigel upstairs. If you agree, of course."

"Agree?" Elaine echoed. "I can't wait to see what he's talking about."

"Neither can I." Jan moved toward the door, motioning for Elaine and Nigel to follow. They made their way up the stairs to the second floor, then walked into the guest room.

Nigel moved toward the closet and opened the door. "Feel the back wall."

Both Jan and Elaine walked to the closet and each placed a palm on the paneled wall.

Jan couldn't believe how cold it felt. "Do we just have bad insulation?"

"I don't think so," Nigel replied. "What's on the other side of this closet??"

"Another closet," Elaine replied. "The one in the sewing room."

"We need to look at that one," Nigel said, this time leading the way out of the guest room.

Jan looked at Elaine, wondering what on earth the closets had to do with anything, but they both walked with him to the sewing room closet and opened the door.

Nigel studied it for a moment. "This one is shallow too, just as I suspected." Then he turned to face them. "It's apparent to me as an architect that the dimensions of these two closets don't match the distance between them."

"And what does that mean?" Elaine asked.

Nigel looked between them. "I think one of these closets leads to a secret passageway."

CHAPTER TWELVE

A secret passageway?" Elaine could barely say the words without laughing. Surely Nigel must be joking. "Do you think it leads to the treasure?"

"It's possible." His expression remained serious. "Or it could simply be a way for someone to move around your house without being seen—a way for them to search for the treasure or a decoded map."

Elaine looked at Jan, still skeptical. "Like the night we heard the intruder but couldn't find anyone?"

"Maybe," Jan said with a shrug. "But I have to see it to believe it."

"I actually made a study of secret passageways and hidey-holes once," Nigel said. "Old manor houses and castles in Europe are full of them. And treasure hunters know about them too. My neighbor used to download blueprints of specific buildings, depending on where their latest treasure hunt was located."

"So you think a member of Finders Keepers may have learned our house had a secret passageway?"

"Anything's possible," Nigel said.

Jan moved a step closer to the closet. "So is this like something from the movies—where we push a lever and a door slides open?"

He smiled. "It could be."

"Well, what are we waiting for?" Elaine said, eagerly leading the way into the closet. There were small storage tubs stacked around the closet floor, but enough room to move around. The back of the closet was made from white paneled boards, each about twenty inches wide. Elaine noticed the side walls of the closet interior were plaster, like the rest of the second floor.

And now that she thought about it, the back of the guest room closet was paneled like this too. But did the panels really conceal a secret passageway, or was this all an assumption on Nigel's part? After all, this wasn't a castle in Europe, she thought with a smile. Yet some part of her was excited by the possibility.

"Now what do we do?" Jan asked him.

Nigel stepped inside the closet and began to tap on each panel with his knuckles. The first two sounded solid, but the third one had a hollow tone to it. "I think this is it."

Elaine watched while he carefully examined the seams of the panel, then he reached one hand up and pushed against the panel. At first it didn't move. Then he pushed again, harder this time, and it opened like a swinging door, revealing a dark, dusty space behind it.

"You were right, Nigel," Jan breathed, her eyes wide with amazement. Then she looked at Elaine. "Can you believe it?"

"No," Elaine said honestly. "But I want to see what's in there."

"We'll need a flashlight," Nigel said. "There's no way to know if there's any kind of light source in there."

"I'll get one," Jan offered, hurrying out of the room.

Elaine stared into the dark passageway, wondering where it led. She could feel the cool air from it wash over her. "Why is it so cold in there?"

"Because there are probably no furnace vents along the passageway," Nigel said. "I'm sure it's sweltering hot in the summer too. The lack of any kind of ventilation contributes to the extreme temperatures." He met Elaine's gaze. "It wouldn't be a fun place to get stuck, that's for sure."

Jan walked back into the room, a flashlight in her hand. "Here you go," she said, handing it to Nigel.

He switched it on, then walked back into the closet, turning sideways to fit through the narrow panel opening. Jan followed after him with Elaine bringing up the rear.

She sneezed, the dust motes tickling her nose. The three of them stood on a landing the width of the closet.

Nigel turned around and knocked on the wall opposite the open panel. "This is the back of the guest room closet." The he pointed the flashlight along the floor, moving it until the beam revealed a narrow set of steep stairs.

In Elaine's mind, creepy didn't even begin to describe this narrow, dusty space full of cobwebs. The narrow wooden steps creaked as they slowly made their way down, one after the other, with Nigel and the flashlight leading the way.

The stairs curved sharply at one point, suggesting that they were heading straight down to Elaine's office. Soon they could hear Archie's voice coming through the wall, followed by the sound of him and Rose laughing in the kitchen.

Down they went, the air growing cooler until they finally reached another landing at the bottom of the stairs. Nigel ran the flashlight beam up and down the paneled wall in front of them, having come to a dead end.

Then he reached out and began tapping on each panel, just as he'd done in the sewing room closet, until he found one that rang hollow. He pushed it open, this one moving easier than the panel on the second floor.

Elaine peeked out, surprised to see they were in one of the storage rooms in the basement, surrounded by shelves of canned goods.

"We're lucky nothing was in front of this panel," Jan said, stepping through the open panel and into the storage room. "Or we might have had to turn around and climb all the way back up."

Nigel was the last one out of the passageway and closed the panel behind him. Then he turned to face Jan and Elaine, the beam from the flashlight lighting the concrete floor of the storage room.

"Wait!" Elaine said, spotting something glittering on the floor. "Keep pointing the flashlight right where it is."

Nigel stood still, the flashlight beam unmoving.

"What is it?" Jan asked behind her.

"I'm not sure." Elaine moved closer to Nigel. Then she leaned down to pick up a small glittering stone.

It was attached to the end of a hair pin.

Elaine stared at it, then turned around to show Jan and Nigel. "We've seen this before."

Jan nodded. "It belongs to Astrid."

CHAPTER THIRTEEN

L ater, Elaine stood outside on the side porch near the back of the house. Despite the afternoon sun spiking the temperature to the mid sixties, Elaine felt a chill deep inside of her. Of all the treasure hunters, Astrid would have been the last on her list she'd suspect of sneaking around the house.

After she, Jan, and Nigel had walked up the stairs from the basement, they'd shared their discovery of the secret passageway—and the bobby pin—with Archie and Rose. Then Nigel had taken Macy home.

Now, Elaine waited. And wondered. Would Astrid have a good excuse for her bobby pin winding up on their cellar floor? She couldn't imagine what it might be—or that she'd believe it.

Soon, the click of high heels against wood sounded near the front of the house, moving closer to her. Elaine squared her shoulders, bracing herself.

"My, this is mysterious," Astrid said as she turned the corner on the porch at the back of the house and saw Elaine waiting for her. "I didn't know what to think when Jan slipped me a secret note at my table to meet someone out here."

Astrid breathed a wistful sigh, the rhinestone-studded bobby pins in her hair sparking in the sunlight. "I hope you don't take offense, but I was hoping this secret rendezvous would be with a handsome man."

"No offense taken," Elaine said, then motioned to one of the tables on the porch. "Shall we sit down?"

"Of course." Astrid settled into a chair while Elaine took the seat across from her. "I can't wait to hear why you wanted to speak to me in private."

Either Astrid was a very good actress, Elaine thought to herself, or she truly had no idea that they suspected her of skulking around their house last night. She showed no fear—and seemingly no concern.

So without saying a word, Elaine removed the bobby pin they'd found outside the passageway and set it on the table between them.

Astrid arched a brow. "Where did you find that?" She reached up one hand to pat her hair down. "Those things are always falling out."

"I found it in a place where no one should be," Elaine said quietly. She didn't want to give Astrid too much information, hoping the woman would incriminate herself.

Astrid stared at her. "Oh dear. I'm in trouble now, aren't I? You have to understand—I didn't realize it was off-limits. I mean, the door was cracked open... and I simply couldn't resist."

Elaine tensed, not sure what to say next. So she decided the best thing to do was stay quiet. Silence made some people nervous and talkative, and Astrid seemed to be one of them. She folded her hands on the table, not saying a word.

And she didn't have to wait long.

"Yes, I admit it," Astrid said at last. "I walked into your screened porch after the tearoom was closed and spent some time with your cat. He's such a dear. And so cuddly!"

Elaine stared at her. That wasn't the confession she was expecting. "And that's really the only time you snuck into our house?"

Astrid's brow crinkled. "Snuck into your house? What exactly are you accusing me of?" She picked up the bobby pin. "Did you find this on the back porch or somewhere else?"

"Somewhere else," Elaine said, meeting her gaze. Astrid did look truly perplexed. If she was acting, she deserved an Oscar for her performance.

Astrid tossed her hands in the air, making her bracelets jingle. "I have no idea what you're talking about."

"Where were you last night, say around midnight?"

"Asleep in my bed," Astrid replied without hesitation. "And my roommate, Millie, can vouch for that. She saw me complete my evening makeup removal routine, and she knows I never step foot out the door after that."

Her story had a ring of truth to it. Add to that, Millie would have easy access to Astrid's bobby pins. It was just as plausible that she could have been the intruder and left the bobby pin behind to cast suspicion on Astrid.

Astrid's expression softened. "Are you saying someone broke into your home last night?"

"Yes," Elaine said, seeing no reason to keep it from her. "And when we found your bobby pin in a…suspicious place, we naturally assumed it was you."

"Well, as I said earlier, my bobby pins are always falling out, so anyone could have picked one up and planted it, I suppose." She frowned. "But who would do such a thing?"

Elaine was surprised at the question. "I assume you're aware that Jan and I know about your Finders Keepers Club and that the four of you are hunting for treasure here."

Astrid plucked a stray thread off of her jacket. "Lawrence did mention that you both knew about our club."

"So does it really surprise you that someone might play dirty in the quest for the treasure?"

"Yes, it does," Astrid said, now sounding hurt. "We do this for fun. I consider us all friends." Then her expression hardened. "Actually, I think I may know who broke into your house."

Elaine sat up in her chair. "Who?"

"It was that bird-watcher. The man who claims he's some kind of doctor." She sniffed. "All I see him do is sit around in trees with his camera. Sometimes I wonder what kind of pictures he's taking. He should have plenty of bird photographs by now."

Elaine let that sink in. Dr. David Zabel hadn't been in the tearoom since that first visit when he'd sat at Astrid's table. It did seem strange that he was spending so much time in Lancaster. Then again, springtime was so lovely here, giving him the opportunity to combine a nice vacation with his photography trip.

"And there's something else," Astrid said, once again breaking the silence between them. "I saw him walking outside last night. I heard a noise outside our door and peeked through the window. He was strolling past our cottage, but I didn't see his camera on him."

"What time was that?" Elaine asked.

"I can't give you the precise time, but I know it was close to eleven." Then Astrid stood up. "If you don't have any other questions, I should really be getting back to my group."

Elaine rose to her feet. "I think you've answered all of them."

Then Astrid held out the bobby pin in her hand. "Here, take this. I don't know if you believe me, but I didn't try to break in. You can even analyze this for fingerprints—if that's possible on something so small."

Elaine smiled. "As much as I love my fingerprint kit, I don't think that would work."

Astrid shrugged. "Well, it's up to you. I understand why you suspected me, so no hard feelings." Then she turned around and walked toward the front of the house.

Elaine watched her go, feeling deep down that Astrid wasn't the culprit. Or maybe she really *was* that good of an actress. She stared at the bobby pin. Either way, this wasn't enough evidence to prove that Astrid had anything to do with sneaking into their house last night.

So they'd just have to keep digging.

THE NEXT DAY, Jan opened the oven door to check on the applesauce muffins, filling the air with the scent of cinnamon and spices. She poked a long toothpick into a muffin then lifted it out, now half covered with a film of batter. "Ten more minutes," she said out loud, closing the door and then adjusting the oven timer.

The tearoom had closed an hour earlier and Elaine had gone out to run some errands, so Jan was alone in the house. She disposed of the toothpick, then headed to the screened porch where Earl Grey sat licking one gray paw.

"Hello there," she greeted him, scooping him up. She held him close for a long moment, hearing his contented purring rumble deep in his chest. He closed his eyes as her hand stroked the thick fur around his ears and head.

Soon it would be time to pack away his winter shelter, although the nights were still cold enough that she and Elaine had decided to leave it in place for a while longer.

She closed her eyes, taking a moment to relax after the events of the last few days. She'd been so distracted she hadn't even had time to practice for the baking contest.

Jan opened her eyes and smiled down at the cat. "I may fail spectacularly, Earl Grey. But you'll still love me, won't you?"

Then she heard the screen door open and looked up to see her son walk inside. "Hi, Brian!" She placed Earl Grey gently on the floor. "This is a wonderful surprise."

"Hi, Mom," Brian walked over to give Jan a hug. His sturdy frame and dark-brown hair and eyes reminded her so much of Peter. At thirty-two, her eldest child had always been protective of her, especially after Peter's death. He'd come back to central Maine after college and now worked a busy job as the manager of an auto parts store in Augusta.

So Jan wasn't expecting to see him in Lancaster on a Tuesday morning. "What are you doing here? Did you take the day off?"

"Afraid not," he said as they walked inside the kitchen. "I needed to make a delivery to an auto shop nearby, so I thought

I'd drop in and say hello." He looked around the porch. "Is everything all right here?"

She placed her hands on her hips. "All right, spill it," she said, knowing her son well enough to sense that this wasn't just a casual visit. "Why are you really here?"

A smile tugged up one corner of his mouth. "Can't I just stop in to see my mom?"

"Absolutely," she said. "But something tells me you're here for another reason."

His smile faded. "I'm worried about you, Mom. Trooper Benson stopped into the shop earlier today to pick up new wiper blades for his truck. He told me what happened here Sunday night." His eyes darkened as he looked at her. "I'm worried about you and Elaine."

"We're both fine," she assured him. "Come in for a bit and I'll tell you all about it. I have muffins baking that are just about ready to come out of the oven. And we can have a cup of tea together."

"You had me at muffins," he teased, following Jan into the kitchen

She washed her hands while Brian took a seat at the table. Then she poured them both a cup of tea just as the oven timer rang.

"That's what I call perfect timing," Brian said.

Jan pulled the muffins from the oven. "We need to let them cool for just a few minutes." Then she brought the teacups over to the table. That's when she noticed the notebook with the notes about the map was still there. She and Elaine had worked again on solving the puzzle last night, but with no success.

After hearing about Elaine's meeting with Astrid, she agreed with her cousin that Astrid probably wasn't to blame. But now Dr. Zabel was on their radar too.

Jan set a mug in front of him. "Did Trooper Benson happen to tell you about the treasure map when he was in your store?"

"As a matter of fact, he did." Brian picked up the mug and blew on the hot tea. "You've been holding out on me, Mom. How am I supposed to care of you when I don't know what's going on?"

She smiled. "It's not your job to take care of me," she said gently. "I'm doing just fine on my own. But I don't want to keep secrets from you either."

Then she spent the next ten minutes filling him in about the events on Sunday night and everything else that had happened. When she'd finished, Brian sat in silence for a long moment.

"I think I need that muffin now," he said at last.

She rose from the table, letting him digest it all while she plated two muffins and carried them to the table. "I think you need two after that story."

"So let me get this straight," he said, splitting one of the muffins in half. "You and Elaine are trying to decode a map? And if you figure it out, that should put a stop to all this trouble?"

"We hope so. Once the treasure is found, there's no reason for the Finders Keepers Club to stick around."

Then she retrieved the map from the office and showed it to him, along with their notes. "The code is a series of numbers, letters, and symbols. We've separated them out in this notebook to give us a different way to look at it."

Brian's gaze moved from the map to the notebook and back again. Then he whistled low. "I don't see how anyone could figure that mess out, but if anyone can, it's you."

Jan smiled. "Thanks, hon."

"Just promise you'll call me right away the next time anything happens," Brian said, setting his empty cup on the counter. "I could have come over here and spent the night last Sunday."

"I know you would have, that's why I didn't call," Jan explained, touched by his concern. "You have a wife and two daughters who need you at home. Elaine and I got along just fine."

Brian sighed. "Will you at least let me know about it next time?" he asked. "So I don't have to hear it from someone else?"

"Okay," she agreed. "I will."

He smiled. "Good." Then he popped the last of the muffin into his mouth before glancing at his watch. "I'd better get back to the shop to close up for the day."

"Say hello to Paula and the girls for us," Jan said, getting up to walk with him to the door. "And we'll see you here for Easter dinner if not sooner."

"Sure thing," Brian said before taking his leave.

Jan watched him until he was out of sight, then headed back into the kitchen. She picked up the dishes off the table and carried them to the sink.

Then the front doorbell rang.

Wiping her hands on a dish towel, she hurried to the front of the house. The doorbell rang a second time just as she reached the door and opened it.

Jerry Huston stood on the other side. He wore a dark suit, neatly pressed, with the double-breasted jacket buttoned over a gray shirt and black tie.

"Oh, hello," she said, surprised to see him.

Jerry didn't return her greeting. He simply held up his wallet and said, "Let's make a deal."

CHAPTER FOURTEEN

"May I come in?" Jerry asked.

Jan hesitated, not sure if she wanted to be alone in the house with one of their top suspects. She knew Elaine would be returning soon but didn't want this chance for a one-on-one with the elusive Jerry to pass her by. So she stepped outside and closed the door behind her. "It's so nice out today. Let's talk in the fresh air, shall we?"

Before he could respond, she led the way to the nearest table on the side porch and took a seat, leaving Jerry with no choice but to join her there.

"Now," she said, "what's this all about?"

Jerry set his brown leather wallet on the table before he sat down. "It's simple enough, Mrs. Blake. I'm here to offer you a sizable sum of money for something I want."

Jan usually tried to see the best in everyone, but there was something about Jerry that she just found abrasive. "And that is?"

"It's twofold. First, you give me any clues you've gleaned so far, of course. And second, that you drop out of the hunt."

"And why would we do that?"

"Well, because I'm going to pay you. You can't win the game if you don't have a strategy, after all."

It suddenly occurred to her that Jerry might provide some of the information they'd been seeking. His bravado might work in her favor if she asked the right questions.

"Well, Mr. Huston, I don't make deals with people I don't know."

"Then let's start by calling me Jerry."

She smiled. "All right, Jerry. And you can call me Jan."

He nodded. "So, Jan, what can I say to make you consider my offer?"

"Before we go there, why don't you tell me something about yourself? Where are you from?"

"Milwaukee," he said. "Born and raised."

"And do you have family there?" The question seemed simple enough to Jan, but she saw a flash of irritation in the man's green eyes.

"Yes, a son."

She waited for him to continue, but Jerry didn't elaborate. That was when she realized he didn't intend to give her any more information about himself than absolutely necessary to get what he wanted.

"I have a son too," she said, "and two daughters. They all live near me, along with my two granddaughters and twin grandsons." She smiled. "I can't imagine traveling all over the country like you Finders Keepers people do. You must find it exciting."

He sat up in his chair, resting both forearms on the table. "I do it because I like to win," he said bluntly. "To be honest with you, I don't like the traveling and I don't care much for the people in the club either. But it's a challenge—and at my age, I find few things that challenge me like hunting for a treasure."

She studied his expression for a long moment. "You make it sound as if the treasure itself doesn't matter. Just the winning."

"Maybe you do know me, Jan." A wry smile curved his mouth. "So now we can get down to business."

"First, tell me why I shouldn't give Lawrence, Astrid, and Millie a chance to bid on what we know and our resignation?"

He arched a brow. "So you want to start a bidding war? I have to admit, I underestimated you."

Jan thought he gave her way too much credit. She simply wanted to draw him out, not drive a hard bargain. There was no way she and Elaine would stop looking for the treasure, and she certainly wouldn't help him find it. Not when both Nigel and Macy had already been hurt because of it.

"Well, here's your answer," Jerry said. "Lawrence doesn't care about the treasure. He's just a lovesick puppy who follows a certain lady around. Astrid could never match the offer I'm planning to make you, so she's out."

"And Millie?"

His mouth thinned. "Millie is my toughest competition. So don't underestimate her. She's like a shark—quiet and always hunting. Millie loves the challenge, you see. She doesn't *want* any help solving the mystery."

The sound of a car approaching made them both look toward the road, where Jan saw Elaine's red Malibu slowing down to turn into the driveway.

"Enough chitchat," Jerry told her. He opened his briefcase and pulled out his checkbook. "I'm willing to write you a check for two thousand dollars." He tapped his pen on the rectangular pad. "Take it or leave it."

Jan was stunned at the amount, although not at all tempted. Besides, he'd be sorely disappointed with their progress in decoding the map and would probably demand the money right back. She swallowed, realizing that someone willing to pay that kind of money for someone else's clues might go to even greater lengths to secure the treasure.

Money seemed to be no object for him—only the victory mattered. "I'm sorry, Jerry, but I'm going to have to leave it."

The man scowled. "Are you sure you don't want time to think about it?" he asked. Then the sound of a car door closing made him point toward the driveway. "Or maybe I should consult with Mrs. Cook?"

"There's no need. She'll agree with me." Jan stood up, signaling that their conversation was over.

A flash of anger shone in Jerry's eyes as he stuffed the checkbook back into his briefcase. Then a small square of paper fluttered out and landed on the ground.

Jan bent down to pick it up. As she held it out to him, she saw that it was a picture of a cute little girl. "Oh, who is this?"

He reached out one hand and, for a moment, Jan thought he was going to snatch it from her. She looked at him with curious eyes.

Instead, he cleared his throat. "That's my granddaughter. Katie."

"She's adorable," Jan said, seeing the first hint of vulnerability on Jerry's face—the first sign that he cared about something other than winning. "How old is she?"

"I believe she's seven now," he said as Jan handed him the picture. He placed it carefully back in his wallet, then tucked the wallet inside his jacket pocket. "I should be going."

Jan walked with him to the front of the house, then he turned to her and said, "Are you sure I can't change your mind?"

"I'm positive," she said firmly.

He nodded, then said, "I should warn you—our group is small, but mighty. We won't stop until one of us finds the treasure."

There was a hint of a threat in the words, but his tone didn't scare her at all. Ever since that picture had fallen out of his wallet, Jerry seemed...deflated.

She watched him leave, then walked into the house, where she found Elaine unloading groceries in the kitchen.

"Hey there," Elaine said, holding a loaf of bread. "Was that Jerry Huston I saw on the porch?"

"It sure was." Jan walked over to the table and pulled a bag of flour out of a grocery sack. "He offered me two thousand dollars to give him any clues we've gleaned from the map so far, and to stop trying to find the treasure."

Elaine blanched. "You have to be kidding."

"No, I'm completely serious." She grabbed a box of baking soda with her other hand, then headed for the pantry, still processing her conversation with Jerry. "And so was he."

"Okay, start from the beginning."

Jan relayed the story as they finished putting away the groceries, then began making lamb stew for supper. Elaine chopped vegetables while Jan cooked a roux on the stovetop, constantly stirring the flour and butter mixture in the large soup pot.

"But according to Lawrence, the treasure is only worth five thousand dollars," Elaine said. "So why would he offer almost half that much?"

"Because all he cares about is winning. And buying us out would get us out of his way." Jan added the rest of the ingredients to the pot before stirring them together with a wooden spoon. Then she remembered the look on his face when he said his granddaughter's name. She glanced over her shoulder at Elaine. "But I don't think that's all he cares about. He handled that picture of his granddaughter like it was his most precious possession."

Elaine looked surprised. "So maybe Jerry actually has a soft spot?"

Jan chuckled. "Well, not for his fellow club members. He made it clear that Astrid and Lawrence are no competition for him, but Millie is another story. He made her sound quite formidable."

Elaine carried a plate of chopped carrots and potatoes over to the stove. "Is it possible we've been underestimating her?"

"It sure sounds like it."

They finished making the stew. An hour later they each carried a bowl upstairs to enjoy in the private sitting area. Once they were settled, Elaine said, "So I stopped at the bank and learned something interesting about one of the treasure hunters. While I was making a deposit, the teller let me know that one of Astrid's checks to us had bounced."

Jan winced. "But her orders have always been under ten dollars."

"I know," Elaine said, "she's either really bad at managing money or she doesn't have any."

Jan considered that new tidbit of information as she took a bite of her stew. They'd all but crossed Astrid off their suspect list, but if she truly was low on funds, then she might be desperate.

And desperate people do desperate things.

"So what should we do about it?" Jan asked, interested to hear Elaine's thoughts.

Her cousin took a bite of stew, chewing thoughtfully before she answered. "The amount of money is so small, but should we let her keep buying tea and pastries here if her checks continue to bounce?"

Jan didn't relish the idea of turning a customer away, but Elaine had a point. Still, maybe it would be better to talk to Astrid about it. It might be a simple banking error on her part that could be easily resolved.

"If she comes in again, one of us should say something," Jan said at last. "I don't want to embarrass her, of course. But she may be unaware that there's a problem."

Elaine nodded. "You're right. It's a delicate matter, but we can't avoid it."

They finished eating, chatting comfortably together. Then Elaine got a phone call, her face lighting up when she looked at the name on the screen. "It's Nathan," she told Jan, rising to her feet. "Do you mind if I take this?"

"Of course not," Jan said, smiling at Elaine's reaction.

After Elaine left the room to chat with Nathan in private, Jan retrieved her latest cross-stitch project and sat down on the sofa.

She began humming softly to herself while she worked, and feeling more relaxed than she had in days. She moved the needle in and out of the cotton mesh fabric, her mind thinking about the day's events. Then it wandered to the upcoming baking contest—and she made a silent promise to herself to practice again tomorrow.

As she stitched, she could hear Elaine's laughter in the other room. Jan smiled to herself, realizing she'd hadn't heard her cousin sound so happy in a long time.

LATER THAT NIGHT, Jan settled into bed and reached for the book on her nightstand. She was close to the end and hadn't read any more about the Wood family or the woolen mill. For the last several months, she and Elaine had looked for clues and information about the sapphire ring found hidden in the wall of their home, but now she was beginning to wonder if they'd ever learn the full story.

Her eyelids already feeling heavy, she turned to the page where she'd left off and began to read.

ELAINE ROLLED OVER in bed and opened her eyes to the darkness that surrounded her. The only light in the room was the green glow of the numbers on the digital clock sitting atop her nightstand.

"Two o'clock," she breathed, stretching her legs under the bedcovers. It wasn't unusual for her to wake up during the night, but she usually fell right back to sleep.

This wasn't one of those nights.

Thoughts began to drift through her mind like clouds in the sky. Did they have enough cream for the tearoom tomorrow? Would Jerry give up on trying to buy their map? She needed to call her mother tomorrow and invite her for Easter dinner if she didn't already have plans...

With a sigh of resignation, she reached over to switch on her bedside lamp, but nothing happened. "Great," Elaine muttered, realizing the lightbulb had burned out. And she'd just used the last spare one yesterday to change a bulb in the sitting room.

She climbed out of bed, her bare feet landing on the rug covering the hardwood floor. The room was warm and a little stuffy, so she walked to the window and slid it open just a crack. Now that March had arrived, the nights varied between too warm for a winter quilt on the bed and too chilly for a summer coverlet.

She closed her eyes as a cool breeze washed over her, and inhaled the crisp, night air, enjoying the nocturnal sound of an owl in the distance. When she opened her eyes, she looked out from the second story, unable to see more than the dark outlines of trees and cottages in the distance.

Then, a pinpoint of light caught her attention. It flashed in and out among the trees.

And it seemed to be moving.

Curious, she leaned her head closer to the window, watching the light. Then it just disappeared.

"Strange," she murmured to herself. It resembled the beam of a flashlight, but she couldn't think of anyone in their right mind who would be out at this time of night.

She sniffed as she closed the window. Then she sniffed again, smelling something strange.

Elaine moved toward her bedroom door, pausing only for a moment to put on her slippers. Then she opened the door and sniffed again.

Something was burning.

CHAPTER FIFTEEN

Elaine hurried over to Jan's bedroom door and started knocking. "Jan?" she called out. "Jan, are you awake?"

There was no answer.

She opened the door and turned on the light. Jan's wasn't in bed, but the sheets and comforter were rumpled. Elaine thought about the intruder sneaking in two nights ago, then she spun around and checked the other rooms on the second floor, calling Jan's name. She didn't see any smoke, but there was definitely something burning.

Elaine hurried downstairs, desperate to find her cousin. When she reached the first floor landing, light from the kitchen illuminated the dark hallway. She half-ran to the kitchen, then stopped in her tracks. Jan was asleep at the table, one arm stretched out in front of her, and once again surrounded by cookbooks.

Then Elaine saw a thin curl of smoke drift up from the oven as the burning smell became more intense. She looked up at the smoke alarm, wondering why it wasn't working. Then it suddenly started to wail.

The noise startled a sleeping Jan, causing her to sit up and look around. "What's going on?" she asked, sounding disoriented.

"Something's burning in the oven," Elaine told her, rushing over to the stove to open it. She was greeted by a cloud of smoke and the acrid smell of burned cookies. An oven mitt lay on the counter and she pulled it on, then reached in to grab the cookie sheet. She placed it on the top of the stove, then closed the oven door.

Jan rose to her feet, her eyes bleary. "My cookies!" Her words were barely audible over the loud, siren-like beeping of the smoke alarm.

Elaine turned on the stove fan while Jan rushed over to the window and cranked it open. After a few seconds, the smoke alarm stopped beeping.

"Oh, Elaine," Jan said, looking distraught, "I'm so sorry."

Elaine walked over and hugged her. "I'm just glad you're all right. Nothing's hurt—except for your cookies, of course." Then she took a step back, meeting Jan's gaze and noticing the circles under her eyes. "What in the world are you doing up at this hour?"

"Apparently, trying to burn down the house," Jan said ruefully. She walked over to the stove, turned it off, and frowned down at the blackened lumps on the pan. "These were supposed to be pumpkin cheesecake cookies. I couldn't sleep and started thinking about the contest—which is this coming Sunday afternoon. So I thought I'd get in some practice."

Elaine knew that Jan must be worried about doing well in the contest if she was baking in the middle of the night. And she really couldn't blame Jan for being preoccupied—there wasn't much time left to prepare.

"Wait a minute," Jan said, jarring Elaine from her thoughts. "I almost forgot to tell you why I couldn't sleep." She hurried over to the table and reached under a thick, open cookbook. Then she pulled out another book. "I read something about the Wood family."

"In Diane's book?"

Jan nodded, her eyes now clear and shining. "Yes, you won't believe it."

They sat down at the table, Elaine now wide awake. "Tell me everything." She knew it could probably wait until morning, but they'd been searching for answers about the sapphire ring for so long that she didn't want to delay another minute.

"Well, we already know that Elmer Wood and Arthur Murphy both boarded here at the same time," Jan began. "It turns out that Bertha was sweet on Arthur at the time. In the book, Diane writes about how upset Bertha was when Arthur was accused of theft at the mill."

"The ring," Elaine said, looking up at Jan. "We found that 1934 newspaper article that said a theft had happened there."

"Right," Jan said, "and Des Murphy told us his grandpa, Arthur Murphy, had a solid alibi, so he was cleared. But Bertha claims in the book that she knew the real culprit. It's what we suspected, Elaine, when we found out that Elmer boarded here at the same time as Arthur."

The answer suddenly seemed obvious to Elaine. "Elmer stole the ring."

Jan nodded. "Yes. Elmer and Arthur were good friends and shared a room here, according to Bertha. But she saw the way Elmer acted after Arthur was accused of theft—and knew in that moment that he'd taken Arthur's key to the mill. She tried to tell Arthur, but he didn't want to hear it. She said Elmer and his family had already been cheated by the banker—so Arthur refused to point the finger at his friend."

Elaine took a moment to process this new information. "We know that the ring was given as collateral to the bank, and that a banker bought the land for a very low price. So he cheated the Wood family?"

"Maybe the banker didn't give the ring back to the Woods," Jan ventured. "That could be what Bertha meant when she said the Wood family was cheated."

"It makes sense," Elaine agreed, some of the pieces falling into place. But she still had more questions. "So why was the ring behind a wall in our house? Why was the Wood family crest and motto etched on to the flue cover? Did the book say anything about that?"

"No," Jan said, sounding disappointed. "And I read it cover to cover. There was only one other mention of the Wood family." She opened the book in front of her and turned toward a page near the back, then began to read. "*Soon Arthur and I lost touch. I later learned that the Wood family had come to a tragic end.*" Jan closed the book and looked up at her. "That's it."

"Well, that doesn't sound good." Elaine thought about the ring—which had been hidden behind the wall for over seventy years—and a wave of sadness washed over her.

"No, it doesn't," Jan said. Then she tapped the book cover with one finger. "But maybe there's more to the story. I'm going to talk to Diane Blanchett and see what else she knows."

Elaine glanced at the clock and yawned. "Not tonight, you aren't," she said with a smile. "We're making a bad habit of burning the midnight oil."

"Or midnight cookies," Jan said, chuckling through her own yawn. "Let's go to bed. I'll clean up that cookie sheet in the morning."

"And let's add lightbulbs to our grocery list," Elaine said, walking over to turn out the light. "I need one for the lamp in my room."

"Agreed," Jan said, walking out of the kitchen and heading toward the staircase. Elaine followed her, talking about Jan's plan to meet with Diane tomorrow and, hopefully, learn the fate of the Wood family.

And Elaine had a plan of her own.

On Wednesday afternoon, Jan parked her car in front of Computer Gal, Diane's small computer shop located just off Main Street. Just about everyone in town brought their computers to Diane for repair, and she also made house calls.

As Jan closed her car door and headed for the shop, she noticed the lights weren't on inside. "I should have called first," she said under her breath. But she'd been so eager to talk to Diane that she'd made her way here at the first opportunity.

Then she saw a notice on the door: *Gone to a conference. Back on Friday.*

"Friday," she groaned, feeling a stab of disappointment. Learning the fate of the Wood family would have to wait for a couple more days. And that was only if Diane knew their fate. It was a long shot, but Jan didn't know where else to look.

As she turned around, she saw Bob walking toward her on the sidewalk, his silver-threaded dark hair shorter than the last time she'd seen him. "Hello," she said, her spirits suddenly lifting. "Fancy meeting you here."

He laughed. "I saw your car when I walked out of A Cut Above and was hoping I could catch you. Do you have time to share a piece of pie with me at Kate's Diner?"

Jan pointed to the sign on Computer Gal's door. "I do now. Diane is gone until Friday."

"Are you having computer problems?"

She shook her head. "No. I'm hoping she can help me with something that happened before the computer age." Then she reached for his hand. "Let's go have some pie and I'll tell you all about it."

An hour later, Jan drove back home and turned her Camry into the driveway. As she climbed out of the driver's seat, she heard footsteps behind her.

"Jan?"

She turned around to see Astrid Shayne standing behind her car. "Oh, hello, Astrid." She glanced at the house, wondering if the woman had just come from the tearoom—and if Elaine had talked to her about the bounced check.

"Here," Astrid said, holding out a small envelope. "I'm so embarrassed. I received an overdraft notice from my bank today and realized the check I wrote you didn't go through."

"There's no reason to be embarrassed," Jan said kindly. She was glad she didn't have to bring it up herself. "These things happen."

Astrid's lower lip quivered. "They didn't use to happen to me," she said. "But now…"

"Won't you come in?" Jan asked gently, "and have a cup of tea with me?"

"No, thank you," Astrid said, then pushed the envelope into Jan's hand. "This money is actually a loan from Millie. I don't know how I'll repay her. I used to do a lot of voice work, but the jobs have dried up." Tears gleamed in her eyes but she blinked them back. "Forgive me for going on like this."

Despite the fact that Astrid was one of the treasure hunters—and suspected of breaking into their house and possibly assaulting Nigel—Jan's heart went out to her. "Is that why you joined Finders Keepers?" she asked kindly. "To supplement your income?"

Astrid stared at her for a long moment, then laughed. "I so wish that was true," she said, wiping away a stray tear. "But membership in Finders Keepers costs much more than it ever returns. Just the travel expenses alone add up quickly."

Astrid smiled, now looking more like the confident woman who had first walked into the tearoom. "I joined Finders Keepers for the adventure—and found so many friends along the way.

I don't have any family left, so the folks in Finders Keepers are just like family to me."

Now that Jan thought about it, that was exactly how Astrid had treated her fellow club members. Even curmudgeonly Jerry was invited to sit at her table.

"You're all so different," Jan said, "in personality, at least."

"Well, that's what makes it so fun," Astrid said. "We've had members come and go over the years, but the four of us are the charter members of our chapter, along with Kiki. She just quit recently, but left us this fun treasure hunt as a bon voyage gift."

"Wait," Jan said. "Are you saying a woman named Kiki planned this treasure hunt? Everything?"

Astrid nodded. "She sure did. Kiki Johnson. Do you know her?"

Jan racked her brain, but couldn't think of any Kiki she knew. "No, I don't think so. But I'll have to check with Elaine."

"Anyway," Astrid continued, "the five of us started the club and now the four of us want to keep it going." She sighed. "I just wish..."

"What?"

Astrid hesitated. "Well, if I have to leave the group, I worry about Millie. She doesn't make friends easily and I know she's been a little upset with me lately. She thinks I've been flirting with Lawrence."

"Millie's jealous?" Jan asked.

"I think so," Astrid said softly, "although she shouldn't be. Lawrence can be a bit moody, if you ask me, and I say that as someone who thinks of him as a brother."

"That's because he's in love with Millie." Jan said the words before she realized it. She put a hand over her mouth, but it was too late to keep from spilling Lawrence's secret.

"Well, what do you know!" Astrid said, looking thoughtful. "He's never said a word about it to me."

"Or to Millie," Jan said, "so please don't tell her what I said. I was told that in confidence."

"I understand," Astrid said, looking more cheerful than when she'd arrived. "And thank you for being so understanding about my situation. I truly appreciate it."

After Astrid left, Jan looked inside the envelope and saw the money owed to them, along with a very generous tip. Then she walked toward the house, thinking about Astrid's claim that the Finders Keepers Club members were her family. That meant she'd never do anything to put that family at risk—like commit criminal acts in pursuit of a treasure.

Maybe it was time to cross Astrid Shayne off their list.

On Thursday evening, Jan sat upstairs in the sitting room, going over her notes for the baking contest. She was due at the TV station for a rehearsal on Saturday morning. The contest itself would be held on the following Sunday afternoon, so time was ticking away.

"Jan!" Elaine called out from the first floor. "Can you come down here?"

"Be right there," Jan called back, closing her notebook. She rose to her feet, stretching a moment, then made her way to the stairs.

As she walked down the steps, she could hear water running in the kitchen, so she headed in that direction. "What do you need?" she asked, walking into the kitchen.

The first thing Jan noticed was Rose putting a small piece of tape on a red streamer. The streamer was hung from the entrance of the kitchen, across over the island, and to the opposite wall.

"Surprise!" cried Avery and Kelly, bursting out from the pantry.

Jan laughed as they ran up to her and embraced her in a group hug.

"Oh my goodness! I'm so happy to see you. What a nice surprise!" Jan said. "What's the occasion?"

"Come look!" Kelly grabbed her hand and started pulling her grandmother farther into the kitchen. They stopped next to Elaine, who was placing magnets on a handmade poster on the front of the refrigerator. It had clearly been created by Avery and Kelly, and the glittery green bubble letters read Grandma's Bake-Off.

"What a beautiful sign," Jan said, although she still wasn't quite certain what was going on. Elaine answered her question before she asked.

"We're having a practice bake-off this afternoon. Avery and Kelly are going to be your judges."

Jan couldn't believe the thoughtfulness of her family and friends, or the timing. Just when she was feeling anxious about the bake-off, Elaine, Rose, Avery, and Kelly showed up to practice with her.

Avery walked over to her, holding out one of Jan's aprons. Jan put on the coral apron, which had spray of wildflowers embroidered on it. The apron had been a gift given to her years ago by Elaine.

Kelly stood by the glittery Grandma's Bake-Off sign and held a hairbrush up to her mouth.

"Hello, everyone. Welcome to our show. It's time for *Grandma's Bake-Off!* Grandma, please go stand by the island," Kelly told her.

Jan moved next to the island, a smile spreading across her face.

Kelly continued, "Now, it's time to see the secret ingredients." Kelly flung out one arm, pointing toward Elaine's office. A moment later, Avery walked out of the office carrying a basket covered with a tea towel.

Elaine and Rose began clapping. They had pulled up a couple chairs and sat down, playing the part of the audience. Jan couldn't stop smiling as she watched the four of them put on this performance just for her.

"Let's count down!" said Avery. "Five, four…"

Elaine, Rose, and Kelly joined in. "Three, two, one!"

Avery pulled the towel off the basket, and then announced the ingredients.

"Today you will make a dessert with the following ingredients: chocolate chips, puffed rice cereal, and jalapenos."

Jan burst out laughing. The anxiety about the baking contest that had been building inside of her suddenly melted away. This was exactly what she needed.

"Jalapenos?" Jan asked, playing along. "Who puts jalapenos in desserts?"

"Grandmas do!" Avery shouted, raising her hands in the air.

"But only this time," Kelly said seriously. "Not when you make your good desserts."

"Got it," Jan said with a wink.

Then she approached the island to look over the ingredients. She didn't often use jalapenos when cooking, especially not in her desserts, so this would be a challenge—and good practice for her to bake in front of an audience.

"You have two hours," Kelly announced. "And the timer starts *now*!"

Jan began pulling bowls out of the cupboard as Kelly and Avery took a seat at the kitchen table with their comic books.

After taking a moment to consider the ingredients, Jan decided to make a chocolate cake. It seemed like the best way to camouflage the jalapenos while, at the same time, giving the cake a bit of a kick.

With one eye on the kitchen timer, Jan began mixing together the basic ingredients for a chocolate cake, pausing only to decide the best way to incorporate the secret ingredients.

After a few false starts, she decided to mince the jalapenos as finely as possible, hoping that the taste wouldn't be too overpowering.

And to counterbalance the heat, she'd add some yogurt to the batter. She knew dairy products contained casein, which could ease the burning sensation from the capsaicin in the jalapenos.

Then she decided to incorporate the puffed rice cereal into the chocolate frosting, providing a nice crunch. She also made a raspberry filling for the cake and used the chocolate chips to make a ganache.

Then Jan heard the oven beep, signaling that it was finished preheating. So far, so good.

"What kind of cake pan will you be using?" Elaine asked from where she sat at the kitchen table.

"Good question," Jan said, knowing the type of pan she used would impact how quickly the cake baked. She wondered how much time she would need to decorate the cake, and then checked her timer. She had finished the batter more quickly than she'd anticipated, so it probably didn't matter which pan she used today.

But this was something she'd definitely need to consider during the real competition. Jan finally opted to go with the two nine-inch cake pans. She greased and floured the pans before pouring in the batter. Then she popped them both into the oven.

After setting the timer, Jan turned around, took a deep breath, and then began gathering supplies to work on making the raspberry filling and the ganache.

Even though Jan had two hours, the time ticked by quickly. Rose and the girls wandered out to the deck to play a game, while Elaine headed to her office to calculate the tearoom's monthly expenses. But Jan knew as soon as the two-hour buzzer sounded, they'd be back to judge her cake.

By the time she'd finished the frosting and filling, the cake was done baking and cooling on a rack. Rose and the girls walked back into the kitchen.

"Kelly," Jan asked her granddaughter, "how much time do I have left?"

"Twelve minutes," Kelly said as Elaine emerged from her office to join them.

Jan began to worry again. This was just practice, but if she could finish on time today, then maybe she would be less nervous on the day of the contest.

She spread the raspberry filling on one layer, then carefully placed the second layer on top.

"Eight minutes," Kelly called out.

Jan was about to start adding the chocolate ganache to the cake, when she suddenly realized that she'd forgotten to add the puffed rice cereal to the frosting.

"Six minutes," Kelly shouted as Avery cheered beside her.

Jan poured the puffed rice cereal into the bowl of frosting and gave it several quick stirs. Then she began frosting the cake.

"Four minutes," Kelly said.

Jan couldn't remember the last time she worked this fast, almost forgetting that this time was just a practice run. She couldn't imagine the amount of pressure she'd feel when it was time for the real thing.

"One minute," Kelly cried out.

"Go, Grandma, go!" Avery shouted, clapping her hands together.

Jan began adding fresh raspberries to the ganache on the top of the cake, feeling a little frantic.

"Time's up!" Kelly announced as Rose and Elaine started applauding.

Jan stepped away from the cake and wiped one hand across her forehead, feeling like she'd just run a marathon. "Whew, that was something!" She laughed. "I didn't know I'd have to go into training for this."

Elaine laughed along with her. "That was quite a workout for you."

Jan stepped back from her cake. She felt relieved to have finished in time, although she'd cut it too close for comfort.

"The cake is so pretty!" said Avery, walking over to the island, her gaze fixed on the cake stand. "Can we eat it now?"

"It does look delicious," Elaine said.

"I agree," Rose added, turning to Jan. "I think you're ready for the real thing."

"Well, let's see how it tastes first," Jan told them.

Elaine pulled a knife out of the drawer and began cutting small slices of the cake, while Jan pulled plates out of the cupboard, and Rose grabbed forks from the drawer.

Avery and Kelly stood near the cake, patiently waiting to receive their share. Jan gave the girls the first two plates and they each walked carefully back to the table. Elaine, Rose, and Jan soon joined them, and they each took their first taste.

"So how do the judges rule?" Jan asked, looking between the four of them. Then she focused on Kelly and Avery. "Do you like the cake?"

"It's yummy!" Kelly said, a smear of chocolate frosting circling her mouth.

"It's really good, Grandma," Avery added.

Elaine took another bite. "It is surprisingly good. I was afraid of the jalapeno in there, but you camouflaged it well. There's just the tiniest kick—but I think I like it."

"Me too," Rose said. "You've outdone yourself, Jan."

Avery reached for the hairbrush, holding it like a microphone. "Grandma wins!"

CHAPTER SIXTEEN

J an walked into Computer Gal on Friday morning, happy to
see Diane seated at her desk. The thirty-year-old computer
whiz wore a headset and was speaking to someone on the other
end. At the same time, she was also typing something on the
computer in front of her.

Diana smiled when she saw her, then held up one finger to
indicate she'd be done with her call soon.

Jan whispered, "Take your time," not wanting to interrupt
her work—especially since this was a personal matter.

Then she took a stroll around the shop, looking at computer equipment, power cords, chargers, and laptop cases for
sale on the shelves. The shop itself was sparse, since Diane
focused more on repairs than sales.

Diane sat in front of three twenty-seven-inch computer
monitors and one keyboard, her fingers flying over the keys as
she conversed in computer lingo over the phone.

Jan heard words like *server, network,* and *cookies.* She didn't
know much about technology, but she knew cookies didn't
refer to the sweet treats they served at Tea for Two.

The large L-shaped desk also served as a front counter, the shorter end bare, while the longer part of the L was utilized as Diane's workspace.

After a few minutes, Diane finished her phone call and swiveled her chair to face Jan. She wore a black top and black slacks, with a sheer floral vest of bright yellows and blues. The effect was striking.

"Sorry about that," Diane said. "I had to solve a computer emergency." She smiled. "Now what can I do for you today, Jan? Are you having computer problems?"

"No, everything is working great," Jan replied, walking close to the front counter. "I actually wanted to talk about your book." She pulled the book out of her purse. "If you have the time."

Diane's face brightened. "You read it?"

"I sure did," Jan said, fanning the pages. "You did a great job. It was almost like I could hear Bertha speaking to me."

Diane's green eyes softened. "Great-Grandma Bertha was ahead of her time. She taught me to play the guitar." She sighed. "We lost her two years ago, and I'm embarrassed to say how long it took me to transcribe those recordings and put together the book."

"I'm sure she'd be proud of you no matter how long it took."

"I think so too," Diane said with a smile. "So was there something specific in the book you wanted to ask me about?"

"As a matter of fact, there is." Jan set her purse and the book on the counter. "We found a sapphire ring behind our wall..."

"Yes, I heard about that," Diane interjected.

"And we've been looking into it since then," Jan told her, "trying to figure out how the ring got there. In the book, Bertha mentions the Wood family, including Elmer Wood. He used to board at my house in the early 1930s, along with Arthur Murphy, Des Murphy's grandfather."

Diane nodded. "Yes, Arthur was her first boyfriend."

"It's actually Elmer Wood that I'm interested in. The last mention in the book says the Wood family came to a tragic end." Jan paused, trying to prepare herself for disappointment. She knew it was a long shot that Diane would have any of the information she sought. "Did Bertha ever tell you what happened to them or why their end was tragic?"

Diane didn't hesitate. "Yes, she did. In fact, she specifically asked me *not* to put those details in the book. Even after all those years, she still had fond memories of Arthur and didn't want to besmirch his friend's memory." Diane's mouth curved into a reminiscent smile. "*Besmirch* was the exact word she used."

Jan leaned forward. "And did she tell you those details?"

Diane thought for a long moment. "So you mentioned Elmer Wood—Arthur's friend. Elmer had a younger brother, Frank. His mother was Mabel, and his father was Jameson."

Jan nodded. "We know they owned a woolen mill at one time that burned down. And it seems that the Wood family gave the bank a sapphire ring as collateral on the loan to keep the mill afloat, before realizing that either way, they couldn't afford it. We discovered that one of the bankers later bought the land at a bargain price, since the Wood family couldn't manage the finances."

Diane nodded. "That banker was Mr. Giles, according to Great-Grandma Bertha, and she certainly didn't have anything nice to say about him. He cheated the Wood family, according to her." Diane leaned forward in her chair. "In fact, to hear her tell it, Mr. Giles used his position and power to buy out a lot of land and other property at 'bargain prices' from people who couldn't make their loan payments."

"So that's why Arthur didn't want to accuse Elmer of stealing his key to the mill office," Jan mused. "But what was the ring doing there in the first place? Did Bertha say anything about that?"

Diane thought for a moment and clicked her phone on. "Let me check my notes." She pulled up what looked like some kind of notes app and began scrolling. "Ah, here it is. According to Great-Grandma, Mr. Giles was running the mill by that time." Diane scrolled a little more. "He'd made enough money buying up cheap property and foreclosures, and wanted to be his own boss, according to Great-Grandma. So he rebuilt the mill, and never returned the ring to the family, despite the fact that, by selling him the land, they had effectively paid back their loan."

Jan let that sink in, picturing the scenario in her mind. Elmer Wood had been forced to work for the unscrupulous banker who had cheated his family and kept their sapphire ring.

"So at some point, Elmer must have snapped," Jan said slowly, "and stolen Arthur's key so he could get the ring back." Then she looked at Diane. "But why put it in the wall of our house behind a flue cover?"

"Because that's part of the tragic end," Diane said solemnly. "Great-Grandma told me that Mr. Giles eventually suspected that Elmer had broken into his office, so he sent the police after him. He was arrested shortly before his brother, Frank, was killed in a car crash just outside of Augusta."

"Oh no," Jan said, finding it hard to imagine such a tragedy.

Diane sighed. "I remember finding this part of the story so scandalous," she said. "My great-grandma clearly did too, because she remembered it all very clearly. She said that Elmer was tried for theft, but he was never convicted, because there was never any proof. The ring was never found. But he died a few years later of a heart attack. Great-Grandma—and I—can't help but wonder if it was caused by stress."

"So that was their tragic end," Jan said softly. She thought about this mystery they'd been investigating for months now. The hidden ring, the family crest, the tragic end… "I think Elmer must have left the ring in the wall for someone in his family to find, as a last-ditch effort. Only there was no one left," she said, almost to herself.

Neither one of them said anything for a long moment. Then Diane looked up at her and said, "Well, that's not quite true."

Jan blinked. "What do you mean?"

"Frank was married to a woman named"—she looked at her notes again—"Ella. The only reason I remember that name is that Great-Grandma Bertha told me Ella was pregnant at the time of Frank's death, and named the baby after both him and her: Frella."

Frella Wood.

Jan's heart skipped a beat. She'd believed the story of the sapphire ring had ended with the deaths of Elmer and Frank.

But maybe it wasn't quite over yet.

ELAINE WALKED INTO the kitchen. "Rose, how many blueberry scones do we have left?"

"Four," Rose said with a smile.

"Great, that's just how many I need for Nigel and Macy," Elaine said. "Do you mind plating them for me, two on each plate, while I make some lemon tea for Emmaline and Evie?"

"Coming right up." Rose reached for two gold-rimmed, vintage dessert plates. "How is Macy doing?"

"Much better today," Elaine said, pouring hot water into a teapot, then adding a strainer full of tea leaves. "She's only using one crutch now."

"Well, that's good to hear," Rose said.

Archie walked into the kitchen, carrying a tray full of dishes. "That group of tourists just left."

"So who do we have left in the tearoom now?" Rose asked him.

"Nigel and Macy, and the Cribbs sisters," he replied. "But I just saw a car pull up before I came in here, so we'll have another table soon."

"I can take that one," Elaine said, placing the blueberry scones on a tray, then adding the teapot. She picked it up and headed out of the hallway just in time to see Astrid and Lawrence walk through the door with a strange woman in tow.

Then Elaine took a second look and realized the strange woman was Millie. She was dressed in a bright-blue pantsuit with a floral silk scarf at her throat. Her short, dark hair had been lightly curled and sported some of Astrid's rhinestone bobby pins, and she was wearing a full regimen of makeup.

The black mascara made Millie's brown eyes pop, and the coral lipstick was a perfect color for her complexion.

"Good morning," Elaine greeted them, still holding the tray. "Please have a seat and I'll be right with you."

"This way, gang," Astrid said, giving Millie a wink as they headed into the east parlor.

Elaine noticed that Millie didn't wink back, just walked stiffly in her black heels behind Astrid and Lawrence.

Turning into the west parlor, Elaine carried the tray over to Emmaline Cribbs's table. "Here we are," she said, setting the plates and teapot on the tablecloth, along with a small pot of honey. "Is there anything else I can get for you?"

"This will do just fine," Emmaline said cheerfully as Evie nodded in agreement.

"Enjoy," Elaine told them, stepping away from the table just as Macy waved her down.

Elaine walked over to their table, anticipating Macy's next comment. "Did you decide to have another pot of tea?"

"No, we'll be leaving soon," Macy said, then leaned closer to Elaine and whispered, "What do you think of Millie's makeover?"

Elaine hesitated. "I almost didn't recognize her."

"Yes, she's really quite striking when she's all made up like that, isn't she? Astrid did a wonderful job."

Nigel arched a brow. "So that was Astrid's idea?"

"It certainly was," Macy replied in a low voice. "She even came to borrow some eye shadow from me, since Millie's coloring is a better match to my own."

That's when Elaine remembered Jan telling her about the conversation she'd had with Astrid in the driveway and letting it slip that Lawrence was in love with Millie. Apparently Astrid had decided to play matchmaker.

"I've never really understood why women go to all the trouble of wearing makeup," Nigel said.

Elaine left them to their conversation and put the tray away. Then she returned to Astrid's table, where Millie sat, head down, working on a spiral-bound puzzle book. Lawrence sat across from her, his gaze on the puzzle book too.

"Are you three ready to order?" Elaine asked.

Astrid raised a hand to her temple. "You know, I woke up with a headache this morning, and now it seems to be coming back." She looked between Millie and Lawrence. "Would you two mind terribly if I went back to my cottage to lie down for a bit? It looks like Nigel and Macy are leaving, so I'm sure I could catch a ride with them."

"We can go too," Millie said, pushing her chair back.

"No, I insist you stay." Astrid rose quickly to her feet. "I don't want to ruin the morning for all three of us." Then she hurried toward the door before either Lawrence or Millie could protest.

"My, that was subtle," Millie said under her breath.

Lawrence cleared his throat. "Well, we can still enjoy some tea and breakfast. How about some of those maple croissants and a pot of chai tea?"

"Yes, fine," Millie said, turning her attention back to the puzzle book.

"Two maple croissants please," Lawrence said, looking up at Elaine. "And the chai."

Elaine nodded, feeling almost as uncomfortable as Lawrence looked. She felt sorry for both of them, yet frustrated too. Part of her wanted to shout at them to just tell each other how they really felt. But the two of them weren't teenagers anymore—even if they were acting like it.

By the time she returned with their order, Millie was almost done with the puzzle. "Two maple croissants," Elaine said, setting the tray on the table.

Millie looked up, then bit her lip as Lawrence reached for the teapot.

"Shall I pour?" he asked.

Millie suddenly rose from her chair. "I'm sorry. I can't do this!" Then she bolted out of the tearoom.

Lawrence looked flummoxed. "What's wrong with her?"

"Oh, Lawrence," Elaine said, sighing. She turned to follow after Millie. She walked outside and found her standing on the porch.

"Are you all right?" Elaine asked her.

Millie dug a tissue out of her pocket, then began wiping away the lipstick on her mouth. "This was such a stupid idea! I look ridiculous." The word ended on a sob, but Millie sucked in a deep breath to collect herself. "I never should have listened to Astrid."

Before Elaine could reply, the front door opened behind them and Lawrence stepped outside. "Millie, I . . ."

Millie spun around to face him. "Lawrence, I'm so sorry you had to witness this farce. This isn't *me*," she said, motioning toward her face and hair. "And it will *never* be me."

"Please stop talking for a moment and listen to me," Lawrence said, taking a step toward her. "You've tied up my heart in knots for so long, I've been afraid it might snap."

She stared at him. "What are you talking about?"

"You," he said simply. "Isn't it obvious?"

Millie looked over at Elaine, then back at Lawrence. "Seriously?"

"Yes, I'm quite serious." He took another step toward Millie. "I think you're beautiful, inside and out. I think I first fell in love with you when you were working a crossword puzzle and asked me if I knew the fifteen letter word for *confused*."

"And you knew the answer," Millie said, sounding a little breathless. *"Discombobulated."*

"Yes, discombobulated," he said, gazing into Millie's shining eyes. "That describes exactly how I feel at this moment."

Elaine took that as her cue to leave, stepping around the couple and quietly making her way to the front door. Once inside, she smiled to herself, glad those two puzzle-masters had finally figured it out.

Maybe love wasn't so confusing after all.

CHAPTER SEVENTEEN

That afternoon, Elaine sat at her computer in the office, with Jan looking over her shoulder.

"It's Frella," Jan told her. "F-R-E-L-L-A. At least, I'm guessing that's how it's spelled, since it's a combination of Frank and Ella."

They'd had so much to tell each other when Jan had returned from her trip to see Diane Blanchett. They'd been able to swap stories over a quick lunch before the tearoom had gotten busy again. Now that it was closed for the day, this was the first time they'd had a chance to sit down and see if they could find Frank Wood's daughter.

Elaine typed the name into the search engine: *Frella Wood.* Then she sat back and waited for the links to appear.

"Well, that's disappointing," Jan said, looking at the screen. "There are no Frella Woods listed." She took a seat in the empty chair next to Elaine's desk. "But let's think about this. She was born in 1934 or '35. That was so long ago—and it's likely she married and took her husband's name."

"Which means I may never find her," Elaine said, fearing the worst.

"But Frella is an unusual name," Jan said. "And Diane told me that Frank Wood was killed in a car crash just outside of Augusta."

Elaine nodded, picking up Jan's thought process. "I see where you're going with this." She typed the words *Frella, Augusta,* and *Maine* into the search engine. Then she sat back in her chair. "Let's see what happens."

It only took a moment for the links to pop up on the computer screen. And the first link was to the obituary page of the Augusta newspaper.

Elaine sat up and clicked on the link. Then she quickly scanned the obituary. "Frella Mabel Hagerty. Born on January 2, 1935, and passed away last year. Survived by daughter and son-in-law, Lisa and Bruce Curry, and three grandchildren."

"Mabel was the name of Frank's mother," Jan said, her eyes wide. "So that has to be the right Frella."

Elaine did a little jig in her office chair, too excited to sit still. "We found her!"

Then she took a deep, calming breath, thinking back to all those months ago when they'd discovered that gorgeous sapphire ring inside a wall of their house.

Elaine was so thankful that they'd finally found the answers they'd been seeking. She closed her eyes for a moment in prayer.

"Can you believe it?" Jan asked, her voice quavering.

Elaine opened her eyes to see Jan blinking back tears. The story of the Wood family had touched both their lives, and their story wasn't finished yet. "We need to contact Lisa Curry."

A SHORT TIME later, Jan walked into the kitchen, still feeling energized from their discoveries about the sapphire ring. They'd done an initial search for Lisa Curry, but didn't have much success. So they'd decided to wait until after the baking contest rehearsal tomorrow to dig a little deeper.

"A simple walk-through rehearsal tomorrow," Jan said to herself, "and the real thing on Sunday afternoon."

Ready or not, it was almost bake-off time.

Elaine was upstairs in the shower, ready to relax after a long week. They planned to enjoy a late supper and then relax with a favorite movie on the DVD player. But Jan didn't think she could relax even if she tried. That's why she was on a cleaning spree now, hoping it would tucker her out so she could get a good night's sleep.

Now that the baking contest was so close, Jan could only hope she had prepared well enough. She certainly did feel more knowledgeable about different flavor profiles, and felt much more confident after the successful—and fun—practice bake-off with Elaine, Rose, Avery, and Kelly.

If only she knew what the secret ingredients would be.

Last night, she'd even had a dream about it. In her dream she'd faced off against a famous chef from France. The contest was sponsored by the Finders Keepers Club, and Astrid had revealed the secret ingredients, which were lobster and popsicles.

Jan chuckled now, recalling the dream, and decided that no matter how the contest turned out, she'd just try to enjoy the experience.

She began filling the sink with water, planning to make quick work of the dishes. She dropped in a handful of silverware, then added some plates. After she finished cleaning up, she might even have time to look through a few more of her cookbooks.

Washing dishes felt second nature to Jan since she had done them countless times throughout her life. She often let her mind wander as she completed this task. So it wasn't until she saw a stream of red water run over the knife she was washing that she realized she had accidentally cut her right index finger.

Then she felt the stinging pain, and instantly dropped the knife into the sink.

Jan stared at the deep slice in her finger. "What have I done?"

As the water ran over her hand, Jan was able to clearly see the exact location of the cut. It ran diagonally across the middle knuckle of her right index finger and then curved to the underside of her finger. As she held it under the water, she tried to hold back tears.

Jan managed to shut off the faucet with her left elbow before quickly walking over to a drawer and grabbing a clean towel. She wrapped it around her cut and applied pressure with her left hand.

Then she took a seat in one of the chairs at the kitchen table. She sat there for a few minutes, continuing to apply pressure while taking deep breaths. Her finger continued to sting painfully. Jan finally decided to take a closer look at the cut so she could begin searching for a bandage that would be big enough to cover it.

She slowly pulled away part of the towel. The cut in her finger was still bleeding, and was bigger than she first realized. It also appeared to be fairly deep. She wrapped the towel back around her finger and held it against her lap as she fumbled to pick up her cell phone with her other hand.

At that moment, Elaine walked into the kitchen, wearing a white terry cloth bathrobe and combing her fingers through her wet hair. She took one look at Jan and said, "What's wrong?"

"I was washing the dishes, and sliced my finger on a knife," Jan said, rocking back and forth in her chair. "It's pretty deep."

Elaine hurried over to her. "Let me see."

Jan lifted part of the towel away, and showed Elaine the cut. "I think I might need stitches." Her voice quavered but she fought back the tears, not wanting to think about what this meant.

"Oh, that looks painful." Elaine winced. "I agree we should go have it looked at." She headed for the hallway. "Just give me a minute to get dressed and we'll be on our way."

Twenty minutes later, Jan walked into the emergency room of MaineGeneral. Elaine had dropped her at the door and was now parking the car.

When the young receptionist at the front desk looked up as Jan entered, she saw the woman's gaze fall to the towel wrapped around Jan's right hand. It was spotted with large drops of blood.

"I accidentally cut my finger on a knife," Jan told the woman, identified by her name tag as Gina. "I think I may need stitches."

"Okay," Gina said. "Your name please?"

Jan gave the receptionist her name and address. Fortunately, her medical information popped up on the screen and Gina asked her only a few more questions just to make certain her information was current.

"Go ahead and take a seat," Gina told Jan. "We'll call you when the doctor is ready for you."

Elaine entered the emergency room just as Jan walked into the waiting area, and they both found a seat together. There were only two other people sitting there, and both of them were called back shortly after they sat down.

Twenty minutes later, Jan was called. She and Elaine followed a nurse back to a small room.

WHEN THEY LEFT Waterville an hour later, Jan had eight stitches in her finger. She had taken a painkiller, but her cut was still sore and now throbbing. As they drove back to their house, she tried to slowly bend the fingers on her right hand. This proved so difficult that she almost cried out in pain.

"It's no use," Jan said, "I can't participate in the baking contest now. I can barely move my finger."

"The doctor said you shouldn't put any pressure on it for three to five days," Elaine said, glancing over at Jan. "I know you're disappointed, but I don't see how you can go through with the baking contest now."

Jan turned toward the window and looked out at the night sky. Tears stung her eyes, but they were tears of disappointment, not pain.

She hadn't asked the doctor about participating in the bake-off, mostly because she knew what his answer would be, given his instructions.

Jan also knew her finger wouldn't heal much between now and Sunday. And getting it wet might risk infection. Even worse, she didn't want her finger to start bleeding while she was preparing food for other people to eat. Even wearing a glove might not prevent the blood from seeping out.

Jan blinked back her tears and faced forward once more. "You're right, Elaine. The contest is off."

"I'm so sorry, Jan," Elaine said, compassion in her voice. "I know how hard you worked to prepare for it."

"It's fine," Jan said sleepily. The painkiller was making her drowsy, so she rested her head against the back of the car seat. "I just feel badly for disappointing you and Rose and the girls—especially after you all helped me with that fun Grandma's Bake-Off."

"Accidents happen," Elaine said gently. "And the Grandma's Bake-Off was so much fun I think we should do it more often." Elaine glanced over and smiled. "Only I want to participate next time too."

"You should...," Jan began, trying to stay awake. But the combination of the car ride and the medication made her drift off into a dreamless sleep.

AFTER THEY ARRIVED back at the house, Elaine made tea and they sat at the kitchen table together. The short nap had revived Jan, and an idea had formed in her head that she wanted to share with Elaine.

"The walk-through at the TV studio is tomorrow and the contest itself will be taped on Sunday afternoon," Jan said. "So it's probably too late for them to find someone to take my place."

"It can't be helped, Jan," Elaine said softly. "They'll just have to make do with two contestants instead of three."

Jan picked up her tea cup with her left hand, a feat more difficult than she expected, and took a small sip. The fragrant tea blend was soothing and just what she'd needed after her roller coaster of a day. Then a new thought occurred to her. "What if Rose takes my place?"

Elaine looked at her. "Is she allowed to take your place?"

Jan nodded. "Remember that night I burned the cookies? Well, I was so worried about the contest, I decided to read every bit of small print on the form they sent me. According to the rules, a replacement can be made in the case of an unforeseen circumstance, as long as the substitute baker has experience working in a licensed eatery in Maine."

Elaine smiled. "Then Rose qualifies."

"She does. The hard part will be getting her to agree to it."

"Well, let's try," Elaine said. "Let me call her and see if she can come by tonight for a late supper. Then we can work on her together."

ROSE ARRIVED A few minutes after eight o'clock that evening. Elaine let her in as Jan sat at the kitchen table that was set for the three of them. Given her finger injury, she'd let Elaine take over the kitchen duties, including making the chicken-and-rice dish that was now baking in the oven.

When Rose and Elaine entered the kitchen, Jan turned around to greet them. "You're right on time," she told Rose. "Dinner should be ready in a few minutes."

"Good, because I'm half-starved," Rose said, hanging her purse over the back of her chair. Then her gaze fell on Jan's bandaged hand. "Oh no! What happened to you?"

"Kitchen accident," Jan replied. "I cut my finger on a knife while washing dishes."

Rose moved closer to her and sat down. "That's terrible. Is it bad?"

"I had to take her to the ER." Elaine said. "Where they gave her eight stitches and strict instructions not to use that finger for several days."

"That's terrible," Rose exclaimed, sympathy shining in her eyes. "Does it hurt?"

"Yes, it's still rather sore," said Jan, "and I can't really bend it."

Then Rose's eyes widened. "But what about the Maine Dessert Competition?"

"I'm out," Jan said bluntly. "This cut is going to prevent me from participating."

"I'm so sorry, Jan," Rose said. "That's terrible. You've been working so hard to prepare for it."

"Yes," Jan said, "but what I am more concerned about is who will fill my empty slot in the baking contest. Who will wear the Tea for Two apron?"

Rose looked back and forth between the cousins, her eyes narrowing. "Wait a minute. You two don't think I..."

"Yes, we do," Elaine interjected. She slipped into the chair next to Rose. "That's why we asked you to come over tonight."

"Well, not the only reason," Jan clarified, not wanting to scare her off. "Elaine has prepared a wonderful supper. And I thought we could talk about the contest and how to prepare for Sunday."

"Whoa!" Rose held up both hands. "I haven't agreed to anything yet. And frankly, I think you two are crazy to even ask me." She smiled at both of them. "You must have a lot more confidence in me than I do."

Jan nodded. "Well, I think that's a given."

"But I'm not prepared at all!" Rose said. "I would definitely mess it up, and when I do, I'll be wearing a Tea for Two apron. That's the last thing you want."

The oven timer dinged, providing a natural pause to their conversation.

Elaine stood up and walked over to the oven, then pulled out the chicken and rice and carried it over to the table, where she set it on the trivet.

Rose peered into the baking dish. "You made one of my favorite meals," she said accusingly, although there was a hint of humor in her tone. "I think you two are just trying to butter me up."

"Oh, speaking of butter," Jan said, "we have some of those angel biscuits you like too—with plenty of fresh butter from Richardson's Dairy."

Rose dissolved into laughter. "Okay, I get it. You think the way to my participating in the baking contest is through my stomach." Her gaze moved eagerly over the food on the table. "Can we eat now?"

Jan sat up straighter in her chair. "First, tell us if you'll do it. Will you take my place at the Maine Dessert Competition?"

CHAPTER EIGHTEEN

Yes, I'll do it," Rose said, laughing as she raised her hands in surrender.

"Wonderful!" Elaine said, clapping her hands together. She looked over at Jan and saw her beaming. She was so glad to see her smiling after dealing with such a brutal disappointment. Jan had been so excited about the contest and worked so hard for it. But it seemed God had other plans.

Sometimes Elaine had trouble trusting that His way was the best. In the aftermath of Ben's sudden death, she'd often questioned why her dear husband had been taken away from her.

But now she looked at life in a different way—not about what was taken from her, but what was given. She had been given the opportunity to live in this beautiful Victorian home and share it with her cousin. They'd opened a tearoom together— fulfilling a dream—and meeting all kinds of people.

And then there was Nathan.

Her heart skipped a beat at the thought of him and the tender kiss they'd shared the other night. She couldn't wait to see him again and they were both happily planning their next date.

"Earth to Elaine," Jan said, leaning forward. "I think we caught you daydreaming."

Elaine smiled. "You sure did." She reached for the bowl of biscuits and placed one on her plate. "What did I miss?"

"I was just telling Rose that she's a wonderful baker and that I know she'll do great."

Rose raked her fork through her chicken and rice. "I'm still not sure."

"I wouldn't want anyone else to take my place, Rose," Jan said. "I'm confident you'll do well."

"And it will be a great experience," Elaine added.

"Yes, I suppose that's true." Rose looked up from her plate. "I only wish I had more time to prepare."

Jan tried to reassure her, "You'll be fine. Trust me, more time would only make you more nervous."

"What do you think the ingredients will be?" Rose asked.

Jan laughed. "I have been driving myself crazy trying to figure that out."

A worry line appeared on Rose's forehead. "Are there any helpful hints you can give me?"

"Well, after I had to use jalapenos during the Grandma's Bake-Off, I decided to study up more on flavor profiles. After dinner, I'll give you some of the information I found if you'd like to look it over."

"Yes, I definitely would," Rose said, sounding relieved. "Thank you."

"Also, don't let me forget to give you all the contest rules and information before you leave," Jan told her. "Like what time you need to arrive for the rehearsal tomorrow and what cooking tools you're allowed to bring with you to the contest. I'll give you the baking supplies I was going to bring along."

Rose paled. "Now I'm starting to feel overwhelmed."

"Don't worry, Rose, we'll help you," Elaine said. "And we'll make sure you have everything you need."

ON SATURDAY AFTERNOON, Jan carried a laundry basket into the tearoom and began preparing the west parlor for Monday. It was a simple job and one she could do with her sore finger.

They'd had a busy Saturday at the tearoom—and a successful one. According to Rose's recent phone call, her rehearsal at the TV studio had gone well also—but she'd sounded even more nervous to Jan than before.

Jan hoped she hadn't pushed Rose too hard. She'd been so proud of the young woman's accomplishments in the kitchen and the fact that Rose had started culinary school. What if something did go horribly wrong for Rose at the contest and set her back?

Then she shook that negative thought out of her head, refusing to worry about things that hadn't happened yet. She had every confidence in Rose and, no matter what happened, Jan and Elaine would always be there to support her.

Jan began to hum a favorite hymn as she laid a freshly laundered white tablecloth on the nearest table and then straightened the chairs around it.

After an extensive computer search early this morning, Elaine had found an Augusta public school Web site that listed both Lisa Curry and Bruce Curry as staff members. And each one had a school e-mail address listed also. So they'd composed a message to Lisa Curry together, explaining they had some property belonging to the late Frank Wood, and to please contact them for further information.

The setting sun in the west window cast a rainbow of colors in the parlor, glinting off the glass of the corner hutch. Jan walked over to it and looked at the Lefton teapot through the glass, wondering if they'd ever figure out who had sent it to them.

Then she turned to resume her work, reaching for another tablecloth from the stack in the laundry basket. She shook it out, then let it flutter over the next table. Jan made sure the edges of the tablecloth were even, then straightened the nearest chair into place.

As she moved it, a spiral-bound book fell on to the floor. Jan picked it up and turned it over to see the front cover. "Word Puzzles for Brainiacs," she said, reading the title out loud.

As someone who loved working puzzles herself, Jan couldn't help but flip through the pages, noticing that some of the puzzles were already solved.

Then she saw a puzzle that made her look twice.

A few moments later, Elaine walked into the west parlor. "Need some help in here?" Then her gaze landed on the book in Jan's hands. "Oh, that belongs to Millie," she said with a smile. "She must have left it here after she and Lawrence walked off hand in hand yesterday."

Jan looked up at her. "I think I just figured out how to decode the treasure map."

A few minutes later, Jan sat with Elaine at the kitchen table with Millie's puzzle book open in front of them, along with the treasure map and their notes.

"When I saw the rebus puzzle in Millie's book," Jan explained, "I realized that might be the first clue into reading the map."

Elaine opened the notebook to a clean page. "Okay, so just so I'm clear, what do you mean?"

Jan tapped the page of the book in front of her. "A rebus puzzle is word play that often uses images or symbols. Like this one: *important = important*."

Elaine studied it for a long moment. "Equally important."

"Right," Jan said, impressed that she'd solved it so quickly. "They can be tricky, but fun." Then she pulled the map closer. "So we have four symbols on this map. A heart, an eye, an ace of spades playing card, and the 'at' sign."

"And they each have letters and numbers around them," Elaine said, "so any ideas how we sort them out?"

Jan stared down at the map for several minutes, then glanced at their open notebook where they'd separated the numbers, letters, and symbols into three columns. There were so many more numbers than symbols and letters.

"Let's ignore the numbers for now," Jan said, "and just focus on the letters and symbols."

Elaine tore out a fresh sheet of paper and set it between them. "Okay, starting from the top down, we have a heart, followed by an *L*, followed by an ace of spades card."

Jan tried to put the three together like a rebus puzzle in her mind. *"Heart L card? Heart L ace? Heartless?"* she looked up at Elaine. "Maybe it means *Heartless?*"

Elaine jotted the word down. "Moving on, we have *L* and a drawing of an eye. *Lie?*"

"Yes, that one's pretty straightforward. So we have *Heartless Lie.*"

Elaine smiled as she wrote that down. "Not the cheeriest message so far."

Jan agreed, but she was too entranced in the puzzle to try to analyze those two words. And they couldn't be certain they had them right. "The next one is *L8.* That has to mean *Late.*"

"Heartless Lie Late," Elaine said, adding the last word to the paper. "So all that's left is *P@. Pat?*"

"I guess so." Jan shook her head. "But *Heartless Lie Late Pat* makes no sense."

"So we've either got the words wrong," Elaine mused, "or we're missing part of the puzzle."

Jan rubbed a hand over her chin, looking at the map again. "There's the number 2 before *L8.* Maybe that's supposed to be: *Too Late.*"

"Heartless Lie Too Late Pat?" Elaine guessed, and then her eyes widened. "Hey, we may be getting somewhere. "How about the number 1 in front of the '*L* eye'? That could be *One Lie.*"

Jan leaned forward, sensing that they were getting closer. It seemed obvious to her that the words were jumbled, so she tried rearranging them to see if they made more sense. *"Pat Too Late One Heartless Lie."* She looked up at Elaine. "Do we know anyone named Pat?"

"Well, there's Patti Garland," Elaine reminded her.

Jan nodded. Patti was the twenty-five-year-old married daughter of Kate Pierce. She also seemed like one of the least likely people to be involved with a treasure map and a valuable teapot.

"I don't think it's her," Elaine said, as if reading Jan's mind. "Maybe it stands for Patrick or Patterson?"

"Let's move on and try to figure that one out later." Jan looked at each symbol individually. "You know," she said slowly, "sometimes the symbol can stand for something else. What if the heart symbol means love?"

"So if we put it together with the *L* and the ace of spades: *Love Lace?*"

"I think it's a name," Jan said. "*Lovelace*. And since the words appear to be scrambled, I think the full name is *Pat Lovelace*."

"Wow, I think you're right." Elaine's brow furrowed. "But who's Pat Lovelace?"

"Maybe if we figure out the rest, we'll find out." Jan pointed to the notepaper. *"1 L 'eye symbol' 2 L8. One Lie Too Late."*

"Bingo!" Elaine cried, writing it down. Then she picked up her cell phone. "Now let's look up Pat Lovelace."

Jan waited while Elaine searched the Internet on her phone. Then she lowered it, her eyes sparkling. "Pat Lovelace is the author of a novel called *One Lie Too Late*, published in 2014."

"Whoa. And 2-0-1-4 are the first four numbers at the top of the map," Jan said as the final pieces clicked into place. "If we take those out, along with the numbers in the title, the 1, the 2, and the 8, then..."

"Then?" Elaine prodded.

"Then I think this is a book cipher. The numbers after 2014 are 103, 8, and 11. That means if we track down the 2014 copy of *One Lie Too Late*, we'll be able to decode the map. The page number will be 103, 8 will be the eighth line on the page, and 11 will be the eleventh word on that line."

"So if we just follow the numbers, we'll eventually come up with a message?" Elaine met Jan's gaze. "A message that tells us where to find the treasure?"

Jan nodded, telling herself not to get her hopes up too high. It was possible the message just might lead them to another puzzle. But something told her they were close—which meant the game might get a lot more dangerous.

CHAPTER NINETEEN

On Sunday afternoon, Jan and Elaine arrived early at the TV station in Portland, wanting to make sure they had prime spectator seats to cheer Rose on.

Elaine had even made hand-held signs with the word *Go* and a picture of a rose on the front. Due to Jan's injured hand, she couldn't help with the sign, but she'd offered plenty of unsolicited advice. She especially liked the gold glitter edging the sign.

Jan had said a prayer in church this morning for Rose, asking the Lord to give her strength and encouragement. As Jan shifted in her seat, she found herself almost as nervous as if she were competing herself. As a mother, she knew that sometimes it was harder to stand by and watch the people she cared about take on a challenge and not be able to pitch in to help than it was to take on the challenge herself. Then she thought about the challenge she and Elaine faced in finding the treasure before anyone else did.

"I'm a little nervous," Jan whispered to her as the lights in the studio dimmed. "How about you?"

"I'm a lot nervous," Elaine said, "but hoping for the best."

Then Jan saw Rose hurrying toward them.

"I can't believe you two are here already!" Rose exclaimed, a wide smile on her face. "And this sign is amazing. When did you have time to make it?"

"Last night," Elaine told her. "We still have gold glitter all over the sewing room floor, but it's worth it. We're so excited to see you compete! Do you feel ready?"

"As ready as I'll ever be," Rose said, a flash of apprehension in her blue eyes.

"Have you met the two chefs you'll be competing against?" Jan asked her.

"Well, that's the good news," Rose said, then wrinkled her nose. "And the bad news. One of the chefs has the flu, so he had to drop out."

"And the other chef?" Elaine asked.

"She's right over there." Rose pointed to a tall brunette, about thirty years old, wearing a crisp white chef's uniform. She stood near the staging area where a modern kitchen had been set up.

"Her name is Jody," Rose told them, "and she's worked in a Bangor bakery for the last ten years. Which means I probably don't have a chance."

"This isn't a Bangor bakery," Jan reminded her, wanting to keep Rose's spirits up. "You're both starting with a basket of unknown ingredients, which levels the playing field in my mind. The judges will be looking for creativity as much as technique, so don't be afraid to take chances."

"Any other tips for me?" Rose asked. "I need all the help I can get."

"Just go with your gut," Jan said calmly. "As soon as you see the ingredients, go with your first idea—don't second-guess yourself. Be confident. Indecision will only waste time."

"Got it." Rose squared her shoulders. "Okay, we're going to start soon, so I better make sure I have my station organized."

"Okay, break a wooden spoon!" Elaine said as Rose walked away. "We'll be cheering for you."

Jan turned to her cousin. "Break a wooden spoon?"

Elaine grinned. "It's an expression. Like telling an actor to break a leg before they go on stage. But cooks should have one too, especially when they're competing."

Jan laughed as the lights around the stage dimmed and the producer called for everyone to be quiet on the set.

Rose smiled at them as she took her position on stage, her cooking supplies spread out in front of her.

"The *Rocky* theme song is playing in my head," Elaine whispered.

Jan smiled, her stomach twisting as she watched the three contest judges stop by the staging area to introduce themselves to Rose and Jody. All three judges were middle-aged women, and probably excellent bakers, Jan thought to herself.

A blush of pride warmed Jan's cheeks as she watched Rose pick up her Tea for Two apron and tie it on.

A few minutes later, a production assistant set a dome-shaped, stainless steel cake stand in front of each contestant. Then the silent countdown to taping began.

It was almost time to reveal the secret ingredients.

One of the judges, a petite blonde, held a microphone and stood in front of the camera.

"Hello, everyone," she said to the camera. "My name is Nan Turner and I'm one of the judges today. With me at the judge's table are Jacie Mandeen and Elinor Bard. Our contestants today are Jody Hassan and Rose Young."

The crowd applauded.

Nan Turner continued, "Our contestants will have two hours to incorporate the secret ingredients into their own recipe. Each contestant must incorporate *all* of the secret ingredients into their dessert, but they may also use any other ingredients available in our pantry and cooler.

"At the end of the two hours, judges will rank the desserts on their presentation, creativity, and taste. The winner will be awarded a brand-new set of culinary pans valued at $1,100 dollars."

She turned toward the contestants. "Now, it's time to reveal the secret ingredients. Elinor, what will our contestants find in their baskets today?"

Elinor stood in front of the cake stand, then she lifted the dome to reveal the items inside. "The three secret ingredients are parsnips, maple syrup, and pumpkin seeds."

"Rose and Jody," the moderator said, "you have two hours to complete your dessert and your time begins *now!*"

Jan watched Rose remove the three ingredients from her stand, study them for a moment, then spring into action. Rose raced toward the pantry and grabbed flour, sugar, and baking powder, along with other items, carrying them back to her station.

Elaine whispered in Jan's ear, "What would you make?"

Jan said, "I'm not sure. I think maybe a bread pudding of some sort, but I don't think that's what Rose would choose."

Jan watched Rose walk over to the shared refrigerator and supply table. She loaded her basket with various ingredients, including canned pumpkin, applesauce, and various spices, as well as items from the cooler.

Her opponent, Jody, selected some of the same ingredients, but also added bacon and coconut. Back at her station, Rose was preheating her oven.

"I love parsnips," Elaine said, "though I rarely cook with them. And I certainly don't use them in a dessert!"

"They could be tough for her," Jan acknowledged. "I think my favorite of the secret ingredients is the maple syrup. Not only is it tasty, but it's just a sweetener, so easy to add to any dessert."

"I am curious to see how they each include the pumpkin seeds."

"Rose needs to toast them," Jan said, "so I hope she leaves time for that. It doesn't take long and really enhances their flavor."

As the time ticked by, the two contestants worked quickly. Rose was soon mixing ingredients in a bowl to form a batter.

"Look, she's set out a muffin tin," Elaine said. "She must be making either cupcakes or muffins. Can you see what Jody is making?"

Jan looked over toward Jody's table. From her vantage point, it was difficult to see everything at her station.

"I can see a pie plate. And it looks like she's rolling out some dough for a crust," Jan said.

Rose added a few more seasonings to her batter, and then began pouring equal portions into the muffin tin. When she had finished she carefully carried the tin over and placed it inside the oven. She set the timer, pressed start, and then walked back to her table.

"Great timing," Jan said, checking the clock.

A few minutes later, Jody placed her pie in the oven to bake.

Rose stood at her counter for just a moment, and took a deep breath. Then she started clearing away some of the supplies she had used for her batter and pulling out some clean bowls and spoons. She made another trip to the supply table to grab cinnamon, and then started mixing together more ingredients.

"She's making a frosting, I think," Jan said to Elaine. "She must be making cupcakes."

"Whatever those two are baking smells delicious. Now I wish *I* were judging."

Jan smiled. "Me too."

Rose had used the parsnips and maple syrup in her batter. She now mixed part of the maple syrup into her frosting. When her oven timer went off, she pulled the cupcakes out of the oven and set them down to cool.

A short time later, Jan watched Jody take her pie out of the oven to cool.

As soon as the cupcakes had cooled, Rose began applying frosting. She used two different decorative frosting tips to make swirling designs on each cupcake.

"Rose has always been good at decorating," Jan said, agreeing with Macy that Rose had artistic talent. "They look beautiful."

"I only hope she'll be able to finish in time," Elaine said.

Jan was surprised when she looked at the timer. There were only three minutes left.

When Rose finished frosting, she began strategically placing toasted pumpkin seeds on top of each cupcake. Her opponent had had a similar idea, it seemed. Jody had sprinkled what appeared to be toasted coconut on her pie after taking it out of the oven, and was now completing a design on the top using the pumpkin seeds.

"One minute left," Nan Turner announced from the judges' table.

Both Rose and Jody carefully arranged their baked creations to present to the judges.

"Time's up," Nan announced, a wide smile on her face. "Let's hear it for our two contestants."

A small but enthusiastic smattering of applause spread over the large room. Then Elaine gave Rose a big thumbs-up. Jan was too nervous to do anything but watch.

"Jody, please bring your creation to the judges' table," Nan Turner said.

Jody walked over with her pie. Each of the three judges looked at it and made notes on their judging sheets. Then pieces were sliced and served to each judge. The judges took a few bites, and then each of them took turns talking with Jody about her flavor choices.

"They like her pie, I think," Jan whispered to Elaine. "One of them even took an extra bite."

"It looks good from here," Elaine conceded. "But so do Rose's cupcakes. I wonder what they'll taste like."

Once Jody had cleared away her dessert, it was Rose's turn.

She presented her cupcakes on a decorative, spiral cupcake holder. As with Jody, the three judges spent a minute examining how the cupcakes looked before tasting them. They each took a few bites of the cupcakes.

"Do you think they like them?" Jan asked Elaine.

"I can't tell. I can't see their faces well enough from here."

The judges spoke with Rose for a couple minutes about her flavor choices, and then Rose took her dessert back to her table.

"Elinor, Jacie, and I will compare our scores," Nan said, "and announce the winner shortly."

"I'm getting so nervous for her," Jan said, rubbing her palms over her legs, "Oh, look! She's looking over at us again."

Jan and Elaine held up their signs again for Rose, smiling and waving at her.

Rose smiled back, but Jan could tell that she was feeling a little nervous as well. After about ten minutes, Jacie announced that they had chosen a winner. She called Rose and Jody to the front of the room and had them stand next to each other.

"Rose and Jody," Jacie began, "you both made delectable desserts with unusual ingredients. Jody created a parsnip coconut pie and Rose made pumpkin parsnip cupcakes. It really was a pleasure trying both of your desserts. However, because they were both so well executed, it was also quite difficult to determine the winner."

Jacie looked straight into the camera. "When the three of us compared our ratings for each contestant, the winner won by only two points. So before I announce the winner I want to thank you both for being here, and say that you two really are amazing bakers."

Jacie reached for the trophy beside her, shaped like a golden whisk. "And today's winner is...Rose Young!"

Jan and Elaine jumped to their feet, clapping and cheering.

Rose looked stunned at first, as if she didn't believe the judge had called her name. Then a slow, wide smile began to spread across her face.

Rose turned and shook hands with Jody. Then the judges presented Rose with the beautiful set of brand-new high-end stainless steel cooking pans.

Jan and Elaine stood proudly by while Rose posed for pictures. Then they ran up to congratulate her.

"You did it!" Jan said, hugging her.

"I can't believe it," Rose said, sounding a little breathless as she turned to hug Elaine. Then she looked over at Jan. "Your advice to make a decision and stick with it really helped me," Rose said, pure joy shining in her eyes. "At first I was second-guessing myself, but then I just decided to be confident and stick with one idea."

"You did so well," Jan said, "Is there any chance we could try one of the leftover cupcakes?"

Rose laughed. "Of course. I hope you like them as much as the judges did. I think I might be more nervous about the two of you trying them."

"I tend to like anything with cake in the name," Elaine said with a smile.

Rose, Jan, and Elaine walked over to the leftover cupcakes and each took one.

"These are amazing," Elaine said after taking a bite.

"I agree," Jan said. "You may have to make some of these for the tearoom sometime."

"I'm glad they turned out so well. It'll be interesting to try making them again without the time pressure," Rose said.

She turned to Jan. "I feel like you deserve the prize. You're the one who entered the contest. I only got to compete today because you asked me."

"Nonsense," Jan told her, "You've earned it. My prize is seeing you do so well—and eating this delicious pumpkin parsnip cupcake."

CHAPTER TWENTY

On Monday morning, Jan walked along the lake after breakfast, enjoying the crisp morning air and watching the geese fly overhead. Her jacket kept her warm, along with the warm glow of happiness from Rose's win at the Maine Dessert Competition yesterday. But she knew even if Rose hadn't won, that glow would still be there simply because Rose had risen to the challenge—and completed it.

As she walked, Jan's mind turned to her newest challenge—decoding the book cipher once they had the book in their hands.

"*One Lie Too Late*," she said out loud, finding the title of the book quite apt. Soon after the Finders Keepers Club members had arrived in Lancaster, she and Elaine had assumed any one of them could be telling lies.

But, surprisingly, in the past two weeks, they'd both grown to like Astrid, Lawrence, and Millie.

And Jan's instincts told her that none of those three had been sneaking around in their secret passageway.

Jerry was another story—his standoffish behavior and win-at-all-costs mentality still made him the prime suspect on her list. And what about Dr. Zabel? She wasn't sure there was anything to Astrid's suspicion, but he remained on her list.

Jan walked through a stand of trees, some of them just beginning to bud. Soon there would be nests with birds' eggs and lush, green leaves filling all the spaces around the bare branches. Then she looked up and saw a branch that wasn't bare.

Dr. David Zabel, as if drawn from her thoughts, was sitting on a branch above her. He wore a khaki jacket and blue jeans, along with a sturdy pair of hiking boots and an Indiana Jones–style fedora. A fancy camera with a long telephoto lens hung from a thick black leather strap around his neck.

"Good morning," he greeted her. "Nice day for a walk."

Jan came to a halt under the tree, watching as he climbed down. That's when she noticed a brown knapsack leaning against the tree trunk. The zipper was half open and she could see a folding shovel inside. "How long have you been out here?"

"Since just before sunrise." He placed the lens cover on his camera, then picked up the knapsack and slung it over one shoulder. "That's when I get some of my best shots. From up there, my telephoto lens can capture a lot of activity—of both animals and humans."

"Any humans in particular?" she asked.

He grinned. "A species called Finders Keepers has always interested me. They find treasures and sometimes leave them lying around or even mark the spot."

Jan blinked, wondering if she understood him right. "So you take them?"

"Don't get me wrong," he continued. "I don't commit any crimes. It's just sometimes those club members get distracted easily—as I'm sure you've noticed. I'm like the frigate bird that feeds itself by snatching food from other seabirds. Finders, keepers, if you will. So if there's a treasure there for the taking..."

"You're there to swoop it up," Jan finished for him. "Or maybe you dig for it, using that shovel in your knapsack. That would explain the hole in our yard—the one that caused Macy's sprained ankle."

"Accidents happen," he said with a shrug, not denying it. "I'm sorry she was hurt, but it's just a game, after all. You may find this hard to believe, but I love what I do—taking bird pictures, I mean. It just doesn't pay enough to keep me in the style to which I'm accustomed. So I supplement my income with a little treasure scavenging along the way."

Jan wondered what else Dr. Zabel had seen from his perch.

"Have you noticed anyone sneak into our house," she asked bluntly, "during one of your...photo shoots?"

He hesitated. "Sorry, I can't help you. And it doesn't matter anyway," he added, then he tilted his head to one side, as if sizing her up. "I think it's a hoax."

She stared up at him. "What do you mean?"

"This supposed treasure—I don't think it exists. I've been sitting in trees for the past two weeks, just watching people search for it. They haven't found a thing. In fact, I think they've given up and just decided to have fun."

That certainly contradicted what Lawrence had said about a ruby necklace worth five thousand dollars. But she wasn't about to share that with him. "So are you giving up too?"

He nodded. "I'm leaving town today. There are other Finders Keepers clubs out there, searching for treasure. And I'll pick the most promising hunt and be on my way." Then he gave her a small salute. "Enjoy the rest of your morning, Mrs. Blake."

Then he walked away, whistling a jaunty tune.

Jan watched him until he disappeared, still surprised he'd been so honest with her about his scavenging ways and the reason for them.

Maybe he was right about the treasure being a hoax too.

LATER THAT MORNING, Elaine emerged from her office and walked into the kitchen, where Jan was setting out plates and teacups on the counter. She could hear Archie rustling around in the pantry. He'd arrived an hour ago and planned to work until early afternoon. Rose had the day off, which she'd definitely earned after her performance yesterday.

"So I just called Bristol at the Bookworm," Elaine told Jan, "to ask them if they had *One Lie Too Late* in stock. And guess what?"

"They have it?" Jan asked hopefully.

"They sure do. Bristol told me someone ordered it a couple of weeks ago, right around the time we received the teapot and map, but never came in to pick it up."

"It sounds like it was ordered for a treasure hunter to find." Jan turned to face her. "Did she say who ordered it?"

"A woman named Kiana—and she didn't give a last name." Elaine smiled. "Sound familiar?"

"Yes," Jan said slowly, the pieces fitting together. "A Kiana stayed at the lake for a week last summer and came to the tearoom almost every day."

Elaine nodded. "She was a world traveler and collector— we had a lot of conversations about Japan."

"And a philanthropist, as I recall. I guess she likes to donate to treasure hunters as well." Jan breathed a wistful sigh. "So Kiki must be short for Kiana. And she's the one who sent us the Lefton teapot and included us in the game, isn't she?"

Elaine nodded. "Now that I'm remembering some of the conversations we had, I'm sure of it. She loved Chickadee Lake and she knew how much I loved teapots and solving mysteries."

Jan smiled, happy to have figured out that little piece of the puzzle. "I'm having lunch at the Grill today with Bob, so I'll stop at the Bookworm and pick the book up. Then maybe we can start getting some answers."

LATER THAT MORNING, Elaine felt a strange restlessness that simply wasn't normal for her. She kept looking at the clock, waiting for noon to arrive so Jan could leave on her lunch date and pick up that book. She simply couldn't wait to see what message they'd discover once they broke the code.

Tamping down her impatience, Elaine turned her attention to the arriving customers in the tearoom. Bristol had promised to hold the book for them and Jan would have it in her possession soon.

She greeted Pastor Mike and Sarah, enjoying a long chat with them as Archie and Jan attended to the other tables. She told the pastor how much she was looking forward to the Easter service and invited the couple to think about joining them for Easter dinner if they didn't have other plans.

Then Elaine walked over to Astrid's table, where she found all four Finders Keepers members seated together, enjoying tea and a variety of pastries. Even Jerry was there, although he didn't look too happy about it.

"How nice to see all of you," Elaine said, noticing that Millie had shed the fancier clothes and hairstyle in favor of her former look. The only remnants that remained of Astrid's makeover were the mascara on Millie's eyelashes and a hint of the coral lipstick.

And yet the woman was glowing. And Lawrence couldn't seem to take his eyes off her.

"This is our fond farewell," Astrid told Elaine. "We'll be leaving Lancaster tomorrow."

Elaine was surprised to hear it. "So no more treasure hunting?"

"This one's a wash," Jerry grumbled. "We've already spent more time here than we usually allow. Time to move on to the next spot. Kiki can retrieve her own treasure."

Elaine glanced at Astrid, wondering if she'd be able to join them, but the former actress just sipped her tea as if she hadn't a care in the world.

The front door opened and Elaine looked up to see Nigel and Macy walk in. Macy was off the crutches and had an almost indiscernible limp.

The pair walked over to Astrid's table. Then Macy reached into her purse and pulled out an envelope. "Here, Jerry," she said, handing it to him. "This came in the mail for you today."

"For me?" he asked, staring at the envelope.

Nigel moved closer to Elaine. "Is Archie working today?"

"Yes, he is," she said with a smile. "You can go on back to the kitchen. I'm sure he'd love to see you."

"Thanks," Nigel said, then turned to Macy. "I'm off to have a chat with Archie—want to make sure we're still on for dinner in Waterville this evening. I'll join you in a bit."

"Take all the time you want," Macy told him. "I'm in no hurry today."

Elaine watched Nigel walk toward the kitchen, so glad that Archie had been able to spend so much time with his old friend these past two weeks.

"So what are you waiting for?" Macy asked Jerry. "Aren't you going to open it?"

Elaine saw Millie and Lawrence exchange a glance, already sharing that silent communication that was so common among couples. Then again, the two of them had been friends for years, so maybe that wasn't surprising.

"It's from Milwaukee," Jerry said, looking at the postmark. Then he tore the seal and pulled out a piece of folded piece of paper.

His mouth gaped as he stared at a crayon drawing of a gold crown. Then he lifted the flap of the homemade card and began to read it out loud. *"Dear Grandpa, Thank you for the princess book and tiara for my birthday. I love you."* His voice cracked and he took a moment to compose himself before continuing. *"Katie."*

"That's very sweet," Millie said. "What book did you send her?"

"I didn't send her anything," Jerry said, his voice raspy. He cleared his throat, then gazed back down at the homemade thank-you card. "I don't understand."

"I did it for you," Astrid said breezily. "Every girl needs a doting grandpa, even if that grandpa is too stubborn to see it." She took a sip of her tea. "So I did a little research and discovered the day of her birthday. Then I sent the gifts and a card in your name." Astrid smiled at him. "Easy-peasy."

Lawrence chuckled. "You're a bit of a busybody, aren't you, Astrid?"

Astrid looked Lawrence and grinned. "I am, and quite successful at it, judging by the two of you."

Millie blushed, but neither she nor Lawrence disagreed.

Jerry turned to Astrid. "Maybe I should hire you as my personal assistant. I've never been great at dealing with... people."

"I accept your job offer and will begin immediately." Astrid smiled. "We can work out the terms later."

Lawrence and Millie started to laugh, and after a few moments, Jerry joined in. "Well, I guess that settles it."

Astrid clapped her hands together. "I think I found my dream job. And there's nothing easier in the world than shopping for a seven-year-old girl. Almost every one of them wants to be a princess." Then she winked at Millie. "And some of us sixty-plus gals wouldn't mind that gig either."

When Elaine returned to the kitchen, she found Nigel seated at the table sipping a cup of tea. Jan stood by the door, her jacket on and her purse slung over her shoulder.

"Are you headed out for your lunch date?" Elaine asked her, setting an empty teapot on the counter.

"Yes, and I thought I'd stop at the market while I was out. Archie's taking a quick inventory of the pantry right now."

"Can you pick up some laundry detergent?" Elaine asked her.

"And some sugar," Archie said from the pantry door. "We're getting low."

"Laundry detergent and sugar," Jan repeated, nodded. "Anything else?"

"Don't forget the lightbulbs," Nigel added.

"Got it," Jan said, then headed out the door.

Elaine watched her leave, so eager to get her hands on that book and solve the code on the treasure map that she could hardly stand it.

And yet, as she continued working in the tearoom, something gnawed at her that she couldn't quite nail down.

WHEN JAN RETURNED from her lunch date an hour later, Elaine was waiting for her in the driveway.

Jan parked her Camry and climbed out of the car. "I got the book," she said, holding up the bag in her hand. Then she saw the expression on Elaine's face. "What's wrong?"

"Nothing," Elaine said, then wrung her hands together. "Well, that's not true. I wanted a chance to talk to you privately."

"About the lightbulbs?" Jan guessed, feeling the same uneasiness in the pit of her stomach that she saw on Elaine's face. "It hit me when I was at lunch with Bob."

"I never mentioned we needed them to anyone," Elaine said. "Did you?"

"No," Jan replied. "Which means the only way that Nigel could know that is if..."

"He was in our house at two o'clock in the morning the night the smoke alarm went off," Elaine finished for her.

Jan didn't want it to be true. She'd been searching for some other explanation, some plausible reason that Nigel would know they needed lightbulbs. But Elaine had only mentioned it that night in the kitchen, so nothing else made sense.

"We could hear Rose and Archie talking while we were in the secret passageway, so Nigel must have been in there that night and heard me mention lightbulbs for our grocery list."

"Yes, but why?"

"I don't know," Elaine told her. "How could it be Nigel? He's one of Archie's dearest friends. He was even *attacked* by one of the treasure hunters."

"But *was* he?" Jan countered. "Or did he just say that so we wouldn't suspect him?"

"If so, it worked," Elaine said softly. "And it gained him access into our home, didn't it? He spent the night in our guest room. And was the first one up the next morning."

"Very early in the morning," Jan said. "Giving him plenty of time to explore the house—and to find that secret passageway. As an architect, he'd know what to look for."

"And he also had time to figure out a way to get in and out without leaving any evidence behind." Then Elaine shook head. "Was he waiting for us to find the treasure—or eaves-dropping so we'd lead him to it? Then he could scoop it up?" She cupped her hands on her face. "Oh, Jan, I don't want this to be true."

"Neither do I," Jan said. "But the only way we'll know for sure is to catch him in the act."

"And how do we do that?"

Jan took a deep breath. "We'll need to set a trap."

CHAPTER TWENTY-ONE

That evening, Elaine walked into the sitting room on the second floor with Jan following close behind her carrying a tea tray. Elaine had the book *One Lie Too Late* in one hand and the notebook in the other. "I can't believe it's finally happening,"

"Neither can I." Jan set the tea tray on the coffee table in front of the blue, plush-covered sofa, then poured them each a cup as Elaine took a seat on one end of the sofa.

Jan joined her there, her blue eyes shining with excitement behind her glasses. "How shall we do this?"

Elaine placed a sofa pillow behind her back, helping her sit up straighter on the sofa. "Why don't you take the book," she said, handing it to Jan, "and I'll read the cipher, and then I'll write down each word after you find it in the books."

"Sounds good." Jan took the book, her gaze scanning the plain red front cover with the title in bold black letters. There was nothing remarkable about it—no illustrations or anything to help them understand why this book was chosen for the cipher.

Elaine knew this would take some time, but they had all evening. They'd eaten an early dinner, neither one of them having much appetite after learning that Nigel was the probable culprit.

So they'd set their trap, with Jan mentioning in the tearoom in front of Nigel and Macy that Bob had bought four tickets to a popular dinner theater in Bangor and was taking Jan, Elaine, and Nathan there as his guests on Thursday evening.

That meant the house would be empty—giving Nigel the perfect opportunity to search it without interruption. They both knew it was possible he might not take the bait, but it was the best plan they had for now.

"I still feel bad," Jan said suddenly, the book sitting on her lap, "for not telling Archie about our suspicions of Nigel. Did we do the right thing?"

"I think so," Elaine replied, feeling a slight twinge of guilt herself. They both liked and respected Archie too much to keep secrets from him, but they wanted to be absolutely certain that Nigel was the culprit before they revealed him to anyone—and that included not only Archie, but Trooper Benson. "We need to see how this plays out first."

"You're right," Jan agreed, placing both hands on the book. "Let's do this."

Elaine turned to the page with the numbers column, then circled every group of three numbers after 2-0-1-4, which they knew was the year the book was published. "Page one hundred and three, line eight, the eleventh word."

"Got it," Jan said, paging through the book until she reached page 103. Then she slid her finger down the page, counting each line. "Here it is," she said. "The eleventh word is *dead*."

"That's a scary start," Elaine said dryly, writing it in the notebook. Then she looked at the next series of three numbers: "Page sixty-eight, line ten, the second word."

Jan turned quickly to the page, and repeated the same process. *"Tree."*

"Tree," Elaine echoed, jotting it down. *"Dead tree.* Well, I suppose that's better than dead person."

The continued deciphering the numbers and finding the matching word until Elaine finally read the last series of three numbers: "Page fifteen, line twenty, the fourth word."

She stared down at the paper, a tingle of excitement running through her as she waited for Jan to find it.

The Jan looked up at her. "The word is *up.*"

Elaine wrote it down, then took a deep breath before reading out loud the secret message on the map. *"Dead tree hollow where warm water ends reach up not down."*

Jan repeated the words softly to herself. *"Dead tree hollow* seems simple enough. We look for a dead hollow tree—there are a few of them around here."

"Where warm water ends," Elaine said, tapping the notebook with her pen. "That has to refer to Chickadee Lake. And the deeper the water, the colder it is. So that must mean the dead hollow tree is near the shallowest part of the lake." Just a little over a month ago, they'd spent some time studying the lake, and knew that there was a particular part that was significantly warmer than the rest—they'd start there.

Jan nodded. "That's sounds right to me." She closed the book and set it on the coffee table. "And when we get there, we *reach up, not down.*"

Elaine stood up, eager to see what they'd find. "Let's go on a treasure hunt."

A SHORT TIME later, Elaine walked alongside Jan toward the shallowest end of the lake. The spot they were looking for wasn't too far from their house and they could follow a well-worn trail most of the way. The sun was just starting to set, and she'd brought a flashlight along, just in case the search for the right tree took longer than they expected.

Elaine zipped up her jacket. The air was growing chilly as the sun moved lower on the horizon. Every once in a while, she looked around, making sure no one was following them.

Jan had told her about meeting Dr. Zabel in the woods. According to Macy, the ornithologist had checked out of his cottage at Green Glade, but that didn't mean he'd actually left the area.

At least they knew Nigel was dining in Waterville with Archie and Gloria this evening, so he wasn't spying on them. A shiver washed over her that had nothing to do with the weather. She still found it hard to believe that Nigel could be so duplicitous.

She didn't intend to let him—or anyone else—scoop up the treasure once they found it.

If they found it.

Elaine told herself not to let her hopes get too high. Dr. Zabel thought the treasure was a hoax, and this whole thing—starting from the moment they'd received the Lofton teapot with the map inside—didn't quite seem to fit. Especially Nigel's interest in the treasure. Had he become intrigued after hearing the Finders Keepers Club talk about their treasure hunt and decided he wanted the treasure himself? Despite only knowing Nigel for two weeks, the pain of his betrayal cut deep.

"We're almost there," Jan said, shivering slightly as they moved closer to Loon Point.

Elaine nodded, picking up the pace. *Where warm water ends* signified that the dead tree wasn't far from the lake itself.

When they reached the edge of the shore, Jan stopped and turned toward the wooded area. Light from the setting sun filtered through the trees and cast long shadows on the ground.

"Let's move closer," Elaine suggested, sliding her hands into the pockets of her jacket. Jan walked along beside her, both of them looking intently at the tree stand in front of them.

Then Jan pointed. "Look, behind that big fir tree. There's a dead tree there."

Elaine saw it, the thick trunk twisted and cracked. "Yes, that might be it."

They hurried toward it, both of them aware that someone could be watching. But at this point, Elaine knew they couldn't hide what they were doing. Better to look for the treasure and find it quickly, before anyone could interfere.

The low, growling call of a moose sounded in the distance as Elaine and Jan approached the dead tree.

"Look there," Jan said, pointing to a hole in the tree trunk about shoulder height. The trunk had split while growing at some point, then come together again, forming a natural cavity.

"I'm not sure I want to stick my hand in there," Jan said in a low voice. "Something might call that home. Something with teeth."

Elaine didn't relish having her fingers bitten by an angry squirrel either. She pulled the flashlight for her pocket and switched it on. Then she moved closer to the tree trunk, shining the beam into the hole.

"I don't see anything dangerous in here," Elaine said, moving the flashlight around inside the hole. "And I don't see any kind of treasure either."

"Maybe someone has already taken it," Jan said, standing behind her.

A wave of disappointment washed over Elaine at that possibility. Then she inserted her right hand into the hole of the trunk and felt around inside it. "Maybe the treasure itself isn't here. Maybe there's a key or another clue. Maybe even another map."

Jan moved a step closer as Elaine felt every inch of the woody cavity.

"Well?" Jan asked at last.

Elaine pulled her hand out, then frowned down at a small splinter in her finger. "There's nothing there."

Jan's shoulder's drooped. "You mean we've done all of this for nothing?"

Elaine wasn't ready to give up yet, not after all the work they'd done to figure out the treasure map. "We must have the wrong tree. We'll keep looking."

Jan nodded, the disappointment on her face now replaced by hope and determination. "Yes, we keep looking."

Elaine stepped away from the tree, and then stopped as something snagged her memory. "The message said to reach up, not down. Maybe I didn't reach up high enough."

Jan's brow crinkled, then her gaze moved up the trunk about eight inches above the hole. "There's a piece of loose bark there," she said, pointing.

Elaine had noticed the same thing. A piece of tree bark had separated from the trunk and jutted out, slightly attached only at the base.

"It's too high for us to reach," Jan said. "We can go back and get a stepladder..."

"Or we can do it the old-fashioned way," Elaine said, lacing her fingers together, palms up, and then holding them out for Jan to step into. "I'll give you a boost."

"Are you sure?" Jan asked, looking between Elaine's interlocked fingers and the loose bark.

"We've come this far," Elaine told her. "Let's see what's in there."

Jan braced one hand on the tree, then placed her left foot in Elaine's hands, pushing off them to lift her a few inches off the ground.

Elaine staggered for a moment under the weight, then leaned against the tree trunk for support. "Are you high enough?"

"Yes," Jan said, pulling the piece of loose bark farther away from the tree. "There's something here, taped to the tree!"

"I'm not saying you're heavy," Elaine said, struggling to hold her up, "but if you could hurry, I might not drop you."

Jan laughed, then Elaine heard the sound of tape ripping. "I've got it."

Elaine lowered her slowly to the ground as Jan moved both her hands along the tree to keep from falling.

"Here it is," Jan said, slightly breathless as she held out a brown lump of tape and plastic only slightly larger than her palm.

Elaine picked it up, noticing that two wide strips of duct tape with a wood-grain pattern covered a small brown water-proof bag. She felt along the bag with her fingers. "It feels like a piece of jewelry. So Kiki really did hide a treasure here."

"Open it," Jan encouraged in a low voice after taking a swift glance around them.

Elaine knew they should wait until they were safely back at the house, but she couldn't resist unsealing the bag to see what was inside.

A large ruby pendant fell into Elaine's hand when she tipped the bag up, attached to a thick gold chain. It looked old. And it really looked expensive.

Jan sucked in a breath at the sight of it. "Oh, Elaine! Look at it!"

Elaine had been so caught up in locating the treasure, she hadn't really envisioned what it would actually look like. "I think we just struck gold."

CHAPTER TWENTY-TWO

Late on wednesday afternoon, Jan stood at the glass counter in one of Waterville's finest jewelry stores, watching as the jeweler, Kenneth Perez, examined the ruby necklace through the loupe magnifying glass he held up to one eye.

"The chain is made of eighteen-karat gold," he said, then turned his attention to the jewels on the necklace. He started with the large ruby pendent in the center, which was surrounded by gold filigree openwork and edged with a sparkling circle of small diamonds.

Three flat, dime-size diamonds hung from the chain on each side of the ruby. After examining each one of the diamonds, he looked at the ruby once more, moving it a few inches closer to the loupe and studying it carefully.

While she waited, Jan thought about their plan this evening, going over it in her mind to make certain they'd considered all possible factors. Bob would pick her and Elaine up at the house at seven o'clock. Then they'd head off in the direction of Bangor. They'd circle around, then head back to a secluded spot with enough trees and brush to conduct a stake out.

Then they'd wait.

She took a deep breath, her stomach twisting now that they were so close to putting the plan into action.

Breathe, she told herself, just as Mr. Perez lowered the magnifying glass.

"This is a 1920s-era necklace in the art deco style," he said, sounding impressed. "The diamonds are all genuine. And so is the ruby. In fact, it's practically flawless. You have quite a treasure here."

The man didn't know how right he was, Jan thought to herself. "That's what we suspected, but we wanted to be sure."

She and Elaine had stayed up late last night, looking at the necklace and trying to determine if it was actually a real ruby. They'd finally decided to have Jan take it to the jewelry store and have it appraised.

The only thing they hadn't discussed yet was what to do with the treasure now that they'd found it.

"Can you tell me the value?" she asked him.

Mr. Perez hesitated. "I'd need to do some research to give you a precise value."

"What's your best educated guess?" Jan prodded, truly curious.

Macy had arrived alone at the tearoom this morning, now fully recovered from her sprained ankle, and announced that the Finders Keepers Club members had checked out and left Lancaster. And that Nigel planned to leave for California tomorrow

"Well, my best educated guess," Mr. Perez said, "is that it's somewhere in the range of five thousand dollars."

So Lawrence had been correct, Jan thought to herself. And Kiki was obviously a very wealthy woman if she could stick a valuable necklace in dead tree.

"Perhaps even more, since it's a vintage piece," Mr. Perez continued. "Often, the story behind it can drive prices up. My guess is that it was custom-designed for someone of wealth and class. If that someone was famous, the value could double."

His words left Jan speechless as he carefully bagged the necklace and then handed it back to her. "Thank you for bringing it in to the store."

"How much do I owe you?" Jan asked, unzipping her purse.

Mr. Perez held up one hand. "No charge," he said with a smile. "I don't often see a piece of that quality and age, so it was a treat for me."

"Well, thank you so much," Jan told him, carefully placing the necklace in her purse. "I'll be sure and stop in again sometime."

"You do that," he said, with a nod. "Have a good day."

As Jan walked out of the shop and into the sunshine, she heard her cell phone buzz. She reached into the pocket of her jacket and pulled it out to look at the screen. There was a notification that a new e-mail had arrived in her inbox.

And it was from Lisa Curry.

THAT NIGHT, ELAINE sat on the hood of Bob's silver Acura MDX and looked through a pair of binoculars. "No sign of anything yet."

Nathan sat beside her, his hands in the pocket of his coat. Jan and Bob sat in the front seat, taking their turn in the heated car, the motor purring softly as they all waited for something to happen.

"Thanks again for helping out," Elaine said, lowering the binoculars and looking over at Nathan. "Sorry to make you sit out in the cold like this."

"Are you kidding?" he asked, a twinkle in his blue eyes. "I feel like one of the Hardy boys on a stake out." He chuckled. "Or maybe I should say the Hardy boys' father."

Elaine laughed, realizing she always had fun when she was with Nathan.

They'd been sitting out here for an hour with a clear view of the house and the grounds surrounding it. They'd left the front and back porch lights on as they usually did when they went out for the night. She just hoped that didn't keep Nigel, or anyone else who might have been breaking into their home, away.

So far, everything had gone according to plan. Bob had picked them up at seven o'clock, spending about ten minutes with them inside the house before escorting them to his car in the driveway.

Then they'd headed to Waterville to pick up Nathan before turning around to drive back toward Chickadee Lake.

Elaine suddenly remembered the other mystery in their life. "Hey, I forgot to tell you," she said, turning to Nathan. "Jan received an e-mail from Lisa Curry today."

"The woman related to the sapphire ring family?"

She nodded. "Lisa would be the granddaughter of Frank Wood, the younger brother. It was Elmer who boarded at the house and put the sapphire ring in the wall."

"So what did her e-mail say?"

"That she's excited to meet with us, but her son just had a tonsillectomy, so it will have to wait a few days until he's recovered."

"How much did you tell her?" he asked.

Elaine placed her hands behind her on the hood and leaned back. "Only that we had some property that belonged to the Wood family. We thought it would be better to tell her the rest in person."

He nodded. "I agree. It's a complicated story."

She smiled. "You can say that again."

An owl hooted nearby and Elaine could hear the rustle of an animal a few yards away. She just hoped it wasn't a skunk.

"Here, let me take a look," Nathan said, reaching for the binoculars.

Elaine wrapped her arms around herself, feeling colder by the minute. She'd enjoy this stakeout a lot more if it were the middle of summer.

She checked her watch, happy to see that it was now their turn inside the car. "Hey, it's our..."

"I see something," Nathan interjected. Then he handed her the binoculars. "Someone with a flashlight is near your house."

Elaine looked through them, taking a moment to adjust the lenses. Then she saw a beam of light bobbing up and down as it lit the ground ahead of the person holding it. Then the flashlight turned off and she saw a man's figure, dressed all in black, illuminated under the porch light before disappearing inside the house.

"He just went in," Elaine gasped, her heart pounding as she reached for her cell phone to call Trooper Benson.

Nathan waited for her to finish the call before jumping off the hood and walking over to tap on the driver's side window.

Bob rolled the window down. "Time to trade?"

"No, time to go," Nathan said, opening the rear car door for Elaine to slide in the backseat. "He's in the house."

CHAPTER TWENTY-THREE

B ob parked his Acura a short distance from the house so the intruder wouldn't hear the car engine or see the headlights. Then they got out and walked the rest of the way.

Adrenaline fueled Jan, helping her keep up with Bob's long stride as the two of them made their way to the back door of the screened-in porch. Elaine and Nathan were going in through the front door as part of their plan to stop the intruder from escaping.

Jan walked into the screened porch, where she'd put Earl Grey in his carrier to keep him safe and out of the way. The cat meowed once, and then grew quiet, as if sensing the seriousness of the situation.

She unlocked the door leading into the kitchen, then let Bob walk in ahead of her before closing the door quietly behind her. The kitchen was dark, and so was the rest of the house.

At the same time, Elaine and Nathan were entering through the front door, then locking it to slow down the intruder if he tried to escape.

Bob and Jan stood in the kitchen, looking around, but didn't see or hear anything unusual.

Then a thump sounded overhead. She looked up at the ceiling and listened. Soon she heard the sound of footsteps.

Elaine's room was right above the kitchen. The intruder was in there, going through her things. Jan suppressed a shudder at the sense of invasion she felt—and knew Elaine would feel it too, at someone rifling through her belongings.

She looked over at Bob and pointed up to the ceiling.

He nodded, then motioned toward the door leading to the hallway. She followed him, the footsteps now moving to another part of the second floor. Perhaps he was in her room now—or the sewing room.

They met Elaine and Nathan in the entrance hall.

"He's upstairs," Jan whispered to them.

Elaine tilted her head up, the footsteps now moving directly overhead. That meant he was in the hallway and Jan wondered if he'd go into her room next or the sitting room.

Please let it be the sitting room, she thought to herself. That's where they'd left the bait—the ruby necklace was back in its waterproof bag with the wood-grain duct tape around it, sitting atop the treasure map on the rosewood desk.

A little obvious, perhaps, but since this would be their one and only chance to catch him in the act, they didn't want him to miss it.

Elaine leaned toward her. "He's up there," she whispered, pointing to the ceiling of the east parlor.

Jan sucked in a deep breath, knowing the confrontation was almost upon them. She hoped Trooper Benson would arrive soon—she feared how the intruder might react when he realized he was caught.

The four of them stood there together, waiting. And waiting. Jan couldn't understand what was taking so long. The treasure was out in the open for the taking. Did the intruder now realize it was a trap?

That thought made her turn to Elaine. "Maybe someone should watch the secret passageway in the basement," she whispered, "just in case he tries to leave that way."

"We'll do it," Elaine volunteered, motioning to Nathan to follow her.

While they headed for the basement, Jan and Bob moved toward the bottom staircase, ready to stop him if he came down that way.

Then a flash of headlights shone through a window, and Jan raced over to see Trooper Benson's truck pull into the driveway. Bob walked quickly to the front door and unlocked it.

The muffled sound of running footsteps above them told Jan that the intruder had seen the trooper's truck too.

"He's headed this way," Bob said, standing protectively in front of Jan as footsteps suddenly pounded down the curved staircase.

As Nigel rounded the corner on the staircase, he blanched when he saw Jan and Bob standing at the bottom.

"There's no way out, Nigel," Jan called out, her heart sinking when she saw that it was really him. She'd been so hoping they were wrong, for Archie's sake.

"Elaine and Nathan are watching the secret passageway," Bob told him. "You can't run—or hide."

At those words, Nigel continued his way down the stairs, wearing a black ski jacket and black pants. "I'm so sorry," he said, looking distraught. "I don't know what got into me."

"You obviously wanted the treasure," Jan said, holding out her hand. She couldn't bear to look in Nigel's eyes and see the anguish there. "May I have it back please?"

Nigel reached into his pocket as Trooper Benson entered the house. A moment later, Nathan and Elaine emerged from the basement, obviously hearing the commotion.

But instead of the duct-taped wrapped necklace, Nigel slowly pulled out the rosewood ring box.

Jan's mouth gaped when she saw it. She and Elaine had hidden it behind a row of books on the bookshelf in the upstairs sitting room. "The ring? You tried to steal the sapphire ring? But why?"

Nigel sighed. "It's a long story."

A SHORT TIME later, after the trooper had read Nigel his rights, the six of them sat at a table in the west parlor.

"I'm not even sure where to begin," Nigel said, staring at the ring box sitting on the center of the table.

Daniel narrowed his gaze on Nigel. "Let me remind you once more, Mr. Fox. Anything you say can be used against you in a court of law."

Nigel nodded. "I know, but Jan and Elaine deserve to hear the truth from me. It's the least I can do."

Daniel shrugged his shoulders, then folded his arms over his chest. "Go ahead."

"As an attorney," Bob said, looking sternly at Nigel, "I want to reiterate Trooper Benson's warning. You may want to hire a lawyer before you say another word."

"I appreciate the warning," Nigel replied. "But I owe it to all of you to come clean—and that's what I intend to do."

Jan knew Nigel risked incriminating himself, but he'd already been caught red-handed. And she needed to know why he'd betrayed them—and Archie—this way.

"I guess I should start at the beginning," Nigel said. "I never intended it to happen this way. I came to Lancaster with the best of intentions—to visit my old friend Archie—and to make an offer to buy the sapphire ring from you."

"But why did you want it?" Elaine asked, confusion swimming in her blue eyes. "There are plenty of sapphire rings in the world to buy."

"I had to have it," Nigel replied. "I couldn't sleep, I couldn't eat, I couldn't focus on anything else until I had it in my possession."

Jan remembered Archie telling them about Nigel's obsessive nature—but this seemed extreme. "Go on."

"Archie had told me how much he loved living in Lancaster and working at your tearoom. We always had fun stories to tell each other, through letters or phone calls. He even briefly mentioned the sapphire ring found in the wall of your house. A story I found intriguing at the time, but quickly forgot about. Until…"

Nigel's voice trailed off and he rubbed one hand over his face.

Jan was a little surprised Archie had told Nigel about the ring, but didn't blame him—it was a great story. Still, she didn't understand what had driven Nigel to do all this. He'd spent the past two weeks trying to "protect" them from the treasure hunters when *he'd* been the culprit all along.

"Until what?" Elaine prompted, her voice sharp. "What made you so determined to deceive us this whole time?"

Nigel sighed as he looked up at them. "I don't know if Archie mentioned it, but I have a tendency to get obsessed about things. After Flora died, I was adrift. She was my anchor in life, you see. So I latched on to something she loved—the silent screen era. I read her thesis again, and began to care about the people in it. The starlets and leading men she wrote about."

Jan and Bob exchanged a glance and she wondered where he was going with this. Nigel sounded truthful, but she had no idea where his story was leading. Or if he was a bit of an actor himself.

"One of those starlets was Amelia Howe. She looked like my wife. I know that sounds crazy, but I started collecting all her films, and read everything I could find about her in old Hollywood newspapers."

"So that's why you planned to go to California," Elaine said, "to feed your obsession."

He winced. "I'm afraid so."

"But why stop in Lancaster first?" Jan asked, ready for Nigel to get to the point. "I still don't understand what all of this has to do with the ring."

"Because I knew that ring had belonged to Amelia," he said, his voice more intense now, "so I had to have it."

Jan stared at him. "But you're wrong. The ring belonged to the Wood family right here in Maine."

"Amelia Howe *was* a member of the Wood family," Nigel told her. "She was a first cousin to Jameson Wood. Amelia Howe was her stage name."

Jan sat back in her chair, stunned. And from the expression on Elaine's face, she was just as surprised.

"How do you know that?" Nathan asked him.

"Because of my interest in Hollywood memorabilia—specifically anything belonging to Amelia. I had an agent purchase a steamer trunk at auction a few months ago—a trunk that used to belong to her. It was full of her belongings, although it wasn't allowed to be opened until it was sold. And when I opened it…"

Nigel's gaze moved across each person seated at the table. "I found all of her journals—spanning from the time she was a teenage girl living near Chickadee Lake until she was at the height of her fame in Hollywood."

Jan met Bob's gaze, and noticed he was paying close attention to every word of Nigel's story. As an attorney, he'd easily notice any inconsistencies. Once again, Jan was so happy to have him in her corner.

"It was her life story—written in her own hand," Nigel continued. "And part of that story was an escape from an abusive stepfather, aided by her cousin Jameson Wood."

He paused a moment, then continued. "Years later, when Amelia had made it big in Hollywood, she'd sent Jameson a sapphire ring as a way to thank him." Nigel's gaze fell on the rosewood box. "She wrote all about it in her journal—and she ended that particular passage with the family motto: For Blood and Love."

Jan met Elaine's gaze, astounded by Nigel's story. Now she was certain he was telling the truth.

"But why the subterfuge?" Elaine asked him, looking bewildered. "Why not just tell us this when you first arrived?"

"I was going to," Nigel said, his voice softer. "I planned to make you a very generous offer to buy the ring. Then I suffered that head injury, so my offer was delayed until the next morning."

Jan suddenly remembered their conversation on the porch the next day, when Nigel had warned them to hide any valuables. "We talked about the ring the morning after you stayed over. You said you were surprised we hadn't sold it."

He nodded. "That was my way of feeling you out. You see, I feared you wouldn't sell it to me. And when you confirmed that fear..."

"You decided to steal it," Elaine said.

"Yes," Nigel replied. "I would have sent you compensation after I got back to London. And when I realized a Finders Keepers chapter was actually looking for a treasure here—it seemed like fate. When you discovered the ring missing, I figured you'd blame them."

"So it became a crime of opportunity," Bob said. "When you fell in the woods, you decided to blame the treasure hunters—to cast suspicion on them."

"Not right away," Nigel countered. "Not until I heard Jan and Elaine say definitively that they'd never sell the ring." He sighed. "That's when I made the stupid decision to call the police and blame my fall on the treasure hunters."

"You committed a crime, Nigel," Jan said, still stunned by his actions over an obsession with a dead actress. It just didn't make sense to her.

"I know." Nigel's shoulders slumped. "But if I'd asked to buy the ring from you, and you'd refused, I would have been out of options. And if I'd taken it after that, I'd be a suspect."

Daniel leaned forward. "So that night you were assaulted—it didn't really happen?"

A flush deepened Nigel's face. "I tripped over a tree root and hit my head. There was no assault, so you can add filing a false police report to my charges."

Nigel sighed. "When I set out for their house, I truly did want a way to warn Jan and Elaine about the treasure hunters—because some of them can be ruthless. Fortunately, the group that came here turned out to be benign."

"That head injury also gave you access to their house," Bob reminded him. "You earned their confidence, and then turned around and betrayed them."

"I did," Nigel said and swallowed hard.

"And you must have planted Astrid's bobby pin too," Elaine said, "to divert suspicion from you after you were in the passageway." Then her brow creased. "But if you were sneaking around there, why tell us about it?"

"I fell in the passage that night you called the police..."

"So that's what we heard," Jan interjected.

He nodded. "You both believed someone was in the house." Nigel gave a small shrug of his shoulders. "I figured if I showed you the secret passageway before someone else discovered it, you'd never suspect me."

"And Astrid's bobby pin was just extra insurance in that regard," Bob said.

Nigel nodded. "I'm more ashamed of myself than you'll ever know. And I betrayed Archie. That's something I'll regret for the rest of my life."

Jan didn't know what to say. A part of her felt sorry for Nigel, who must have been so lonely and devastated after his wife's death that he invented a fantasy woman to fill his heart. A fantasy that had ultimately led to his arrest.

Daniel stood up and pulled a pair of handcuffs out of his belt. "I believe I've given you enough leeway, Mr. Fox. It's time to take you in."

CHAPTER TWENTY-FOUR

On Sunday afternoon, Elaine sat on the side porch, enjoying a cup of tea with Jan. The sun was out, the breeze was warm, and the temperature was teetering on seventy degrees, a sign that March going out like a lamb.

"There's Archie," Elaine said as a blue car drove past the house, then turned into the driveway. He'd called them shortly after they'd returned from church and asked if he could stop by later.

Telling Archie about Nigel's arrest had been one of the hardest things Elaine had ever done. Jan had felt the same way, and they'd both cried a bit afterward. But like a true friend, Archie had come to Nigel's aid in his darkest hour.

After hearing Nigel's heartfelt apology and contrition, he'd forgiven Nigel and promised to assist him in getting the help he needed.

Heavy footsteps sounded on the porch and a moment later, Archie appeared around the corner. "Good afternoon," he greeted them, his thick white hair slightly ruffled by the breeze.

"Please join us," Jan said, reaching for the third teacup they'd set on the table earlier. "We have some hot dosha chai tea if you're interested."

"That sounds delightful," he replied, taking a seat. "I wanted to give you an update on Nigel."

Elaine leaned forward, half-fearing what he might say. "And?"

He smiled. "Since you and Jan decided not to press charges, the DA agreed to reduce the charges to misdemeanors. Nigel will pay a hefty fine and undergo counseling when he returns to England." Archie took a sip of his tea. "There are jurisdiction issues of course, but Nigel has already contacted his physician at home to set up some sessions."

"I hope he gets the help he needs," Elaine said quietly.

"He will," Archie said. "I'll make sure of it."

Jan sighed. "Grief can affect some people in strange ways."

Archie nodded. "For Nigel, his interest in the life of a Hollywood starlet from the 1920s took over his life and his good judgment. He tried to use it as a bandage to cover his grief, but..."

"It only made it worse for him," Jan said softly.

Archie looked between Jan and Elaine. "I want to apologize again for bringing this to your door. If I'd known..."

Jan held up one hand. "There is no need for an apology, Archie," she interjected. "You had no idea—and it's all worked out well in the end. If Nigel hadn't come to Lancaster, we never would have learned the full history of the sapphire ring."

"That's right," Elaine agreed, looking forward to a visit by Lisa Curry later in the day. They'd finally found a time to get together. "So it's a happy ending all around."

He chuckled, reaching for his cup. "I won't argue with that. In fact, Nigel insisted on giving over the money he would have sent you for the sapphire ring."

"We'd never take it," Jan said.

Archie nodded. "I know. That's why I told him to send it to a local charity here." He smiled. "Just like you told me you're planning to do with the proceeds from the sale of the ruby necklace."

Elaine smiled as she looked over at Jan. "In honor of Amelia."

"And the Wood family," Jan said.

The three of them sat together on the porch, chatting about the events of the past few weeks and sharing their plans for Easter, which was now only a week away.

And Elaine silently counted her blessings, including the two blessings who were seated at the table with her.

"So this ring belonged to a Hollywood actress?" Lisa Curry asked later that afternoon, staring in disbelief at the open rosewood box in her hand.

Jan could see that this was a lot for Lisa to take in. In her late forties, Lisa had auburn hair that brushed her shoulders and clear green eyes, along with a light sprinkle of freckles across her nose and cheeks.

She'd arrived at their home almost an hour ago and listened patiently as Jan and Elaine had taken turns telling her the long story of finding the sapphire ring in the wall and their long investigation into learning the story behind it.

A story that had led to her.

"Yes, to an actress named Amelia Howe. That was her stage name," Jan clarified. "Her real name was Amelia Wood. She was a starlet during the silent screen era and made several films. And she was a first cousin to your great-grandfather, Jameson Wood."

Lisa's eyes softened. "How I wish my mother was still alive to hear this story. She grew up never knowing her father, Frank. Although her stepfather treated her like his own."

"So your mother, Frella, and her mother, Ella, never knew about the sapphire ring? That it was in this house?"

Lisa shook her head. "No, Mom always said Grandma Ella blamed my great-uncle Elmer for Frank's death. You see, he'd sent an urgent wire to Frank, begging him to come to Lancaster as soon as possible. Grandma Ella said Frank dropped everything and sped away." Lisa grew quiet for a moment. "He was killed in a car crash that day just a few miles outside of Augusta. He never made it to Lancaster, and never got to see his baby daughter, Frella, born a few months later."

"And Elmer never tried to contact his sister-in-law after he was arrested?" Jan asked. "Never told her about the sapphire ring?"

"He may have," Lisa said. "According to my mom, Grandma Ella burned any letters Elmer sent her and refused to visit him."

Then Lisa carefully picked up the ring and held it in her hand. "This is so beautiful." She lifted her gaze, her green eyes shining with tears. "But even more beautiful is the connection it gives me to a part of my family I thought was lost forever. I never knew my Grandpa Frank—only the sad stories told about him and his brother and parents. Now I know my great-grandpa Jameson was a good man who helped his cousin. And that Uncle Elmer tried to do right by his family by getting the sapphire ring back, even if he was wrong and suffered for it."

Her words made Elaine's own eyes well with tears and she blinked them back.

"We're so glad we found you," Jan said warmly, giving Lisa a smile. Then she reached for another small box and handed it to the woman. "This doesn't have any monetary value, but it's another piece of your family history."

Lisa opened the box lid and looked at the old flue cover nestled inside. "*For Blood and Love.*" She looked between Elaine and Jan. "This is the Wood family crest and motto."

"That was Elmer's last message to his brother," Elaine said softly. "A message that Amelia Wood echoed in one of her journals. The man who bought those journals has agreed to send them to you, along with her old steamer trunk and the other belongings in it."

"Thank you so much," Lisa said, her voice tight. "I'll treasure this forever."

A WEEK LATER, friends and family gathered at Jan and Elaine's house for Easter dinner.

Jan rushed around the kitchen, putting the finishing touches on the food. The savory roast lamb made her mouth water and she couldn't wait to taste the pumpkin parsnip cake that Rose had made as one of the desserts. Rose had brought her father for dinner too, and she could hear Clifton Young laughing with Nathan.

Bob was out on the porch talking to Brian and Paula while the girls played a game of croquet on the lawn. He'd told Jan he wanted to talk to her later, in private. And she couldn't help but worry this was about that job offer in Baltimore. He hadn't said anything about it since returning from his trip, and she hadn't asked, wanting it all to just go away.

Jan took a deep, calming breath, telling herself not to let worry cloud her day. Then she said a silent prayer of thanks, so grateful for the love surrounding her, all the blessings in her life, and the beautiful day that God had made.

She expected more folks to arrive soon, so she hurried over to the stove to check on the dinner rolls baking there.

"Grandma," Max said, the five-year-old bouncing into the kitchen with his twin brother, Riley, by his side. "When can we hunt for Easter eggs?"

Elaine walked out of the dining room, where she was prepping the table, and swooped him up in her arms. "Easter eggs?" she teased. "I think Earl Grey ate them all."

"No, he didn't," Riley said, giggling as Elaine reached out to tickle him.

"The Easter egg hunt will be right after lunch," Jan told her grandsons as more guests arrived, spilling into the kitchen, chatting and laughing.

Elaine looked over at Jan. "I don't think we ever need to hunt for treasure. We have it right here."

Jan smiled at her cousin. "Hallelujah."

ABOUT THE AUTHOR

Kristin Eckhardt is the author of more than forty-five books, including twenty-four books for Guideposts. She's won two national awards for her writing and her first book was made into a TV movie. Kristin enjoys quilting, traveling, and spending time with family and friends.

ROSE'S BLACK FOREST COOKIES

1 cup all-purpose flour

2 tablespoons unsweetened
  cocoa powder

1 teaspoon baking
  powder

½ teaspoon salt

8 ounces. semisweet
  chocolate, chopped

½ cup unsalted butter, cut in
  pieces

½ cup sugar

¼ cup brown sugar, packed

2 eggs

12 ounces semisweet
  chocolate chunks

1½ cups dried cherries

Preheat oven to 350 degrees. Line three baking sheets with parchment. In a medium bowl, whisk together flour, cocoa, baking powder, and salt. Set aside. Place chopped chocolate and butter in a large heat-proof bowl set over a pan of simmering water. Stir until melted and smooth. Remove from heat. Whisk in sugars, then eggs until smooth.

Whisk in the dry ingredients just until combined (be careful not to overmix). Fold in chocolate chunks and dried cherries. Press plastic wrap on to the surface of the dough and refrigerate for thirty to forty-five minutes. Drop mounds of dough (equal to two level tablespoons), leaving about two inches between, on to prepared sheets. Bake just until edges are firm, eleven to thirteen minutes. Cool on baking sheets for two to three minutes; then transfer to a wire rack to cool completely.

READ ON FOR AN EXCITING SNEAK PEEK
INTO THE NEXT VOLUME OF TEAROOM MYSTERIES!

Trouble Brewing

Jan Blake placed a yardstick and a notebook on the back-seat of her car. Her cousin, Elaine Cook, got in on the passenger side and set a bulging tote bag on the floor.

"Got everything?" Jan asked.

"I think so."

Jan backed out of the garage and headed for their little church. They had a lot of work to do to prepare for Lancaster Community Church's Mother-Daughter Tea the following week. Their tearoom on the lakeshore had been busy that morning, but Rose and Archie, their hired servers, had assured them that they would be fine for the next hour or two. Since they didn't serve full meals, fewer customers came into Tea for Two during the noon hour most days.

They would have gotten away a little earlier, but Elaine's twenty-six-year-old daughter had called minutes before they planned to walk out the door. Jan didn't mind. She and

Elaine adapted to each other's schedules and whims. Jan, for instance, had gotten up at 5:30 a.m. to bake fresh scones and cream puffs for the day's customers. She liked to be up early and get her baking done well before opening. She usually had time for devotions on the screened-in back porch or the deck down near the water in nice weather. She loved that still time of day when the sun was rising and, if it wasn't windy, the water was absolutely flat. Elaine, on the other hand, preferred to sit up at night and read, then get up a little later than Jan in the morning.

"So, what did Sasha have to say?" Jan asked in the car.

"She's flying up here Tuesday for a few days."

"Wonderful!" Jan said. "Will you have to drive to Portland to pick her up?"

"No," Elaine said. "She's renting a car."

"She could use one of ours." Jan was ever mindful of expenses.

"It's all right," Elaine said. "I think she'd rather do it this way. She's got to drive over to Sugarloaf Thursday. She's meeting with the management to set up a biathlon event there in the fall."

Jan nodded. Sasha was an Olympic-class biathlete. Elaine could hardly wait to see her compete, and Jan caught the excitement whenever she talked about it.

"Do you think we can get tickets to the event?"

Elaine smiled. "I sure hope so. It would be so much fun." The biggest ski area in Maine, Sugarloaf, hosted many winter sports events, and the prospect of seeing her daughter ski and shoot there made Elaine's eyes glow. She glanced at Jan. "So how was your date with Bob last night?"

Jan nodded, but didn't smile. "It was good." To tell the truth, she was a little worried. Her old school friend, Bob, who had over the last year become her romantic interest, had a job offer that would move him out of state.

"He hasn't made up his mind about the job yet?" Elaine asked.

"Not yet." Bob was an attorney with a practice in the nearby city of Waterville. He was usually decisive, and the fact that he had not yet made a firm decision about the job change was stressful for Jan.

"Here we are." The short drive was over, and Jan pulled into the church parking lot. "Just keep praying about it, okay?"

"I will."

They climbed out of the car, and Jan looked toward the church's side door, at the top of the handicapped ramp. "I wonder if Pastor Mike's in his study."

"I think we should go knock at the parsonage," Elaine said, reaching for her tote. "Besides, we brought them cookies." She led the way across the lot.

The maple trees on the edge of the yard were leafing out, and the sun shone on the tender spring grass. Jan pulled in a deep breath. "I love spring."

"Me too." Elaine stepped up to the front door of the pastor's house and pushed the doorbell. A few seconds later, Sarah Ryder opened the door and surveyed them with pleasure.

"Hello, ladies! What can I do for you?"

"I hope we're not interrupting your lunch," Jan said. "We'd like to get into the fellowship hall so we can firm up our plans for the Mother-Daughter Tea."

Elaine held out a small cardboard box. "Some of yesterday's leftover cookies and a couple of fresh scones."

"Oh!" Sarah's whole face lit. "Yum! Thank you. I'll get the key for you."

From inside, they heard a chair scrape the floor, and Pastor Mike came to the doorway. "No need for that. I unlocked the side door this morning. The Murphy boys were cleaning up the lawn, and I opened it in case they needed to get trash bags or use the restroom."

"Oh, all right," Elaine said. "Thanks, and enjoy the cookies."

Pastor Mike grinned. "I'm sure we will."

They walked across to the parking lot again, and Jan looked toward the church's front lawn. "The boys must have finished and gone home. The yard looks nice though."

"Yes," Elaine said. "They've moved the branches that were on the lawn, and the gravel the snowplow shoved off into the grass too."

Jan smiled as they walked up the ramp. "Those twins are hard workers."

"And they weeded the flower beds," Elaine said, nodding toward the tulips that would soon be blooming in the bed below the ramp. She reached out for the knob on the side door and turned it.

They stepped into a dim entry and went down the back stairs to the cool basement fellowship hall. Inside it was dim, with light coming through a few small, high windows in the foundation. Jan flipped the light switch.

Elaine gasped.

They both stood staring at the mess in the fellowship hall. At first glance, Jan saw two tables overturned, and folding chairs removed from their racks and thrown around the room. Paper towels and tablecloths lay crumpled on the floor. A broom, dustpan, and other cleaning implements were strewn about. Worst of all, someone had spilled cleansing powder and dishwasher detergent all about, making it impossible to cross the room without stepping in it.

Jan looked at her cousin.

Elaine wore a shocked expression. "Someone's ransacked the church."

"WE'D BETTER GET Pastor Mike," Elaine said. Jan's cheeks were pale and her eyes wide as she surveyed the damage.

"Maybe I should run home and get our fingerprint kit," Jan said.

Elaine looked inspired for a moment, but then she frowned. "No, we should tell Pastor Mike first."

"You're right. Come on." Jan turned on her heel, and Elaine followed her.

They scurried up the stairs, out the door, and across the parking lot to the parsonage. This time the pastor answered their ringing of the bell. His gray eyes surveyed them in surprise, and his eyebrows arched.

"Hello again. What's up?"

Nine-year-old Caleb peeked out from under his tall father's elbow. He had one of Jan's cookies in his hand.

"We need you to come over to the church," Elaine said, not wanting to alarm the whole family.

"Oh?" Pastor Mike picked up on her concern immediately. He turned and called over his shoulder, "Sarah, I'm going over to the church for a minute."

"That's fine," Sarah replied from near the sink. "Caleb, sit down and finish your lunch."

"Sorry to take you away from your meal," Elaine said as the three of them hurried across to the church.

"Is something wrong?"

"I'm afraid so," Elaine said.

"Very wrong," Jan added. "In the big room downstairs."

The pastor's mouth set in a grim line as he flung the side door open and descended the steps. He walked into the large room and stopped, gazing about. Nothing had changed. Elaine watched his expression fade from mild concern to deep dismay.

"Well." He shook his head. "Who could have done this?" he asked.

"I have no idea," Elaine said.

"Me neither," Jan added. "You said Des and Jo Murphy's boys worked here this morning?"

He nodded. "Outside. I guess we'll have to ask them if they came in here."

"You don't think Nick and Chris would do this, do you?" Elaine frowned as she looked around again and noticed more items tossed from their usual places. A trash can lay on its side near the door to the kitchen, with wads of paper spilling out of it. A box of straws had been scattered, and a framed Bible verse lay on the floor, the glass cracked. The Murphy twins worked in their parents' store, and she found it hard to believe they would make such a mess when they knew how hard it was to keep the general store shipshape.

"I wouldn't have thought so, but they may have seen something. I'd better call the store and talk to Des right away." Pastor Mike patted his pockets. "I left my cell at home. I'll call from the office." He headed up the stairs, toward where his office lay behind the auditorium.

Jan looked bleakly at Elaine. "Should we clean up?"

"I don't know. He might want someone else to see it first."

Jan walked cautiously closer to an area covered with greenish powdered cleanser. "Look. There are footprints right through it."

"You're right. Don't touch it."

"Don't worry about me." Jan had her cell phone out and raised it to eye level.

"Good idea," Elaine said as Jan popped off a photograph.

Elaine turned toward the stairway as Pastor Mike's "Oh no" reached them. She hurried up the stairs, calling, "What is it, Pastor?"

"They've been in here too."

FROM THE
GUIDEPOSTS ARCHIVE

This story, by Ginger Galloway of Sacramento, California, originally appeared in *Guideposts*.

It was missing. The beautiful ring that had belonged to my mother was gone.

A deep-blue sapphire surrounded by twelve tiny diamonds, lifted high in a platinum setting on an 18-carat gold band, it was passed to me after Mom had died during Thanksgiving week.

Mom's fingers had been a little chubbier than mine, so I decided to have the band made smaller. I put the ring in a small plastic bag with several other pieces of her jewelry that needed repair, intending to take it all to the jewelers when the bustle of the Christmas holidays was past.

A month later I finally had time to go to the jewelers. But I couldn't remember where I had put the bag. I knew it was somewhere in the house, so I figured I would look for it later.

In early spring my friend Ruth announced she was having a garage sale and wondered if we had anything we wanted to sell. She would take 10 percent of the proceeds for setting up and doing the selling. It sounded like a good deal since she lived on a busy thoroughfare and most everything would probably be purchased.

As I quickly gathered assorted baby clothes and household items, I thought of the old chest of drawers we didn't need any-more—"Might as well take that too," I called to my husband. He hauled everything to Ruth's house so she and her husband could set up for Friday.

Friday evening Ruth's husband called to report on the sale. "There was quite a crowd," he said. "I was there when some-body bought your watch."

Watch? "Oh, no," I panicked. "Did you find it in a small plastic bag?"

"Yes," he replied, "along with some other things; it was tucked in that old chest of drawers."

The house seemed to collapse around me as I realized where I had absentmindedly placed my heirloom jewelry. The other things weren't that important—but Mom's ring!

"Please let me talk to Ruth," I pleaded. When I asked her about the jewelry she said, "Yes, I sold a few items."

"And the ring?" I asked apprehensively. "You didn't sell the sapphire ring, did you?"

"Oh, yes," she said. "Somebody took it for three dollars. Why, is there anything wrong?"

I was so stunned I couldn't speak for a moment, then stam-mered my mistake. I couldn't believe I had been so careless and stupid.

"It's okay," she interrupted. "The lady I sold the ring to also bought some power tools and we exchanged telephone numbers. Don't worry, Ginger," she soothed, "I'll just call and explain what happened. I'm sure she'll return it."

I waited anxiously. Finally Ruth called to say she had phoned the woman several times. "She says she can't find the ring," said Ruth. "She wonders if your story about the sapphire belonging to your mother is believable. She thinks you might just be another shopper trying to get your hands on a good purchase. Nothing I said could change her mind."

"Let me call her," I cried.

Ruth gave me the woman's name and number. I phoned and breathlessly explained the situation. But the woman—I'll call her Daisy Lee—still was skeptical about my story.

Daisy Lee maintained the ring was still missing. "I'm not sure where it is," she said vaguely. When I pressed her, she said, "Let me think more about this."

My husband, Don, a minister, was sure his influence would change her mind. He called but it didn't work. Desperate, I telephoned again, reiterated the sentimental value of the ring and offered to buy her something in exchange for it. Again, she wanted to think about it.

After a few anxious months of not hearing, I gave up. But resentment seething within me boiled into anger. How dare that woman keep what was rightfully mine!

The anger permeated me; it spilled out in my voice and actions. Don tried to soothe me. "Ginger," he said, "I know how you feel, but try to remember it was only a worldly possession.

"Keep in mind what Jesus says about holding on to things," he went on. "'Whatever you bind on earth will be bound in heaven, and whatever you loose on earth will be loosed in heaven'" (Matthew 16:19).

He put his arms around me. "I know it's hard, honey," he said. "But let it go."

Tears filled my eyes as I realized he was right. *God, You know the ache in my heart,* I prayed, *and how important that ring is to me. But I know I shouldn't cling to it. I place it in Your hands.*

Letting go was difficult, but slowly I began to feel better and accepted the fact I would never see the ring again.

Two years passed and one spring morning when yellow daffodils blossomed outside our door, the phone rang. I was surprised to hear Daisy Lee's voice. She said her mother had recently died. But because Daisy Lee was suffering excruciating back pain, she had been unable to leave her bed to attend her mother's funeral. "It's so bad that we've even had to hire an aide to help me and do the household chores," she said.

As I listened my anger was replaced by sympathy. I wondered if she was recalling my story of my mom's death. "I'm sorry to hear about your mother and your illness," I said.

"Thank you," she said, her voice quavering, "but here's why I'm really calling. You know that ring?" She was silent for a moment. "Well, I knew where it was when we talked before. I still do. I've kept it in a dresser drawer, and if your offer to give me something in exchange for it is still good, I'd like to do it."

My heart soared. I went to the jewelry store and found a nice ring for thirty dollars.

Because of Daisy Lee's bereavement, I let a week pass before going to see her. Then I drove to her address at a mobile home park.

Much to my surprise Daisy Lee met me at the door and appeared in good health. I handed her the ring I had purchased, along with the receipt in case she wanted to exchange it.

She invited me in for coffee and proceeded to tell me her husband had been on disability and they had had hard times for several years. As she talked, I thought perhaps her bitterness over difficult circumstances had made her hold on to my ring to make up for the hurts in her life.

Then as she handed me my own precious ring, her face brightened. "Ginger, the most amazing thing," she said. "As soon as I called you to come and get your ring, the excruciating pain in my back disappeared! I began feeling better from that moment on."

Daisy Lee and I became friends. I shared my faith with her and answered her many questions about God. Later, as my husband and I prepared to move to another state, Daisy Lee invited me to lunch in a nice restaurant. Her husband joined us and she ended the meal with a surprise. She presented me with a few other pieces of mother's old jewelry she had bought at that garage sale. She had taken them to a jeweler, who had repaired and polished them.

It all happened twenty years ago. Daisy Lee and I still write to each other and she attends my former church in the city where I used to live. My mother's sapphire ring rarely leaves my finger. It's a constant reminder of the power of letting go and letting God, and how He surprises us with answers, even after we've given up.

A NOTE FROM THE EDITORS

We hope you enjoyed Tearoom Mysteries, published by the Books and Inspirational Media Division of Guideposts, a nonprofit organization that touches millions of lives every day through products and services that inspire, encourage, help you grow in your faith, and celebrate God's love.

Thank you for making a difference with your purchase of this book, which helps fund our many outreach programs to military personnel, prisons, hospitals, nursing homes, and educational institutions.

We also create many useful and uplifting online resources. Visit Guideposts.org to read true stories of hope and inspiration, access OurPrayer network, sign up for free newsletters, download free e-books, join our Facebook community, and follow our stimulating blogs.

To learn about other Guideposts publications, including the best-selling devotional *Daily Guideposts*, go to Guideposts.org/Shop, call (800) 932-2145, or write to Guideposts, PO Box 5815, Harlan, Iowa 51593.

Sign up for the
Guideposts Fiction Newsletter

and stay up-to-date on the fiction you love!

You'll get sneak peeks of new releases, recommendations from other Guideposts readers, and special offers just for you . . .

And it's FREE!

Just go to Guideposts.org/Newsletters today to sign up.

Guideposts   Visit Guideposts.org/Shop
                        or call (800) 932-2145

Find more inspiring fiction in these best-loved Guideposts series!

Sugarcreek Amish Mysteries

Be intrigued by the suspense and joyful "aha" moments in these delightful stories. Each book in the series brings together two women of vastly different backgrounds and traditions, who realize there's much more to the "simple life" than meets the eye.

Miracles of Marble Cove

Follow four women who are drawn together to face life's challenges, support one another in faith, and experience God's amazing grace as they encounter mysterious events in the small town of Marble Cove.

Secrets of Mary's Bookshop

Delve into a cozy mystery where Mary, the owner of Mary's Mystery Bookshop, finds herself using sleuthing skills that she didn't realize she had. There are quirky characters and lots of unexpected twists and turns.

Patchwork Mysteries

Discover that life's little mysteries often have a common thread in a series where every novel contains an intriguing mystery centered around a quilt located in a beautiful New England town.

Mysteries of Silver Peak

Escape to the historic mining town of Silver Peak, Colorado, and discover how one woman's love of antiques helps her solve mysteries buried deep in the town's checkered past.

To learn more about these books, visit Guideposts.org/Shop